ARTIFACT

Also by George H. Monahan

Biodiesel: A Novel

ARTIFACT

A Novel

George H. Monahan

Northfield Books
www.northfieldbooks.com

All characters and events appearing in this work are fictitious and are the product of the author's imagination. Any resemblance to actual events or real persons, living or dead, is purely coincidental.

Cover photo courtesy of iStockphoto LP, 200 - 1240 20 AVE SE, Calgary, Alberta, T2G 1M8 Canada

ISBN: 0985462620
ISBN-13: 978-0-9854626-2-8

For Sally

PROLOGUE

Three members of the Makanhassett Tribal Council stood on the edge of the woods in anxious silence. "He's ten minutes late," one of council members observed. "I wish he'd get here."

The youngest member of the group looked up. "Here he comes now."

A man approached on foot and after the customary handshakes, the spokesman for the council got straight to business. "So, what's your decision?"

The man looked around suspiciously. "Where's the Chief?" he asked.

"He's in great pain. He sent me in his place."

"Is he going to be OK?"

"He'll live. So, what's it going to be? Do we have a deal?"

The man gazed around the clearing and inhaled deeply. He really wanted this land. He decided he'd pay the tribal council's price—but only if they stood firm. Yet, something in his Yankee soul compelled him to tender one final counter-offer.

"I'll give you seven hundred and fifty for the whole parcel," the man said.

"What? Are you trying to cheat us? That wasn't the price you and my brother discussed."

"Well, he's not here, and that's my offer. Seven fifty."

"That's an insult," the youngest of the council replied.

"Forget it, then," the man said, pressing his gamble.

. "Wait!" the spokesman interjected. "Give us a moment to discuss your offer."

The members of the tribal council walked off a short distance, and after discussing the matter a few minutes, returned.

"Eight hundred," the spokesman said with resolve.

"Hmmm…" the man intoned.

"Come on. It's a steal—even at this price."

The man frowned. Inwardly, he exulted in triumph. "You got a deal," he said. "But what about the other members of the tribal council? Will they approve the sale?"

"Yes, if the Chief agrees to the price. The rest of the council will go along with his decision."

"Then I must know the Chief's mind—today."

The spokesman for the group pulled out his cell phone and punched in a number. "Hey, Bix. It's Ralph. How are you making out?"

"Talk fast, Ralph," Chief Bix Fairchild said. "The dentist just shot me full of Novocain and my lips are going numb."

"Vincent Tremayne has agreed to pay eight hundred thousand for the parcel."

"Eight hundred grand? I thought we had that deadbeat hooked for eight fifty?"

Ralph Fairchild nodded reassuringly as Vincent Tremayne looked on. "Listen, Bix. He's here right now and wants to know if we have a deal or not. Would you like to speak with him?"

"No, I don't want to talk to that fink! Hold on—the dentist is coming back…"

Through the phone, Ralph could hear his brother being reprimanded. "I'm an oral surgeon, not a dentist. And you're about to have root-canal, so turn off that damn phone."

"I gotta glow," Bix slurred. "I can't pfeel my pflace. My plips…"

"Wait! What about Mr. Tremayne? Are we on for eight hundred thousand?"

"Thlake thle money and thlun," Bix slobbered into the phone. "Thle dope don't thknow when he's peeing had,"

"Shut up or you'll bite your tongue off," Ralph overheard the oral surgeon warn.

"I… caplhaa… ahhhh!!!" Bix said before the line went dead.

Vincent Tremayne looked on expectantly. "So? Is it a deal?"

"It's a deal," Ralph Fairchild replied. "We'll sell for eight hundred thousand dollars."

"Excellent! I'll contact my lawyer. If it's OK with you folks, we can probably go to closing this Friday."

The members of the tribal council nodded. "That should work for us," Ralph said.

Vincent Tremayne climbed back in his Porsche and sped off.

"Can you believe it?" Sol Pharaoh, the youngest of the council chortled. "Eight hundred grand!"

Ralph Fairchild chuckled as he passed out cigars. "He *must* know half that acreage turns to marshland in the spring."

"Well, you know what they say about a fool and his money…" Lance, the third of the Fairchild brothers remarked.

"That's *his* problem," Ralph said as he bit off the end of his cigar.

Sol Pharaoh blew a cloud of smoke into the air. "What a schmuck!"

CHAPTER 1

Dr. Thomas Aquinas McGrath, Professor of Anthropology, bent over the laptop in his cluttered study. Piles of loose papers, teetering stacks of open books, and an odd assortment of whalebone awls and broken pottery shards completely covered the surface of his desk. He had been writing feverishly since before sunrise and was thoroughly absorbed in his work. Somewhere far-off, a voice called his name.

"Thomas…"

"Uh?" he grunted, not looking up from his computer.

"Thomas," the voice repeated with greater urgency.

He didn't respond, but continued working until he heard his name called a third time, accompanied by a sharp slap to the back of the head. He spun around to face his assailant.

"Thomas! For crying out loud!"

"Good morning, Roxy," Thomas said, befuddled. "How long have you been up?"

"About an hour and a half," Roxanne McGrath replied testily. "I'm leaving for work in a few minutes."

"What about breakfast? I'll make us eggs."

"I already made us breakfast, but I went ahead and ate without you. I've got to go to work."

"How about some coffee? Do you have time for a cup?"

"No. I brought you coffee half an hour ago," Roxanne said, pointing to a mug next to the laptop.

"Thanks," he replied and took a swig of the tepid brown liquid. Looking up, he noticed his wife's disapproving frown.

"Thomas, I'm worried about you. You've been working around the clock for days. This isn't normal."

Thomas sighed. "Roxy, the publisher wants this manuscript before the Fall semester begins. It's already August and I still have three more chapters to write."

Roxanne cast a glance over the clutter on Thomas' desk and pursed her lips. The status of her husband's book had been a source of contention between them for the last few years, when, after receiving a modest advance from the publisher, he began writing a book about North American archaeology with fervid determination. After a few weeks of intense labor, though, Thomas grew bored and the project languished. Roxanne's gentle coaxing to get back in the saddle turned to angry prodding when she realized his procrastination might prevent the job from ever getting done. Then suddenly, just a few weeks ago, he resumed writing in earnest. She was delighted at first, but her joy turned to concern when she realized Thomas' new-found zeal lacked moderation.

"You're an odd bird, Thomas," Roxanne said in her West Texas accent. "Either you're goofing off or working like a madman. There's no balance to your life."

"But Roxy, I need to get this done."

"I'm all for it, but they way you've been acting isn't normal. You've let this project sit for years, and now, all of a sudden, you're working like a demon. What's the rush?"

"I'm planning to put in for a sabbatical next year. Didn't we talk about this?"

"We've talked about your sabbatical many times. But what does that have to do with this?"

Thomas yawned and rubbed his eyes. "The college trustees love it when a faculty member publishes a book. It's good for the prestige of the college."

"So what?" Roxanne challenged.

"So, with this book on my resume, the college trustees will have a hard time turning down my sabbatical request."

"Oh, Thomas. I know you want a sabbatical, but…"

"Don't worry, Roxy. I'm rounding the home stretch. If I keep working like this for another week or two, I'll…"

"You'll burn out!" Roxanne cried. "You need some rest, doll. As your doctor, I'm giving you a medical order—take a break."

"But… but…"

"Just look at yourself! You haven't shaved in days and you're as pale as a ghost. You stink too. When was the last time you showered?"

"But Roxy…"

"Not another word!" Roxanne chided. "I *order* you to take a break. Is that understood?"

Thomas was about to protest, but sensing her concern, relented. "Yes ma'am. I'll take a break. I'll go shower right now."

"Good. But first, help carry my things to the boat."

The island on which Thomas and Roxanne lived was described by the early explorers as shaped something like a fish with elongated tail fins. The fins, two peninsulas actually, jutted off the island's east end and were known simply as the North and South Forks. It was Thomas and Roxanne's good fortune to live in a large cedar-shingled farmhouse on the North Fork, along an unpaved private road, overlooking an expansive bay.

Thomas hefted two canvas tote-bags filled with medical charts and followed Roxanne along the short grassy path from the house towards their private dock. He looked around the fallow farmyard and squinted as his eyes adjusted to the bright morning sunlight. Roxanne's departure for work usually followed the same routine every day. Her duties as medical director of the Makanhassett Tribal Clinic required a daily commute to the Makanhassett Reservation located across the bay on the South Fork. Rather than drive the long distance around, she preferred to cross the bay by boat, and Thomas usually helped her cast off.

"I'm serious about you taking a break, Thomas," Roxanne said as they approached the tidal creek that served as their boat basin. "You need to get some fresh air. Why don't you go for a walk in the woods?"

The unpaved private road along which Thomas and Roxanne lived was bordered on one side by a thicket of woods that stretched about a quarter of a mile towards the Main Road. Covering about twenty acres, the woods afforded a natural barrier between the beachfront houses along the private unpaved road and the busy Main Road that led into the seaside village of Stirling Harbor. Thomas enjoyed strolling its web of footpaths and Roxanne thought the exercise would do him good.

Arriving at the dock, Thomas assisted Roxanne as she climbed aboard her twenty-five foot Boston Whaler. Thomas passed the tote bags over the gunwale to her and set about untying the spring lines while Roxanne started the twin outboard motors, setting them at a low idle. When all was ready, Thomas gave the boat a gentle push. Roxanne donned a yellow life vest and hauled the fenders onboard. As the boat drifted towards the middle of the channel, she looked back towards her husband with concern.

"I promise I'm going to relax," he called over the low purr of the engines. "I'm heading up to Silvio's Café for some coffee with the boys and then I'll go for a walk in the woods. I might even take a swim this afternoon."

Satisfied that all was well, Roxanne smiled and shifted the throttle forward. Thomas waved as she slowly maneuvered the boat down the narrow channel towards the open water of the bay. Once clear of the tidal creek, Roxanne throttled up to full speed, leaving a white, foamy wake. Thomas sprightly retraced his steps towards the house and watched from their private beach as Roxanne's boat faded on the horizon into a shimmering dot. He knew that in less than ten minutes she'd be tying up at the Makanhassett Tribal Marina.

Thomas hadn't been to Silvio's Café for days and was looking forward to a *good* cup of coffee. He maneuvered his pickup truck around the potholes and ruts of the unpaved private road as he made his way towards the Main Road into town. As he drove, he noticed a pink plastic ribbon tied around the base of a sapling along the edge of the woods. A few yards further on, he spotted another one tied to the low bow of a scrub oak. Perplexed, he counted at least two dozen day-glow pink ribbons tied to trees along the edge of the woods before turning onto the Main Road to town.

Thomas parked across from Silvio's Café and caught the aroma of roasting coffee in the still summer air. Inside, he found Silvio hunched over the roaster intently scrutinizing a sample of beans.

"Hi, Silvio," Thomas said as he crossed the threshold.

Silvio looked up and squinted against the morning light. "So, you've finally decided to grace us with your presence. Did you run out of coffee at home?"

"Roxy ordered me to take a break. She thinks I'm working too hard."

"You're a college professor. You don't *work*."

Thomas rolled his eyes. Jibes like this were all too familiar from those outside his profession.

"Your friends are out back on the patio," Silvio added.

Thomas wended his way towards the double doors that opened onto the patio behind the café. From here, over a low hedge, one could look out across the village park towards the expansive bay just beyond the docks. Jack and Fergus sat at their usual table in the shade of an old locust tree.

"Well, look who's here!" Fergus said with mock surprise.

Jack Hancock glanced up from his newspaper, and recognizing his friend, frowned with concern. "Where've you been, Thomas? We were getting ready to send out a search party."

"Oh, come on, guys. I've only been out of circulation a couple of days. You know I'm trying to finish my book before the Fall semester begins."

"It's been over a week since we've seen you," Fergus said. "Didn't you suffer caffeine withdrawal?"

"Roxy keeps me well medicated."

"How's the book going?" Jack asked. "Are you making any progress?"

"Slow but sure. Just a few more chapters and I'll be finished."

"How long should that take?" Fergus asked.

Thomas considered the question. "Three or four weeks—if I keep at it."

"You'll be back teaching by then," Jack observed.

Thomas winced at the thought of returning to his job at the college. He imagined all those bored freshmen he'd soon face whose only interest in attending college was to qualify for something a little higher than minimum wage. He'd long since given up any idealistic notion that college—much less community college—was the intellectual nursery for scholars. It depressed him so much he decided to change the subject. "Have you been fishing lately, Fergus? I was thinking about doing a little surf-casting this afternoon."

Fergus, an old salt, found semi-regular employment with the baymen of the Makanhassett Tribe. "Not lately. Things have slowed down since Bix was elected chief. He's been too busy with tribal business these last few weeks to work the bay."

"I thought Lance would take over the boat while Bix is chief," Thomas remarked.

"Aye, he has," Fergus replied. "But Lance is also on the tribal council and they've all been busy negotiating that big real estate transaction out near your place. We should be getting back to work now that they've closed the deal."

"What real estate transaction?" Thomas asked.

"Haven't you seen the paper?" Jack asked. "The Makanhassetts just sold that parcel of land between your place and the Main Road to Vincent Tremayne."

Instantly, Thomas understood the reason for all those pink ribbons along the edge of the woods.

"He's planning to clear-cut the woods and put up condominiums. The whole story is right here," Jack added, handing Thomas the business section of the local newspaper.

Thomas snatched the paper and scanned it with nervous, bloodshot eyes. He grew increasingly agitated as he read.

By nature, Thomas was not someone who went looking for a quarrel. As best he could, he tried to mind his own business, especially when dealing with coworkers and neighbors. However, try as he might, there were obnoxious people in life he just could not avoid—and Vincent Tremayne was one of them. A few years earlier, along with a local heating oil business, Tremayne inherited a picturesque seaside cottage a little further down the private road from the McGrath's farmhouse. No sooner had he taken possession of the stately old house when he bulldozed it and built in its place an utterly tasteless pink stucco mansion.

Thomas and Roxanne never got over their sense of loss over the destruction of the old cottage, but thankfully they had very little to do with their boorish neighbor. Occasionally, though, the McGraths and the other householders living along the private road needed to confer over matters having to do with snow plowing and pothole repair, and their interaction with Tremayne in this regard had always been properly businesslike. The McGraths preferred to keep it that way, but circumstances of late caused Thomas and Vincent Tremayne to cross paths more frequently, and with far less amicable disregard.

"I thought Tremayne was in the oil business," Thomas said, throwing down the paper.

"Apparently he's branching out," Jack replied.

"Well, he can't just cut down the woods. It's not right!"

"I'm afraid he can. It's a question of private property rights. If a developer owns land, as long as he's acting within the law, he can do just about anything he wants with it."

Thomas' head swirled with thoughts of utter dread. He and Roxanne prized their peaceful isolation, living along the unpaved private dirt road that dead-ended at a stone jetty. This tranquility was made possible by the thicket of woods that separated their bay-front house from the busy Main Road that led into Stirling Harbor. Without the woods, they'd be able to see straight out to the Main Road from their back steps and hear the noisy parade of traffic that became almost intolerable on weekends during the tourist season. Worse still, Thomas envisioned a garish cluster of tightly packed condominiums and all the loud, uncouth people they would house immediately adjacent to his bayside spread. The thought of this was almost more than he could bear.

"But nobody *owns* the woods," Thomas cried. "They're like the beach or the bay. The trees belong right where they are."

Jack chuckled when he considered his friend's naiveté. "I'm afraid you're wrong, Thomas. The trees are on private property. Tremayne can do what he wants with them."

"Good God! What am I going to do?"

"Why don't you go to the hearing?" Jack asked. "Maybe you can persuade the judge…"

"What hearing?" Thomas begged.

"The zoning and permit hearing."

Thomas shrugged with incomprehension.

Jack took a deep breath. "The zoning laws require a public hearing before a builder begins any construction. This gives concerned citizens, such as yourself, a chance to challenge the legality of the project. If you can come up with a legitimate argument why the project should be stopped, the court might reject Tremayne's application for a building permit."

"When is the hearing?"

"It said something about it in the article…" Jack replied, taking up the paper. "Here," he said, tapping the page. "It's next Thursday, 10:00 a.m."

Thomas jabbed his fist into the air. "That's it!" he exclaimed through gritted teeth. "That's what you need to do, Jack. Get in there and persuade the judge to stop the development."

"Hold on," Jack replied.

"Fight him on constitutional grounds. Threaten to take the case to the Supreme Court if you have to."

"Stop right there! The Constitution has nothing to do with this."

"You'll come up with something else, then. You know every legal trick in the book."

Jack rolled his eyes and sighed. Although he worked around town as a handyman, Jack Hancock was no ordinary manual laborer. Tracing his ancestry back to the *Mayflower*, he was actually one of the wealthiest men on the North Fork, and though he didn't need to *earn* a living, the ethical code he lived by taught that hard work, in itself, was a virtue. After attending one of the finest prep schools in the country, Jack went on to study philosophy and economics at Oxford. Not technically a lawyer, he was nonetheless an expert in both civil and constitutional law and had the reputation of being a ruthless amateur litigant. Thomas knew that if there was any way to put a stop to the development, Jack was the man to figure it out.

"I can't go to the hearing," Jack advised.

Thomas gasped. "You're going to leave me to fend for myself?"

"No. I'll advise you as best I can. But you're going to have to speak at the hearing on your own behalf. I can't be there."

"Why not?"

"Because I'm taking Lauren and Parker to Boston next week," Jack explained. "We're visiting the Freedom Trail, and from there we're flying to London. We'll be gone until October."

Jack had been a confirmed bachelor until he met Lauren Wasserman, a widowed heiress, for whom he'd recently worked as a handyman. Jack had taken on Lauren's teenage son Parker as an assistant and the boy came to look upon him as something of a surrogate father. For his part, Jack was fond of both mother and son and found himself enjoying a conventional domesticity he'd always sought to avoid.

"October?" Thomas asked. "Doesn't the kid start school in a few weeks?"

"Lauren's decided to homeschool Parker for his senior year," Jack replied. "She asked if I'd mentor him in History and Political Philosophy. This is an educational trip."

"Wow! This relationship is getting serious."

"More than you know," Jack said solemnly.

Just then, Silvio approached with a serving tray. "So, Thomas," he said, placing three cups of coffee on the table. "I hear you're getting new neighbors soon."

Thomas grumbled an obscenity.

"Maybe they'll let you use their swimming pool," Silvio added as he retreated inside.

"Who cares about a swimming pool?" Thomas barked. "I have my own beach, damn it!" Thomas cast an angry eye towards Fergus. "You knew about all this, didn't you? Every day—fishing with Bix and Lance—you knew the Makanhassetts were going to sell that land to Tremayne."

"Thomas, I'm just a deck hand, not a member of the tribe. I'm not privy to all their business."

"But you knew about the land sale. You said so yourself."

"Yeah, I knew they were selling some real estate, but I didn't know *where*. Besides, who knew the Makanhassetts owned land on the North Fork? I thought all the tribal land was located on the other side of the bay."

"Wait a second," Jack interjected, grasping Thomas by the arm. "Tribal land… *tribal land…*" he repeated contemplatively.

"What? Does that matter somehow?" Thomas asked.

"It might," Jack replied. "Let me give this a little thought."

Thomas looked down at his coffee and sulked. The three men sat in uneasy silence until at last Thomas rose. "I'm going home."

"Don't lose hope, Thomas," Jack said. "We'll figure something out."

Thomas just waved as he departed.

Thomas sped the entire distance home. As he approached the turnoff to the private dirt road, he noticed someone had put up a large billboard along the edge of the woods in the time he'd been gone. Thomas swerved across the double yellow line and skidded to a stop just in front of the atrocious eyesore. Jumping from his pickup, he stood before the giant sign with mouth agape.

Coming Soon! Country Squire Condominiums, the sign read above an artist's rendering of a grotesque cluster of neo-colonial human hives. In an attempt to heighten the appeal of this proposed dystopia, the image included a horrible, multi-tiered fountain as a centerpiece. Thomas' worst fears were compounded when he looked to the lower left corner of the billboard, where, as an inset, he noticed a head-shot photograph of a Barbie doll blond flashing a contrived smile. Underneath the woman's photo ran a caption—*Daphne Tremayne, Senior Sales Agent.*

CHAPTER 2

Tremayne Fuels had been a fixture on the island's east end for years. Started by Vincent's grandfather as a mom and pop operation, the business took off during the housing boom of the 1950s. Inheriting a stable business, Vincent's father build a sizable personal war-chest with which he dabbled in real estate, thereby compounding the family fortune. A heart attack took him in his early sixties, leaving Vincent in charge of a small business empire. To stay on easy street, all Vincent need do was steer an even course and minimize risk. Yet Vincent dreamed of bigger riches. Impatient, and with an inherent competitive streak, he yearned to make his *own* mark in the business world. Although risky, his expansion into experimental biofuels and renewable energy showed great promise, and in spite of some recent business setbacks, he was poised to delve into the *terra incognita* of commercial real estate.

The Tremayne Fuels service yard at the edge of the Stirling Harbor business district was in a part of town not usually frequented by tourists. A parking area for two dozen oil delivery trucks took up most of the yard along with two large storage tanks and a filling platform. Rising on a gentle knoll opposite the tanks, surrounded by a narrow perimeter of grass and shrubbery, stood a two story building housing the company offices. The executive office suite occupied a first-floor corner overlooking the service yard. Vincent had scheduled a meeting for ten o'clock that morning, the main order of business being to appoint a president for his new sideline, the Country Squire Development Corporation. Half an hour before the meeting, Vincent's secretary alerted him that his attorney Martin Farquhar had arrived.

"You're here early," Vincent observed.

Martin Farquhar grunted as he took a seat. "Vincent…" he said gravely, "we need to talk."

Vincent checked his watch. "Can't this wait? Candice Brennan will be here soon."

"All the more reason for you to hear me out. I wouldn't want to say this in front of anyone else."

Vincent hated the way Martin had a knack for making him feel like a naughty schoolboy. He valued the older man's legal acumen, but believed age had turned him into an overly cautious fuddy-duddy. Vincent wasn't interested in listening to a sermon, but he couldn't cow Martin the way he did his oil company underlings. Like it or not, he'd have to listen to what the old man had to say. "What's on your mind?" Vincent asked.

"I have serious misgivings about this whole project."

Vincent leaned forward. "What's the problem?" he asked with a condescending smirk.

"For starters, you paid too much for that land."

Vincent shook his head dismissively. "I don't think so. Even if I did, I'm going to make a huge profit selling condos."

"I'm not so sure," Martin said skeptically. "Real estate is not a good investment right now."

"What are you talking about? You and my father made a bundle in real estate."

"That's true. But the market was booming back then. Things are different now."

"But the North Fork is still a hot market," Vincent rejoined. "Did you know Stirling Harbor made the *Forbes List of Prettiest Towns* last year?"

"Yes, yes. That's all fine and dandy. But I think the area is overbuilt. I'm afraid you're not going to make nearly the kind of money you expect on this venture."

"Martin, when I start selling condos…"

"Stop right there. You're putting the cart *way out* in front of the horse. It's going to be at least a year—maybe two—before you sell a single unit."

"I don't think it should take that long. Once we're up and running, Country Squire is going to be the hottest address on the North Fork. We'll make a fortune."

The elderly lawyer sighed with careworn weariness. "The way you're talking proves my point. You really haven't got a clue what you're doing."

Vincent smirked. "I'm not exactly new at this. I've bought and sold a few properties, you know."

"Flipping foreclosures is an amateur's game," Martin quipped. "A development project of this sort is not something you can dabble in like a hobby. You're already talking about selling condos, but haven't even secured the building permits yet."

"That's a mere formality," Vincent said dismissively.

"You also need to get approval for your architectural plans… hire the contractors… the carpenters, the electricians, the plumbers…"

"Yes, Martin. Duly noted. All those things *should* be handled by a professional. That's why I'm bringing in Candice Brennan as president of the Country Squire Development Corporation."

Martin Farquhar threw his hands up in frustration. "Is there no getting through to you?"

"I thought you liked Candice Brennan."

"I do," Martin replied. "I've worked with Candice on other projects and she's a competent professional."

"Then what's the problem?"

"The problem is people like Candice don't come cheap. And I guarantee you you're going to sink a lot of money into this project before you sell a single condo. I'm worried about your staying power."

"I appreciate your concern, Martin, but isn't that what banks are for?"

"For commercial loans? Yes, but you'd be lucky to get one. Even if you did, the interest rate would be sky high."

"Nonsense. My credit rating is excellent."

"It used to be, but it's not anymore. You have a serious cash-flow problem at the present time. Your biofuels business has taken a serious downturn since last month's… uh… *mishap*… and you still have a number of lawsuits hanging over you. Have you considered your financial position lately?"

Vincent swiveled in his chair and peered out the window overlooking the service yard. He hated to admit it, but the old man was right. When plans for this development project began taking shape months earlier, he expected to be swimming in cash by now. Everything looked rosy as he was poised to break into the financial big leagues at the helm of an expanding, eco-friendly biofuels business and a cutting-edge carbon credit marketing enterprise. However, just as his star was on the rise, everything came crashing down. For reasons that were still under investigation, an industrial accident resulted in the release of a particularly noxious batch of biofuel onto a group of VIP partygoers at a corporate publicity event. The whole mishap spawned multiple lawsuits and the bad publicity resulted in a substantial loss of market share for Tremayne Fuels. Money was tight, and securing a business loan was going to be much more difficult in light of all the litigation.

As Vincent mulled matters over the intercom buzzed. "Mr. Tremayne," the secretary said. "The Vice President of Public Relations is holding on line two. She says it's urgent."

"And that's another thing we need to talk about," Martin advised. "You must do something about Daphne."

Vincent swiveled in his chair to face the older man. "I assure you, Martin, everything's under control."

“Is it?” Martin asked, holding up the business section of the local paper. “I’m assuming this story isn’t your doing. Do you realize how much trouble this could cause?”

“Mr. Tremayne,” the secretary beckoned again. “The Vice President of Public Relations…”

Vincent groaned wearily. “Tell her I’m in a meeting and I’ll call her after lunch.”

“She’s only going to call again in ten minutes, Mr. Tremayne.”

Vincent looked at Martin with an expression of bewildered exasperation. “That’s got to be the tenth time she’s called this morning.”

“Don’t come to me for sympathy. I advised you not to marry her in the first place. You never did get her to sign that prenup, did you?”

“Please, Martin. Don’t twist the knife.”

“Well, whatever the case, this article spells trouble. Now, every tree-hugger on the North Fork knows about your plans. I expect the hearing this Thursday is going to be packed.”

“Oh, come on! What’s the big deal? You know nobody ever goes to those hearings.”

“Normally they don’t. But this article confirms your plans to clear-cut twenty acres of old-growth forest adjacent to an environmentally sensitive wetland.”

“People were going to find out sooner or later.”

"Yes, but you have to *time* this sort of thing so you don't draw attention to yourself. It would have been preferable for this story to come out *after* the hearing on Thursday."

"Maybe," Vincent admitted grudgingly.

"Mr. Tremayne," the secretary said. "Your wife just called to say she's on her way down."

"Damn it, Martin!" Vincent exclaimed. "She's driving me crazy! If I could just set her up in an office on the other side of town, then I can…"

"That's another thing we need to discuss. Why in the world did you name her *Senior Sales Agent*?"

"I don't know. It was Daphne's idea. She said she liked the sound of it."

"But she has no experience. Do you realize the damage she could cause if she tries to assert her *seniority*?"

"That's not going to happen. Don't forget—we're here today to put Candice Brennan in charge. Daphne's only responsibility will be to decorate the model condo and show around perspective buyers."

"Does Daphne know you're bringing Candice in as president of the development corporation?"

"Well…" Vincent began.

Before he could explain, the intercom buzzed again. "Mr. Tremayne, the Vice President of Public Relations urgently wishes to speak with you—right away."

"For God's sake, tell her I'm busy!"

"Mr. Tremayne, she's standing right here," the secretary advised. "She said she's coming in."

"No!" Vincent shouted just as the inner door to the executive office swung open.

Daphne Tremayne strode in wearing a navy blue knee-length skirt, white blouse, and a bright red waistcoat. She wore a red and white silk scarf tied loosely around the neck, and her hair was piled into a classic Brigitte Bardot half-up beehive. "Vincent, I need to know your opinion. Should we go with the red or the blue jackets?"

"What…?" Vincent grumbled with unconcealed aggravation. "What are you talking about?"

"For the company uniform. I can't decide if my sales agents should wear red or blue."

Vincent glanced at Martin Farquhar, who smirked at the younger man's predicament.

"I really have no opinion," Vincent replied. "Wear whatever you want."

Daphne glanced over, noticing Martin Farquhar. "Oh, hello, Martin," she purred seductively. "What do *you* think? Do you prefer the red jacket?" As she spoke, she spun around and walked a few paces across the carpeted office before turning back towards the elderly lawyer.

"Why don't you get both?" he suggested. "You can wear different colored blazers on alternate days of the week."

"That's a fantastic idea! What do you think of the crest?"

"What crest?" the elderly lawyer inquired.

"The Country Squire Coat of Arms," Daphne responded. "I designed it to be worn over the left breast pocket as part of the uniform." Daphne looked down and realized the crest was missing.

"Daphne, please," Vincent said. "Mr. Farquhar and I are in the middle of an important meeting. Can't we discuss this later?"

"I must have left it on my desk," Daphne said. "You need to see the uniform with the crest in order to get the full effect. I'll be right back."

Before Vincent could dissuade her from returning, she left.

"I can't take it anymore," Vincent confided. "I've got to get her out of here."

"Mr. Tremayne," the secretary called through the intercom. "Ms. Brennan is here for your 10 o'clock meeting. Shall I show her in?"

As Candice Brennan took the seat next to Martin, Vincent couldn't help notice her long, slender legs. She dressed in a stylish, yet conservative, woman's business suit topped smartly by a single string of pearls. Vincent thought her about the same age as himself, and very attractive. She held her head high and bore the faintest of smiles as he made the introductions.

"So, Martin tells me you've worked together before," Vincent said.

"Yes," Candice replied with casual confidence. "Most recently on the *Von Däniken Village* project."

"Vincent and I were just talking about how smoothly the Von Däniken project went," Martin fudged. "You were up and running in… what was it… eighteen months?"

"About that," Candice replied. "Everything was working in our favor, though."

"Well, we're very happy you've agreed to head up Country Squire," Vincent said unctuously. "As president of the development corporation, I bet we'll have units on the market within a year."

Candice chuckled and cast a skeptical glance towards Martin. "That's highly unlikely. Country Squire is a far more complicated project."

"Why is that?" Vincent asked.

"Zoning. The Von Däniken property is in the middle of the Pine Barrens, in an unincorporated part of the county. There were no neighbors to raise objections, so obtaining permits was a breeze. Your land, on the other hand, is within the limits of the incorporated Village of Stirling Harbor, along the Main Road into town."

"You think that poses a problem?"

"Not if we finesse things the right way at the permit hearing," Candice replied. "It would be best if we kept things low key right now so as to not attract public attention. When is the hearing, by the way?"

"Next Thursday," Martin replied, surmising Candice was unaware of the article in the local paper.

"So, if we get the right permits this Thursday we can break ground next week?" Vincent asked.

"Good heavens, no," Candice replied. "That's just the preliminary hearing. At best we might secure a permit just to survey the building site. We're going to have to get the architectural plans approved before we break ground. That'll mean *another* hearing, months from now. And then there's the…"

"Wait a second," Vincent interrupted. "I thought we already had the site surveyed?"

"That was just a property line survey," Martin advised. "You still need to plot out the actual construction site. Everything has to fit the local zoning codes."

"So the point is," Candice added, "we've got a long road to travel before any condo units hit the market."

"And that brings up another point," Martin remarked. "Considering how much there is to do before breaking ground, I think it would be prudent if we tried to keep costs at a minimum. Don't you think, Vincent?"

"Uh… yes," Vincent stammered, dreading any discussion of his financial situation. "That's just until we secure our commercial loan."

Candice arched an eyebrow. "You mean you haven't closed the loan yet? You're going to need lots of capital to get things rolling. And that's before we drive a single nail."

"Of course, of course. It's all been approved," Vincent bluffed. "We're just waiting to sign the paperwork. We expect to close on the loan next week."

Candice nodded thoughtfully as she considered this.

Just then the intercom buzzed. "Mr. Tremayne, the Vice President of Public Relations is back. She's coming in."

"No!" Vincent shouted angrily. "We're in a meeting!"

"I can't stop her," the secretary said.

Daphne strode into the room, this time wearing a blue blazer. She walked right up to Martin Farquhar, and bending forward, thrust her chest towards his face. "What do you think of the crest?" she asked.

Martin examined the emblem through his bifocals. "Outstanding," he replied with merry condescension.

Daphne accepted the compliment with girlish giggles. Glancing sideways, she noticed an attractive woman looking at her with quizzical amusement. Her eyes narrowed as they fixed upon her. "Who are you?" Daphne inquired with unconcealed distaste.

"Uh… How great of you to drop by, Daphne," Vincent said. "I was hoping to introduce the two of you."

"Oh, God," Martin whispered as he turned away.

"Candice, this is my wife Daphne," Vincent said with a forced smile. "And Daphne, this is Candice Brennan. She's just joined our team."

Daphne took Candice's proffered hand as though covered with leprous sores. "Are you a secretary or a bookkeeper?" Daphne asked with affected hauteur.

"Ah, no… no," Vincent stammered awkwardly. "Candice is coming on board as president of the development corporation."

Anger flashed in Daphne's eyes. "What development corporation?"

"The *Country Squire* Development Corporation," Vincent clarified. "The two of you will be working together."

Daphne regally lifted her chin and jutted it towards Candice. "I'm the Senior Sales Agent," she announced, looking down her nose.

"Excuse me?" Candice asked, nonplussed. She glanced towards Vincent who grinned idiotically. Martin, having withdrawn from the conversation, was wagging his head in rueful meditation. She turned to face the young woman once again who now thrust her chest forward.

"*Senior* Sales Agent," Daphne repeated with pronounced emphasis, thumbing the crest on her lapel.

CHAPTER 3

By the time Thomas arrived home he was so filled with rage he could hardly think straight. He slammed the screen door and stomped across the kitchen into the living room and back again three times, for no apparent reason. Finally, he found himself looking out the kitchen window, beyond his fallow farmyard, towards the line of thick green trees in the distance. His eyes darted back and forth across this sylvan vista and in his mind's eye the woods instantly transformed into a row of faux colonial, vinyl-sided duplexes. Thomas drew a deep breath, arched forward, and from the depths of his being roared so loudly the glass in the window pane rattled.

Thomas' outburst left him physically drained and slightly stunned. He found himself turned about, staring at the ringing telephone on the kitchen countertop. It rang a second time before the answering machine kicked on. After the usual instructions, Thomas heard the caller leaving a message.

"Thomas, it's Roz," the caller said in a gravely voice. "Give me a call as soon as you get this message. It's urgent..."

Coming to his senses, Thomas recognized his department chair's voice and picked up the phone. "Roz, I'm here. I couldn't get to the phone in time."

"Listen," Roz snapped. "Don't give me any crap about calling you during the summer, understand?"

"Yeah. So, what do you want?"

"I've emailed you six times in the past three days with no response. Are you sick, or something?"

"I've been busy writing. Would you please come to the point?"

"You got to get in here, Thomas."

"To the college? Forget it. I'm on vacation."

"I'm not joking. You've got to clear some of that junk out of your office—today."

"Are you nuts?"

"Listen. We're getting new carpeting and desks," Roz confided. "The facilities manager says you have too much junk in your office for the workmen to work around. You've got to clear out some of that crap."

Thomas could hardly believe his ears. "You mean to tell me that while the county is on austerity, the college is spending money on new office furniture?"

"It's what the college trustees want. I'm just reporting the news, so don't get sassy with me."

"Do you realize the faculty hasn't had a cost-of-living raise in over five years?"

"Take that up with the union. So, what time can you get here?"

Thomas recoiled at Roz's presumption he'd actually come to the college on his own time. "Hmmm..." he murmured theatrically. "Let me check my appointment book."

"Cut the crap! Get in here and clear some of that junk out of your office."

"Alright. I'll be in sometime this afternoon."

"Good," Roz snorted. "And make sure you stop by my office before you leave. We need to talk."

"What about?"

"It's a bit involved," she confided. "I'll explain everything when you get here. OK?"

"Fine," Thomas grumbled.

"Don't be such a mope," Roz said. "It's good news for a change."

Thomas arrived on campus around noon and parked close to the faculty offices. Since classes were not in session, the only people working were a handful of administrators and secretaries. He stopped by Roz's office and noticed a note taped to her door—*Out to Lunch. Back at 12:30.* Thomas checked his watch and realized he had some time to kill.

Amidst sections of rolled-up carpeting and five gallon buckets of flooring epoxy, boxes of books and other personal belongings from the faculty offices crowded the hallway. The whole building smelled of new vinyl and contact cement. Thomas fished for his keys as he approached his office, but was surprised to find his door already open. Inside, two workmen were preparing to shuffle his old desk into the hallway.

"Hi, Professor McGrath," the senior workman said. "I'm glad you're here. We were hoping you could take some of your stuff home, at least until we're done with the renovation."

Thomas surveyed the situation from the portal of his office. He noticed that other professors in the building had much more of their stuff piled in the hallway than he actually had inside his office. "I don't understand," he said, somewhat miffed. "I hardly have anything. Why couldn't you just stack my stuff in the hall?"

"We were going to move your books, but it's that stuff over there I thought you'd want to take home," the senior workman said, gesturing to a cardboard box. "We thought it might be too valuable to just leave laying around out in the hall."

Thomas glanced inside the box and smirked. The trip to the office, Thomas knew, hadn't been necessary after all, but he couldn't fault the workmen for their concern. To their untrained eye, the box's contents appeared an invaluable collection of Neolithic artifacts.

"Those things must really be worth something," the workman said with reverence. "We didn't want to leave them out where someone might steal them."

"Is this all you need me to move?" Thomas asked hopefully.

"That's it, Professor. We'll move your books into the hallway. I don't think anyone is interested in those."

Thomas didn't have the heart to tell the workmen the box actually contained worthless knockoffs, so he thanked them for their concern and took the fake artifacts with him.

Carrying his box, Thomas ambled down the corridor and discovered Roz had returned from lunch. "Hi," he said, popping his head into her office. "So, what's so important you needed to see me in person?"

"Sit down, smart ass," Roz directed. "I got a call yesterday from the college president, and…" Thomas' box of stone tools caught Roz's attention. "What have you got there?"

"Projectile points," Thomas replied. He fished out a flaked stone spearhead about the size of a butter dish and handed it to her.

Roz rubbed her thumb along the napped edge. "So, this is what the cavemen used to hunt dinosaurs?"

Thomas weighed whether or not to inform her that dinosaurs had become extinct long before the appearance of humans. "Well…"

"This has got to be a couple of million years old, right?" Roz asked, appraising the spearhead from different angles.

"No. It's just a knockoff. It's only a few years old."

"No kidding? How'd you come by it?"

"I made it," Thomas explained. "I demonstrate stone knapping in Anthropology 101 every semester."

"Wow!" Roz exclaimed, admiring his handiwork. "Is it worth anything?"

"I don't think so. Any trained anthropologist would spot it as a fake. Besides, I…"

"You should try selling it on Ebay," Roz suggested. "I bet you could make a few bucks."

Thomas nodded as he pretended to consider the suggestion. Inwardly, he marveled at the odd administrative structure of Peconic Community College, where, as the only anthropology professor, he found himself subordinate to the chair of the Business and Accounting Department. Thomas wasn't adverse to making money, but he found Roz's tendency to reduce *everything* to a commercial transaction as tawdry. He conspicuously checked his watch. "Listen, Roz. I've got stuff to do. What is it you wanted to see me about?"

"Right," she said, handing back the stone spearhead. "Let's get down to business. We're going to set you up as the faculty advisor for a new student archaeology club. The college president…"

Thomas was aghast at the mere suggestion he take charge of a student club. "Forget it!" he snapped. "Student clubs are a joke. Every time I've tried getting one off the ground it falls apart after the first meeting."

"Yeah, yeah. But this is different. Listen, Thomas. The college president…"

"I'm not doing it," Thomas said firmly. "I'll wind up spending my time organizing activities that no one shows up for. Count me out."

"Shut up and listen, big shot," Roz barked. "I got a call from the college president yesterday afternoon. He said that a *highly* motivated group of NonTrads approached him, practically *demanding* the college organize an archaeology club for them. They seemed to know about your work and asked that you'd take charge of it."

"NonTrads?" Thomas asked, suddenly intrigued.

"As in students of *nontraditional* age. You know—mothers of school-aged children... senior citizens... Don't tell me you haven't heard the term before."

"I know what NonTrads are. It's just..."

"You got something against NonTrads?" Roz challenged.

"No," Thomas replied. "NonTrads are great. They usually make the best students."

"So what's the problem?"

"It's just... I don't get it. All of a sudden, a gaggle of geriatrics shows up out of the blue demanding that I organize archaeology club for them? That's a bit strange, don't you think?"

"Not when you consider the agreement the college signed back in April with *Von Däniken Village*."

"*Von Däniken Village*?" Thomas mumbled confusedly, trying to jog his memory.

"The retirement community out on County Road 51—remember? Oh, for crying out loud, Thomas! I must have sent you a dozen emails about it."

"I've been a little busy, Roz. You'll have to remind me."

The department chair rolled her eyes in frustration. "Well, if you'd read your email, you'd know the college is supporting the governor's 'Life Long Learner' tuition assistance program. We've agreed to run a shuttle bus between *Von Däniken Village* and the college so that the residents can more easily attend classes."

"The college is in the red and *we're* providing a shuttle bus for *them*?" Thomas asked. "Why?"

"Because under the governor's initiative, senior citizens qualify for full tuition reimbursement. It's a win-win situation."

"How so?"

"Well, just think about it—instead of sitting around doing jigsaw puzzles, bored seniors can attend college classes for nothing. The governor buys the senior citizen vote by paying their tuition and we get all the money. The cost of running a shuttle bus is a drop in the bucket and everybody comes out ahead in the end."

"Except the taxpayers," Thomas grumbled.

"Hey! Asses in chairs equals money. If you want to get paid, the college has to rake in more dough."

Thomas thought about the new furniture and carpeting in his office and marveled. He had long since given up trying to understand the logic of college administrators. He checked his watch again. "Let's get back to this archaeology club you mentioned."

"Yeah. So, the president told them you'd run it."

Thomas thought for a moment. The possibility of advising a club of mature archaeology enthusiasts intrigued him, and he pondered how gratifying it might be to finally lecture to a group that actually *wanted* to learn something about ancient civilizations. This seemed all the more appealing when he considered how, in just a few weeks, most of his time would be taken up lecturing to recent high school grads entirely disinterested in anything scholarly. Yet, as appealing as this seemed, Thomas was miffed that the college president and his department chair assumed he'd take on the responsibility without first being asked.

"By the way," Roz interjected, "your first meeting is this Tuesday."

"That's unacceptable!" Thomas snapped, rising to his feet. "You people can't order me about this way!"

"Sit down," Roz advised.

"Don't tell me what to do! I am not an *employee*. I am a scholar—a tenured member of the teaching faculty. Neither you nor the college president can order me around like some underling!"

"You should think this through, boy-o."

"And may I remind you that it's still summer? The nerve that you'd think I'd do this on my own time!"

"I think it would be in your best interest to reconsider," Roz said. "The president is really committed to accommodating those codgers from *Von Däniken Village*."

"Tell the president *I* said he can go chase himself," Thomas replied indignantly.

Roz leaned back in her swivel chair and smiled. "OK," she said with a malevolent twinkle in her eye. "I'll tell the president you've declined."

Thomas was about to launch into another tirade but caught himself. As Roz's words sunk in, he felt both a sense of triumph and a faint twinge of disappointment, since a part of him had warmed to the idea of working with mature adults. Yet, on principle, he couldn't let the college administrators push him around and he was unsure how he should respond. "Well…" he stammered, "OK then."

Roz nodded reassuringly. "I'll inform the president of your decision. He'll be disappointed, but I'm sure he'll understand."

Thomas looked at her blankly. "Is that it? We're done?"

"We're done. I'll see you in September. Enjoy the rest of your vacation."

"Yeah," Thomas murmured as he turned towards the door. "I'll see you next month."

"Don't forget your box of rocks," Roz said, pointing to the collection of projectile points.

Thomas was disappointed that the verbal jousting ended. He enjoyed those rare times he got to vent his spleen with the higher-ups, and Roz's easy acquiescence left him crestfallen. He was almost out the door when Roz called to him. "There's one more thing," she said without looking up from her paperwork. "You're putting in for a sabbatical, aren't you?"

"That's right," he replied cautiously.

"Well, I just want to remind you the application must be submitted by October 1st."

"So soon? You realize I'm taking my sabbatical *next* year, don't you?"

"Yes, I know. But the college president needs time to review your paperwork before making his recommendation to the board of trustees. The board must approve it before the Spring semester so we'll have enough time to find a 'temp' for next fall."

Thomas cringed. He hated when Roz used corporate terminology about academic matters.

"Of course," she continued, "there's no guarantee the board of trustees will approve your sabbatical."

Thomas was taken aback. "Just what are you getting at? Why wouldn't the board approve my sabbatical?"

"Well, from what I understand, the board is reluctant to grant sabbaticals since they place a financial burden on the college. Of course, if the president is batting for you, everything should go smoothly."

Thomas realized his predicament. If he wanted his sabbatical, he couldn't afford to slight the college president. Moreover, he regretted the impulsive way he rejected the offer to advise the archaeology club. After all, here was a group of mature adults—active retirees, perhaps not much older than himself—who shared his interests in archaeology and were genuinely enthusiastic about attending his lectures. Why, then, was he so quick to rebuff this opportunity? If he went along, he knew for certain the president would have no choice but to endorse his sabbatical request. What's more, he knew if he secured the president's good will, Roz would have very little leverage over him in other matters. He now pondered how he might acquiesce and still save face.

"Well," Thomas said with nonchalance. "I'll submit the paperwork as soon as the semester begins."

"That will be fine," Roz replied, stone-faced. "See you in September."

Thomas turned towards the door but stopped short. "By the way," he said over his shoulder, "I'm almost done writing my book."

"Good for you," Roz said, sorting through a pile of papers on her desk. "Do you think you'll sell any copies?"

"Well, I was just thinking. Perhaps it might not be a bad idea to meet with this new archaeology club. The publisher expects me to hit the lecture circuit and this group might serve as a good springboard."

"That's not a bad idea," Roz said, playing along. "You could use the new archaeology club as a focus group to refine your sales pitch. Those old folks must know other people interested in buying a book about bones and rocks and maybe they can help you do a little networking."

Thomas fought back every impulse to say something snide. "Those are my thoughts exactly."

"So you'll take on the archaeology club?"

"Yes," Thomas replied guardedly. "It might prove intellectually rewarding."

"That's great!" Roz remarked triumphantly. "I'll let the president know. As I said, your first meeting is Tuesday, seven p.m."

Thomas placed the box of faux artifacts on the passenger seat and climbed behind the wheel of his pickup. Suddenly, he felt overwhelmingly fatigued. He placed the key in the ignition but could not muster up the energy to start the truck. So far, this had not been the relaxing day Roxanne had prescribed. Between the stress of overwork, the alarming news of Tremayne's real estate development, and now, this contentious meeting with Roz, Thomas was about to crash. He took a deep breath and closed his eyes. *So much to do*, he thought. *The book deadline… the court hearing… now this…* Thomas drifted into sleep, if only for a few minutes. The sound of his own snoring roused him, and, waking with a start, he grabbed the steering wheel and jamming his foot on the break. Confused, he looked around and realized he was motionless in the college parking lot. He looked down again at the box of bogus artifacts and breathed a sigh of relief.

Thomas was plagued by vexing thoughts as he drove home. *Tremayne… Book deadline… Archaeology club…* "Archaeology club," Thomas uttered aloud. He thought about the upcoming meeting with the NonTrads from *Von Däniken Village* and smiled. In spite of herself, Roz was probably right. The archaeology club *was* good news for a change. He knew nothing about the demographics of *Von Däniken Village*, but he envisioned a conference table surrounded by well-dressed, well-read and well-off adults in early retirement. Rubbing shoulders with these scholarly enthusiasts would prove a welcome change from the post-adolescent dullards who made up the majority of the student body. Thomas allowed his mind to wander over a range of gratifying possibilities. *Museum visits... Guest lecturers... I could even organize a local dig.* "An archaeological dig," Thomas mused, thinking of his planned sabbatical and of the excavation he hoped to conduct in New Mexico. "Grant money to fund my field work," he remarked aloud. "I bet these folks have deep pockets."

Thomas happily daydreamed, and for a while, forgot about his troubles.

CHAPTER 4

Daphne glanced back and forth between the computer screen and a glossy coffee-table book titled *Italian Art and Architecture.* She spent the morning surfing the internet looking for the perfect image and for the last half hour had been cutting and pasting, clicking and dragging, and now everything was almost perfect.

"Rococo," Daphne repeated aloud as she worked. "Rococo… Rococo…" She manipulated the mouse and elongated the rectangular picture on the screen. She resized the image a few more times and considered the different aspect ratios. "Rrrrrrrrrococo…" she trilled. "Rrrrrrrrrrrro—Coo—Cooooooooo…" Achieving the perfect balance between width and height, she pressed the enter key and saved the changes. Daphne leaned back and sighed. "Exquisite," she said, admiring her work.

"Did you call my name?" a secretary from across the room whined loud enough to be heard over the faulty air conditioner fan.

"No," Daphne called back, her reverie broken. "I don't even know your name."

"I'm Rayette," the secretary honked through inflamed sinuses. "I thought you called my name."

"No. I said 'rococo'."

"Oh. I don't know anyone named Rococo. I'm Rayette."

"Got it."

"My grandmother was named Rayette."

"Great!" Daphne said, turning her back on the woman.

The office of the Country Squire Development Corporation was located in a nondescript professional building on the edge of Stirling Harbor, sandwiched between a dog groomer and a tax prep office. The only indication the address was occupied was a placard taped to the inside of a grimy plate glass window that simply read *DBA CSDC.* The inside bore little resemblance to the traditional image of a corporate headquarters, given the shabby walls, threadbare carpeting and folding tables that served as desks. Daphne hated the drab surroundings and looked forward to sprucing things up. Proper desks, a coat of paint and new carpeting were all in order. And a new sign too! That ugly little DBA placard would have to go. Country Squire was worthy of much better, and Daphne prepared to spare no expense. An entire office makeover was necessary, but that cow Candice Brennan wouldn't even consider it. She'd only been with the company a few days and already acted like she was in charge. Anyway, Candice would be here soon, and Daphne planned to let her know who was boss.

"Hi, Rayette," Candice said as she entered. She noticed Daphne standing a few feet away, casting an angry scowl. Candice decided she was in no mood. "Hey, Daphne," she said striding past. "Why don't you take the day off? We'll call you when we need you."

Daphne gasped. "You… You… I have a bone to pick with you!" she stammered, following Candice towards the back office.

"Not today. I'm busy."

Daphne caught up to Candice at her makeshift desk. "Listen, Candice," she said, wagging a finger. "It's time you realized your place. *I'm* the Senior Sales Agent."

Candice was intently searching amidst a pile of papers she'd pulled from a document portfolio. "We have nothing to sell yet," she said without looking up. "Go home."

"That's just the point," Daphne rejoined. "How can we sell anything if you keep wrecking all my hard work?"

Candice found the papers and looked them over again. She made a few corrections in pencil before finally looking up. "What in the world are you talking about?"

"I want to know what you did with my sign," Daphne demanded.

"I had it taken down. We don't want the publicity."

"We'll never sell anything with an attitude like that!"

"Listen, Daphne. We've got a very important permit hearing on Thursday and it would be good for Country Squire if you took a vacation until then. Better yet, why not take the rest of the month off?"

The thought of being dismissed from her own business filled Daphne with rage. "And who put you in charge, bossy?"

"Your husband, Vincent," Candice replied.

"Oh? Well, you ought to know I had a little talk with Vincent. I told him all about how bossy you are and how you try to run everything."

"That's what a president does, Daphne."

"Yes, well Vincent told me you're only supposed to be in charge of little things like hiring construction workers and putting in sewers. He said you're supposed to handle all the minor details but that I'm the Senior Sales Agent."

"Right. Remind me again—what is it we sell?" Candice asked, feigning ignorance.

"Condos!" Daphne shrieked in frustration. "Country Squire Condominiums!"

"But there *are* no Country Squire Condominiums. And do you know why?"

"OK smarty pants, why?"

"Because they haven't been built yet."

"See! That's because you're not doing your job," Daphne cried. "Vincent told me you're supposed to hurry up and finish so I can get down to what's important. So, lets get going. Chop-chop!"

"Get out of my way," Candice said, pushing past on her way to the front office. Intent on explaining to Rayette the changes she needed to make to the documents, Candice noticed a van in the front parking lot and a delivery man hefting boxes onto a hand truck. As he approached, Rayette, mustering some effort, squeezed out of her chair and assisted by holding the door open.

"Good morning," the man said as he maneuvered the hand truck inside. He double-checked the invoice on his clipboard and skeptically looked around the sparse office. "I'm not sure this is the right place. Is this Country Squire?"

"Who are you?" Candice demanded.

"Stirling Printers. I've had a hell of a time finding you. I've got a delivery for Daphne Tremayne."

"I'm Daphne Tremayne, the Senior Sales Agent."

"Great," he said, handing her the invoice. "Sign here."

Daphne grabbed the clipboard and scribbled her signature.

"What's all this?" Candice asked.

"Postcards," the delivery man said as he slid the hand truck from under the boxes. "Five thousand of 'em."

Daphne gleefully ripped open the top box and withdrew a handful of postcards. She gasped in admiration while Candice chased after the delivery man. "Hold on, fella!" Candice demanded. "Get these things out of here!"

"Sorry, ma'am. That girl already signed for them." He was gone in a flash.

Candice stormed back inside. "Let me see that," she said, snatching up a postcard. Candice recognized that the card bore the same picture as the Country Squire sign she had taken down. "What crap!" she exclaimed.

"You obviously don't know anything about advertising," Daphne rejoined.

"I know bad artwork when I see it," Candice quipped. "This is a catastrophe. Did you design this?"

"I most certainly did. I learned AutoCAD in college."

"You studied drafting?"

"Marketing," Daphne corrected. "*I* have an Associates Degree."

Candice scrutinized the image on the card more closely. "This looks like a cartoon drawing of a neo-colonial mini-storage. And what's with this ridiculous fountain?"

"It's a replica of the *Fontana di Nettuno* in Bologna," Daphne replied with affected Italian pronunciation. "It is a model example of the Mannerist taste of the courtly elite in the mid-sixteenth century," she haltingly added, repeating a description she'd memorized word for word.

"Good Lord!" Candice exclaimed. "It's a white elephant."

"No, it's King Neptune standing atop a pedestal surrounded by cherubs and nereids," Daphne corrected with the air of the *cognoscenti*. "It's rococo."

"But it's out of place. It doesn't belong here."

Daphne rolled her eyes. "Duh! King Neptune is the god of the sea. We're on an island, remember?"

"But architecturally it doesn't fit. We're planning to go with a colonial motif for Country Squire. What's a classical fountain doing here?"

"It's rococo," Daphne corrected.

"It doesn't matter. The two styles clash. They don't belong together."

"That just shows how little you know. If you studied art, then you'd know it's entirely possible because rococo comes before colonial. It's a proven fact."

"So what?" Candice challenged.

"So, that means rococo and colonial won't clash, just so long as rococo comes *first*," Daphne said, believing she'd scored a victory.

Candice was impassive. "I still don't get your point."

Daphne heaved a sigh. "Rococo came first, right?" she posited Socratically.

"Right."

"Well, imagine the rococo fountain was built there first, and then people came along a hundred years later and built condominiums around it. That way it fits. If you did it the other way it would be an anarchism."

Candice took all this in, trying to wrap her brain around Daphne's logic. "An *anarchism*?" she asked.

"Yes," Daphne replied with self-assurance. "Colonial buildings couldn't possibly come before anything rococo. That would be an anarchism."

Could she mean 'an anachronism'? Candice thought. She reconsidered Daphne's bizarre logic and found the whole proposition too convoluted to sort out. "Well, whatever the case, you'd better leave this sort of thing to the professionals. After our architects consult with the Water Department engineers they might decide against including a fountain in the final plans."

"No, no!" Daphne corrected. "Vincent told me I could have any kind of fountain I wanted—and I told him I wanted the most beautiful fountain in the world."

"But Daphne, we haven't even decided what architect we're using, let alone any final design plans. This talk about a fountain is premature."

Daphne began turning red. "That fountain is going to be our biggest selling point. And since I'm the Senior Sales Agent, it's up to me. We're going to have a fountain. It's going to be rococo… and its going to be the *Fontana di Nettuno*. And that's final!"

"We'll see," Candice said. "In the meantime, don't mail any of these postcards."

Daphne smirked. Inwardly, she gloated knowing these postcards were actually the second shipment in an order of ten thousand. She'd already mailed the first lot from the corporate offices of Tremayne Fuels a week earlier.

"And stop wasting money on crap like this." Candice looked at her watch. "I have an appointment with the Village Assessor in twenty minutes. What did I do with those papers?"

"Don't look at me," Daphne said in a huff.

"Damn, I had them just a few minutes ago." Candice gave a quick look around the sparsely furnished office. "Rayette, look around and see if you can find those papers."

"What papers?" Rayette asked.

"It's a copy of the strategic development plan from the *Von Däniken Village* project," Candice replied. "I've added a few things we're going to have to do differently for Country Squire."

"What should I do when I find them?" Rayette asked.

"Just edit in the changes and save it on CSDC letterhead. I'll probably have to fine tune it a little before sending it to Mr. Tremayne." Candice checked her watch again. "I've got to go," she said as she made for the door. "And Daphne, don't do anything while I'm gone."

Daphne's nostrils flared as Candice drove off. Rayette immediately began rummaging through the odd papers and workplace detritus that littered the sparse office. "Help me look for those papers," she said. "Are you sure you haven't seen them?"

Daphne still hadn't regained her composure. "Who are *you* to give orders? I'm the Senior Sales Agent!"

"Oh," Rayette honked innocently. "I just thought maybe you could help."

"I've got far more important things to do!" Snatching up her invoices and a handful of postcards, Daphne headed towards her workstation.

Daphne thought she'd call Vincent and complain about Candice, but she remembered the phone system in this miserable little office hadn't been hooked up yet. She could use her cell phone, but for some reason her calls always dumped into the Tremayne Fuels voicemail system. She thought about driving across town to pay Vincent a visit, but then… on second thought… she felt so listless. Maybe she should take a break and play *Cake Mania* for a while. As she considered her options, Daphne began doodling on one of the invoices. The big-eyed image of an *anime* fairy soon took up half the page. She'd become so engrossed in sketching the billowing folds of the fairy's flowing cape that she almost completely shaded in the text across the top of the page. She squinted to read what was underneath her artwork. *Von Däniken Development Corp. Strategic Plan*, the headline ran. *Wait a second*, she thought. *These are Candice's papers!* Daphne craned her neck and saw Rayette still fussing about. She coyly looked back to the document and casually scanned its contents. Although her artwork made reading more difficult, she realized she'd accidentally come to possess a detailed list and timetable of everything needed to complete the construction phase of Country Squire. The document ran on for three pages and contained a number changes written in pencil. Daphne marveled at her good fortune. *With these instructions, who needs Candice Brennan?* she mused. *I can do all this myself.*

Daphne thumbed deeper into Candice's papers, finding a printout of an email from Martin Farquhar dated the day before. In it, Martin advised that certain "delays" had arisen regarding the capital loan and that until matters were straightened out, "necessary work on the development must proceed," but that it was of the utmost importance to "cut costs and keep expenses low." Daphne pondered what this meant. She didn't know exactly what a capital loan was, but Martin's instructions were clear enough: *necessary work must proceed.* As Senior Sales Agent, she resolved to follow Martin's instructions, even if it meant finding a way around Candice's procrastination. She stealthily stuffed the papers into her *Louis Vuitton* bag.

Daphne had settled into a captivating session of *Farm Frenzy* when her cell phone rang.

"Is this Country Squire Condominiums?" a woman asked unceremoniously. Daphne sensed an edge of urgency beneath the woman's southern accent.

"Yes!" Daphne vivaciously replied. "This is Country Squire. I'm Daphne, the Senior Sales Agent."

The woman at the other end muttered something unintelligible.

"Excuse me?" Daphne begged.

"Yeah… I just got this postcard and I want to know a few things," the woman said in a clipped drawl.

"Certainly," Daphne chimed officiously. "Are you interested in a one or two bedroom unit?"

"Just tell me when you plan to start building. You haven't started yet, have you?"

"Well…" Daphne began haltingly. She was so angry at Candice for all the needless delays. Here was her first customer and she didn't even have a model condo to show.

"Come on! Out with it!" the woman on the phone barked. "Are you building yet or not?"

"Not exactly," Daphne hedged. "You see…"

"What do you mean 'not exactly'? Give it to me straight."

"We're going to put in the fountain first. That's our number one priority."

"The fountain?" the woman on the phone gasped. "You mean this thing on the postcard?"

"Yes," Daphne gushed. "Isn't it lovely? It's going to be the artistic centerpiece of Country Squire."

"Good God!" the woman exclaimed. "You're not joking. This thing's for real?"

"Oh, it's real alright. It's a replica of the *Fontana di Nettuno* in Bologna. It's rococo."

The woman on the other end of the phone grumbled unintelligibly again.

"I'm sorry," Daphne said. "I missed that."

"How big is it?"

"Well… It's going to be *really* big."

"How big, dammit?" the woman demanded.

Finally, Daphne thought, here was someone who shared her passionate for art. Given the woman's agitated tone, Daphne surmised she harbored fears that the fountain might be of inadequate proportions, and thus, not visible from every condo unit. She thought fast and pressed her bluff. "It'll be bigger than the original in Bologna. By the way, that's in Italy, in case you were wondering." Daphne could hear the woman muttering what might have been curse words.

The woman on the other end of the phone cleared her throat. "So, when are ya'll going to erect that thang?"

Daphne realized she had to act fast if she hoped to close the deal. "Any day now," she said with conviction. "And I promise, once the fountain is in, you'll have no problem seeing it from the furthest edge of the Country Squire property. Once we cut down all the trees…"

"Cut down all the trees?" the woman shrieked.

"Yes," Daphne assured. "Once all the trees are gone and the area is cleared, there'll be nothing to block a clear view of the fountain—even from beyond the property line."

"I can't believe this!" the woman exclaimed.

"It's true! Really! And you have my word I'm going to personally see to it that we install the fountain this week. Would you like to set up an appointment for me to show you around?"

"Make an appointment? You've got to be kidding?"

"No, ma'am. The customer always comes first at Country Squire," Daphne said inanely. "I'll be happy to call and set up an appointment just as soon as…"

"Don't bother! You'll be hearing from *me* real soon!" With that the call abruptly ended.

Daphne was disappointed that she let a prospective customer wiggle off the hook. One thing was certain—that fountain was a major selling point. The whole Country Squire enterprise couldn't afford to go another day without it. The time had come to take action.

Daphne withdrew Candice's papers from her bag and examined Martin Farquhar's email again. *"All necessary work on the development must proceed, but it is of the utmost importance to cut costs and keep expenses low,"* she mumbled.

CHAPTER 5

Thomas shuddered with unease as Roxanne paced the kitchen floor and barked into the telephone. She clenched an oversized postcard in her hand and glanced back and forth between it and Thomas as she spoke. It was uncharacteristic for Roxanne to swear, and Thomas found her murmured vulgarities disconcerting. At length, after an awkwardly contentious exchange, she slammed down the phone. She spun towards Thomas with rage in her eyes.

"This postcard came in the mail on Friday!" Roxanne barked. "Why didn't you show it to me sooner?"

"I'm sorry, Roxy. I've been so busy lately I haven't paid much attention to the mail."

"I've noticed. You've taken to just tossing it in a pile by the phone and leaving it for me to sort out." She waived the postcard angrily in her clenched fist. "My God, Thomas! I never realized it could be as bad as this."

Thomas took the postcard and examined the picture on the obverse side. "That's the same picture that was on that billboard on the Main Road."

"Just look at that," Roxanne remarked as she snatched the card back from him. "That *hombre* with the pitch fork is buck naked!"

"I think they call that a trident," Thomas said.

"And there's a gang of naked boys messing around beneath him," Roxanne observed. "What sort of twisted pederasty is this?"

Thomas shook his head woefully.

"Those Tremaynes must be real perverts," Roxanne continued. "Just look at that close-up!"

Thomas scrutinized the detailed inset on the postcard.

"That mermaid's bosoms are as big as beach balls," Roxanne cried. "And there's water jetting from out them udders. My God, Thomas! If I'm to be assaulted with pornography like this when I look out from my porch, I'm fixin' to clear off and move back to El Paso."

Roxanne's home state of Texas appealed to Thomas, but he was not willing to retire to the dusty plains for good. "Let's not do anything rash," he cautioned.

"Thomas, you're about as even tempered as a fart in a fryin' pan. When I got home from work on Friday, you were fit to be tied over them cutting down the woods. The next day I find you slung in a hammock reading some nonsense about skeletons in New Guinea. How can you be so blasé about this?"

"I'm just saying not to panic. This might all come to nothing."

"How can you say that?"

"I noticed yesterday that they took down that billboard," he responded. "Maybe Tremayne got cold feet and changed his mind about the development."

"Oh yeah? Well I just got off the phone with that bimbo wife of his, and she said they're planning to put up that monstrous fountain sometime this week. It's full steam ahead, Thomas."

"Good heavens!" he muttered gravely.

Roxanne looked at her watch. "I'm going to be late for work. Help carry my stuff to the boat."

Thomas followed Roxanne as she strode quickly down the short path from the house to the tidal creek where the boat was docked. He waited until she was aboard before passing the tote bags across the gunwales to her. She lowered the twin outboards into the water and set them at idle as Thomas untied the spring lines.

"What are you planning to do today?" Roxanne queried as the boat slowly drifted from the dock.

"My first order of business is coffee at Silvio's. I'm going to talk to Jack."

"That anarchist?" Roxanne cried. "I thought he skipped town."

"Not yet. He said he might have some legal advice for us about stopping the development."

"You'd be better off trying to press more neighbors into showing up on Thursday," Roxanne advised. "There's strength in numbers."

"I'll do my best," Thomas vowed.

"And don't forget to pick up those pamphlets at the print shop," she called as she shifted the engines into forward. "We need to enlist more people into the coalition."

"Will do!" Thomas said, flashing two thumbs up. He watched as she deftly maneuvered through the narrow boat channel towards the open water. Once clear of the tidal creek, she throttled up, casting a foamy wake as she set course for the Makanhassett reservation on the other side of the bay.

Thomas met Jack at Silvio's Café early on Monday morning as planned. The aroma of roasting coffee filled the air, dispelling some of the melancholy Thomas still harbored. After greeting Silvio, he wended his way towards the back and found Jack at their usual table on the patio.

"Where's Fergus?" Thomas asked.

"Fishing, I think," Jack replied. "How was your weekend?"

"Miserable. When Roxy found out about the development project, she immediately went to work organizing the *Save the Bayview Woods Coalition.* When she wasn't on the phone, she was dragging me all over the neighborhood, knocking on doors. I couldn't get any other work done."

"Other work? Knowing you, I'm surprised you could set your mind on anything else. The way you tore out of here on Friday I thought Roxanne might have to sedate you."

"I have certain academic commitments, you know," Thomas replied with umbrage.

"How could you possibly think about your book at a time like this?"

"It's not the book," Thomas explained. "I'm organizing a student archaeology club. We're meeting for the first time tomorrow and I'm trying to put together an introductory lecture."

Jack looked puzzled. "But it's still summer."

"It's a long story. Anyway, I think Tremayne must have heard about Roxy organizing the *Save the Bayview Woods Coalition* because he took down the billboard along the Main Road. At first I thought he might have gotten cold feet and abandoned the project."

"I wouldn't count on that," Jack advised. "Someone must have convinced Tremayne of the need to avoid publicity. He's probably just trying to cover his tracks before the hearing on Thursday."

Thomas exhaled deeply and slumped in his chair. "You're right," he conceded. "Roxy managed to get through to that idiot Daphne Tremayne on the phone this morning. From what she found out, the development project is moving into high gear. Good heavens, Jack. What am I going to do?"

"I've been giving this some serious thought. Your only hope is to put in a good showing at that hearing on Thursday and make a legitimate argument why the judge should deny Tremayne his building permits."

Thomas sat upright and nodded. "We're going to put in a good showing, alright," he affirmed. "Roxy already persuaded about a hundred people to join the *Save the Bayview Woods Coalition* and most of them said they'd come to the hearing. Surely the judge will see we outnumber Tremayne and put a stop…"

"No, Thomas. That's not what I meant," Jack explained. "Having supporters at the hearing is indeed a good thing, but you must remember this is not a popularity contest. The court is not interested in the democratic will of the majority, nor should it be."

"Why not? This *is* a democracy, isn't it?"

"It's a republic, actually," Jack lectured. "Now listen! Before going into that hearing, you need to get a few things into your head. You must be aware that our whole theory of jurisprudence is rooted in the ancient principle of Natural Law, and in this system an individual has a natural and inalienable right to own property."

"So what exactly does that mean?"

"It means that anybody, even a scoundrel like Tremayne, has the right to do whatever he wants with his own property—no matter what an angry, pitchfork wielding mob like the *Save the Bayview Woods Coalition* thinks."

"Then what hope do I have?"

Jack took a swig of coffee and produced a yellow legal pad from under his folded newspaper. "I did a little research, and as I see it, you don't have many options. I found nothing in Article Nine of the Uniform Commercial Code that can help you, and I wouldn't even bother trying to make a case under the State Code concerning Real Property."

"Why not?"

"Because the Real Property Code actually works in Tremayne's favor."

"Well… What about the Constitution?" Thomas whined desperately. "Isn't there some way we can nail Tremayne on a civil rights violation?"

"I already told you the Constitution has nothing to do with this," Jack said firmly. "If you even mention it during the hearing, the judge is liable to hold you in contempt simply for wasting his time."

"Then it's hopeless! I'm doomed!"

"Get a hold of yourself."

"But you said I have no options."

"I said you don't have *many* options. But you do have a few, and I think I've stumbled across your best bet."

"What is it?" Thomas begged. "Tell me what I can do to put a stop to this."

"Alright. I think Roxanne and her 'save the woods' group should try their hardest to convince the judge that Tremayne will do irreparable damage to the environment if the court allows him to cut down all those trees. Tell her they should to come up with some story about the need to save the habitat of the great northern chipmunk or some other balderdash like that."

"You think that'll work?" Thomas asked skeptically.

"Probably not. But it might be worth a try. Of course, Tremayne's lawyers will be ready for that line of argument."

Thomas arched an eyebrow quizzically. "You really think that's our best bet?"

"No, that's just your opening move. If the judge doesn't buy the 'endangered sparrow' argument, then you move on to Plan B and hit him with the heavy artillery."

"Which is what?"

"Do you remember our conversation with Fergus last Friday?" Jack asked. "He mentioned that he hadn't been out fishing with the Fairchild brothers because the Makanhassett councilmen were all tied up with the sale of *tribal land*."

"Right. Which they sold to that rat bastard Tremayne, who wants to clear-cut it and ruin my life."

"Yes. Well, I came across something very interesting in the State Code you might fall back on."

"But you just said the State Code works to Tremayne's advantage."

"That was the article having to do with Real Property. This is from Article Eighteen, Section Eleven, titled 'Parks, Recreation and Historic Preservation'."

Thomas sensed Jack was on to something. "Tell me more."

Jack scanned the notes on his legal pad. "Listen to this. The State Code says, and I quote, '*any lawfully constituted state, county or municipal court may review and comment upon any action under its jurisdiction requiring permits or variances, pursuant to Section One Hundred Six of the National Historic Preservation Act of 1966'…*"

"Save the poetry," Thomas said wearily. "Just cut to the chase."

"Alright. Here's the important part... '*upon completion of any cultural impact assessment deemed necessary by the court, the court may uphold, rescind or nullify all permits and variances as otherwise provided by law where it appears that any aspect of the action may or will cause any change, beneficial or adverse, in the quality of the historic, architectural, archeological or cultural character of places deemed historic or cultural as listed in Section One Hundred Six, Paragraph Twelve of the National Historic Preservation Act*'..."

Thomas tried to process the significance of all this. He was about to ask a question when Jack held up a silencing finger.

"Before you say anything," Jack advised, "I must add one important point. I reviewed the appropriate sections of the National Historic Preservation Act, especially where it defines historic and cultural landmarks. The list contains things you'd expect like cemeteries, battlefields, and public monuments. Guess what else it includes."

"Tell me."

"'*Land, monuments or gravesites associated with any aboriginal person or persons, groups or tribes*'," Jack quoted, "'*including, but not limited to, those defined as American Indian, Eskimo, Inuit, Hawaiian or Pacific Islander*'..."

Thomas gasped as the significance of Jack's council became clear. "Let me see if I got this straight. Are you telling me that the court is going to shut down this development fiasco because Tremayne is planning to build on what *used* to be Makanhassett tribal land?"

"Not exactly," Jack replied. "What I'm saying is that the judge has the authority to delay the issuance of any permits until a Cultural Impact Survey of the building site is completed."

"And if the survey reveals anything of historical or cultural significance, the court can close the development down for good?"

"Exactly. It's not a sure bet that the court will go to that extent, but it might order the reduction of Tremayne's buildable footprint."

"Why didn't I think of this myself? I don't know anything about the legal mumbo jumbo you just quoted, but I do know something about Cultural Impact Surveys—the field work portion, I mean. It's something my guys do."

"You mean your fellow anthropologists?" Jack clarified.

"Yes. Specifically, the professional archaeologists. I assisted in a few surveys during my graduate school days, but I always thought courts order them *after* something significant was uncovered."

"I think that only applies to accidental discoveries on land not clearly associated with any aboriginal group. Let's face it, the Indians were everywhere, and people nowadays are bound to turn stuff up unexpectedly."

"You don't know the half of it!" Thomas grumbled. "Most Indian grave goods on the black market come from plundered sites that were uncovered accidentally."

"Is that right?" Jack asked.

"Sure. You always hope that backyard gardeners and construction workers will do the right thing and report any surreptitious finds, but sometimes greed and self-interest get the better of people. I've even heard rumors about a group of workers on the South Fork who uncovered human remains while digging a foundation. Rather than report the find and face delays, the foreman tossed the bones into the wet cement and told his crew to keep quiet about it."

"That's terrible," Jack said. "But in this case, you don't have to wait for something to turn up in order to petition the judge for a Cultural Impact Survey of the woods. That land undisputedly belonged to the Makanhassett Tribe up until a few weeks ago. If you raise this point during the hearing on Thursday and request a Cultural Impact Survey, I can't see how the judge can deny it."

Thomas gave this some thought. "So far, so good. But what happens if the court orders a survey and nothing culturally significant turns up? What then?"

"Well, that could be a problem. If the survey doesn't turn up anything, then Tremayne can reapply for his permits, and there'll be no reason for the court to deny their issuance."

Thomas heaved a sigh. "So, it's all a big gamble then. The results of the survey might come up snake-eyes."

"Yes. But you have to remember—by asking for this survey you're going to delay Tremayne's building plans for God knows how long. Take it from me. In the construction business, delays cost money. If you're able to drag things out long enough,

Tremayne might think it worthwhile to cut his losses and abandon the project."

"But then again, he might be willing to wait things out."

"Well, we can only speculate. But as I said before, you don't have many options, and I think this one is your best bet."

Thomas nodded his assent. "Alright. Then that's the hand I'm going to play."

"I wish I could be there to petition the judge for you," Jack said. "But we're leaving for Boston tomorrow morning. I've got reservations for the eight o'clock ferry."

"I wish you could be there too, but you've been more than helpful. At least now I have a good plan for going up against Tremayne."

"The best of luck to you!" Jack said as he raised his coffee cup and belted back the last dram.

Thomas returned the toast by doing the same. "If there's any way I can repay you for all the legal advice, please…"

"There is," Jack said gruffly. "Buy us another round of coffee."

CHAPTER 6

In an overgrown meadow, less than twenty yards from the edge of the North Road, a gnome leered from behind a tangle of raspberry briars. His gaze was transfixed on a demure toad sitting cross-legged with lady-like poise on a grotesquely disproportioned mushroom partially obscured by tufts of sea grass. A short path led further through the unruly undergrowth to a neglected lily-pond, across which lay a narrow causeway camouflaged to resemble the arched back of a sea dragon. Nearby, shrouded by encroaching bows of holly, stood Merlin in weatherworn raiment bedecked with fading crescents and stars, as if frozen since the moment of his entrapment by the Lady of the Lake. The wizard's sad plight was surveyed at a distance by a pointed-eared pixie from her perch atop a moss covered windmill, long rendered motionless through disuse. Brambles and vines enclosed the surrounding acre, slowly swallowing the scattered griffins and kelpies that once enchanted visitors to this glade. Standing watch over all, like a motte and bailey castle along the frontier of this otherworldly realm, stood an enormous, icing covered cupcake. A sign that once greeted wayfarers still stood in front of this pastry donjon bearing a faded but still visible salutation—*Welcome to the Fairy Glen Miniature Golf and Family Fun Center.*

A man wearing a white tee shirt and jeans lurked among the elves. In a remote corner of the Fairy Glen, he hacked at a stand of chokeberry with a pair of pruning shears until, after much effort, a long forgotten púca sprung forth to prance the earth again. The man mopped his sweaty brow before bending to clear away the ivy that entangled the hooves of the equine sprite.

Inside the cupcake a gaunt man sat before a Formica desk upon which were arranged at least a dozen Bakelite rotary telephones. Wires cascaded over the side of the desk, connecting the whole array to a cluster of phone jacks at the base of the concave, faux wood-paneled wall. Beside the desk, a bay window afforded a nearly panoramic view of the bramble-covered golf course. Condensation from a poorly mounted air conditioner beaded down the wall and saturated the discolored carpet, filling the interior of the cupcake with the aroma of mildew. Except for the rattle of the air conditioner compressor, the room was silent. The old man for the moment had nothing to do but wait. After some time, the man with the pruning shears pushed open the Dutch door and entered the cupcake, disrupting the old man's vigil.

"Boss, this no work," the man said, holding forth the pruning shears.

The old man reached up and adjusted his loose dentures. "What's wrong with it?" he asked through gritted false teeth.

"It's no cutting," the man replied. "Better to smite grasses with the whacker, no?"

"The weed whacker is busted," the hunched, skeletal man said. "Make do with that."

"It needs to sharp first," the workman advised.

The emaciated man grumbled as he considered the dilemma. "Alright. There's a file around here somewhere."

Both men began searching around the circular room when one of the telephones rang. It took three tries before the old man answered the correct one. "Yeah?" he growled into the mouthpiece, omitting the customary salutation.

"Is this Louis Nickels Cut-Rate Excavations?" a woman inquired.

"Yeah," the man said, adjusting his dentures again. "This is Louis Nickels. Who is this?"

"I'm Daphne Tremayne, Senior Sales Agent at Country Squire Condominiums. I got your name out of the phone book."

"What do you want?" Louis Nickels demanded.

"We're rapidly moving forward with our construction project and we need a wooded area cleared. Can your firm do that?"

"Yeah. When do you want it done?"

"Right away. We're installing the *Fontana di Nettuno* this week and we must clear out some trees. It's an exact replica of an exquisite rococo masterpiece from Italy and it's going to be the centerpiece of our development. Perhaps you've received our advertisement in the mail?"

"No," Louis Nickels replied curtly. "How big of an area do you want cleared?"

"Uh... I don't know. Pretty big, I guess."

"Well, from the sound of it, it ain't gonna be cheap."

"But your ad in the phone book promises you'll undercut the competition. Are you really a cut-rate excavator or not?"

"Cut-rate excavations—that's what we do!" Louis Nickels snapped. "But we charge by the square foot and we don't work for free. Get the point?"

"Clearly. But we need the work done right away. Can you do it?"

"Yeah. If you show me what you want done we'll get right on it."

"Today?" Daphne asked optimistically.

"I just said 'yeah,' didn't I? Are you gonna show me at the jobsite or not?"

Daphne gave him directions to the woods and suggested that they meet in about an hour. "Is that OK?"

"Yeah," Louis Nickels replied. "Now listen! Let's get one thing straight. Time is money. There'll be a surcharge if you keep us waiting around—and don't even think of stiffing us! Got it?" Satisfied with the woman's promise to be on time, he hung up.

"Hey boss, the file avoids to finding," the younger man said after searching around the circular room.

"Forget that, Moon," Louis Nickels said. "We just got a job."

"What kind of job?" Moon asked excitedly.

"Excavating," Louis Nickels responded as he doffed his Homburg. "Where's the Bobcat?"

"Behind Stonehenge. What to do now?"

"Roll it onto the trailer. I'll drive the Edsel around back and we'll hook it on to the ball-hitch."

Daphne was beside herself with excitement. Finally, things were moving forward—and no thanks to that cow Candice. She thought a momentous occasion such as this should be marked with fanfare, like a ribbon cutting ceremony or something. But what if Candice found out? Surely she'd try to put a stop to it simply out of jealously. But Candice wasn't here, and chances are she wouldn't find out about everything until it was too late. Maybe she should call that reporter from the paper and get her to run another story. Ha! Wouldn't that be a hoot? Candice would be green with envy. And what about Vincent? It would be great to surprise him with the news of the groundbreaking, but was it really fair to leave him out of something so special? No, Vincent should definitely be at the ceremony. Daphne checked the time. She needed to make a few calls before meeting with Louis Nickels.

Vincent was looking over the Tremayne Fuels monthly expense reports when the intercom buzzed. "You have a call from Candice Brennan on line one," the secretary announced.

"Hi, Candice. What's up?" Vincent said as he took the call.

"Hello, Vincent. I'm on my way to a meeting at the Village Assessor's office, but I need to discuss a few things with you first."

"Listen, I really want you to play hardball with those bean counters in the Assessor's office. It would mean a significant reduction in our property taxes if you could get them to reassess the Country Squire property for less than it's worth."

"Martin is going to press that issue with them. But that's not why I called. It's about Daphne."

Vincent winced. "Oh, yes," he cooed. "I'm really happy you've agreed to take her under your wing. She was telling me just yesterday how much she loves working with you."

"With all due respect, Vincent, you're full of crap. And I never agreed to take Daphne 'under my wing,' as you say."

"But she is the Senior Sales Agent at Country Squire. Couldn't you just..."

"No! Now listen," Candice interrupted. "You hired me to manage the construction phase of Country Squire because you know I'm damn good at what I do."

"That's right."

"Well, I'm telling you it's almost impossible for me to get any work done with Daphne underfoot. I've been on the job less than a week and it seems like I've spent half that time arguing with her over what color to paint the office bathroom."

"She's always had a knack for interior decorating," Vincent replied.

"I don't care. It would be amusing to have her around if she stuck to silly things like picking out curtains for the model condo. But she's meddling in sensitive matters. If something isn't done to reel her in, she could shipwreck our chances of getting the permits we need."

"Oh, come on. You make it sound so ominous. What has she done that's so bad?"

"Well, for starters there was that poorly timed newspaper story she leaked. Then there was that ugly billboard she posted out on the Main Road. Publicity like that is our worst enemy at this stage since it's sure to bring out the opposition."

"You took the sign down, didn't you?"

"Yes, but not before that stupid thing tipped our hand to the public. And then there's all those ridiculous postcard advertisements she was planning to send. Thank goodness I caught her before she mailed them."

"But direct mail advertising will serve as an effective sales strategy, don't you think? Daphne *is* the Senior Sales Agent, so what's wrong with her planning a future sales campaign?"

"Listen, I agreed to head this project during the construction phase. I really don't care who you put in charge of sales down the road. But, as I reminded your wife, you're not going to have anything to sell unless we first get our permits and then line up the contractors."

"And I'm sure you're going to do a great job in that regard."

"Not if I have to spend all my time babysitting Daphne, I won't," Candice replied.

Vincent sighed. "I'll talk to her."

"And there's another thing. What's up with your capital loan? I got an email from Martin yesterday. He said you've run into delays."

"It's nothing to worry about," Vincent said reassuringly. "Everything is moving forward and we expect to close any day now."

"Let's hope so. Anyway, expenses are going to start piling up, you know?"

Vincent glanced down at the Tremayne Fuels monthly expense reports and cringed. Cash was indeed very tight. "Have no worries," he said. "Everything's covered." Vincent noticed the flashing light on his telephone. "I'm getting another call, Candice. Let me know how things go with the Assessor." Without saying goodbye he cut her off and pressed the intercom button. "What's up?" he asked the secretary.

"Mr. Tremayne, I'm sorry to bother you, but your wife just called."

Vincent reclined in his chair and took up the expense reports again. "What is it now?" he asked with utter disinterest.

"Forgive me, Mr. Tremayne, but she was speaking fast and I'm not sure I caught all of it. She said something about you not wanting to miss the ribbon cutting ceremony today at the Country Squire building site."

"What ribbon cutting ceremony?"

"I thought *you* might know. She also said you might want to prepare a speech in honor of the groundbreaking since the press will be there."

Vincent sat bolt upright. "What groundbreaking?"

"I'm not sure. She said something about clearing a place for a fountain."

"Goddammit!" Vincent cried as he leapt to his feet and ran towards the outer office. "I'll be back," he called over his shoulder as he bolted past the secretary and made for the exit.

As Daphne waited in her SUV for the excavators to arrive, she intently studied the draft of the strategic plan she'd accidently appropriated from Candice earlier that morning. *So much to do*, she thought as she tried to commit its contents to memory. Daphne looked up periodically, eventually catching sight of an approaching black 1950s vintage automobile. She could see the vehicle towed a small bulldozer. As it pulled onto the shoulder alongside her, Daphne noticed a magnetic sign affixed to the driver's side door which read *Louis Nickels Cut-Rate Excavators.* Beneath that, in smaller lettering, ran the company motto: *We Undercut The Competition.*

"I'm Daphne Tremayne, Senior Sales Agent at Country Squire," she said as she stepped out of her SUV. "Which one of you is Louis Nickels?"

"I'm Louis Nickels," the man wearing the black trench coat and hat said though gritted teeth. "Let's get this show on the road."

"Could we wait for just a few minutes? I'm expecting some important people to arrive. We're going to commemorate this very special event by..."

"Listen up, lady," Louis Nickels interjected. "I got a business to run. Show us the area you want cleared, and make it snappy!"

Daphne found it difficult walking through the tall grass in high heels, but managed to show the two men the general area she wanted cleared.

"Alright, Moon," Louis Nickels said, turning towards the younger man. "Get to work."

Moon backed the Bobcat off the trailer and began crawling towards the edge of the woods. Daphne and Louis Nickels watched as he disappeared behind a screen of leaves and a few moments later, the sound of cracking trees could be heard over the roar of the bulldozer's diesel engine. Daphne clapped her hands and jumped up and down gleefully as she regarded Moon's progress. The arrival of a large van on the shoulder of the road nearby diverted her attention from the deforestation. "Fantastic!" Daphne cried. "The caterers are here."

Vincent tore out of Tremayne Fuels' parking lot and sped through the business district of Stirling Harbor. Once on the Main Road, he floored the Porsche and soon came upon a cluster of vehicles parked near the woods. He searched for Daphne among the small crowd that milled about and found her standing next to a well provisioned buffet table.

"Daphne! What the hell is going on here? Who are all these people?"

Daphne was startled by her husband's sudden appearance. "Oh, Vincent! Isn't it wonderful?" she gushed, throwing her arms around his neck. "I'm so glad you could make it. Did you prepare a speech?"

Vincent looked about in angry confusion, trying to make sense of what was happening. He half-listened to Daphne's prattling as he surveyed the scene when seemingly out of nowhere, a wizened man wearing a black hat and trench coat joined them near the buffet. "We're almost done," the man said to Daphne.

Vincent turned to regard the skeletal figure with suspicion. "Who are you?" he asked rudely.

The man in the Homburg returned Vincent's inquisitorial glare with a scowl. He was about to speak when a fit of coughing overtook him. Hunching forward, the man's chest heaved violently as each wheezy exhalation dislodged another oyster-like bolus of phlegm from his respiratory system. At length, he regained his composure and began fishing around in his pockets with both hands simultaneously producing a handkerchief and a business card, the latter of which he handed to Vincent.

Vincent held the card close to read the small lettering. "*Louis Nickels Cut-Rate Cremations*," he read aloud. "*Service with a Smile.*" Vincent looked up from the card to see the man staring back at him through black horn-rimmed glasses. The thick lenses made his pupils appear the size of half dollars. Vincent looked quizzically between the old man and Daphne. "Who died?"

"Vincent, this is Louis Nickels," Daphne explained. "His firm is handling the excavation of the fountain site."

Vincent groped for words as the faint growl of a diesel engine began growing louder, accompanied by the sight and sound of cracking limbs and falling trees. A bulldozer suddenly emerged from the woods and turned towards the buffet table. The driver parked the machine a few yards away and climbed down before helping himself to a plateful of deviled eggs and stuffed endive.

"Are you done yet, Moon?" Louis Nickels asked.

"Mostly," Moon said with a mouth full of food. "Very much clearing of half acre is completion. Nice and flat. But there are stumps."

"Stumps?" Daphne said in dismay.

"Oh, yes," Moon said gravely as he popped an egg into his mouth. "There is one of great mightiness. I strive against it, but it prevails."

Louis Nickels frowned as he considered the options. "Alright, Moon," he said at length. "I want you to go back to the cupcake and get the dynamite."

"No!" Vincent exclaimed. "That won't be necessary."

"Are you trying to tell me my business, mister?" Louis Nickels challenged.

"No, no. Not at all. The stumps are fine where they are. I think you fellows have done enough work for today."

"But it needs to be totally cleared for the fountain," Daphne whined.

"Excuse us," Vincent said to Louis Nickels as he led Daphne away by the arm. "We need to talk."

Vincent took Daphne out of earshot. "What the hell do you think you're doing?"

Daphne sensed Vincent's anger. "Vincent, how do you expect me to sell any condos if there's nothing here for people to see?"

"We need to get permits before we do any construction. We can't afford to attract any attention to ourselves before the hearing."

Daphne demonstrably folded her arms across her chest. "Now you sound like that old hag Candice."

"But Candice is right, Daphne. We've got to keep a low profile."

"Fine! Take her side. Meanwhile, I'm the one who has to turn away customers because we have nothing to show them."

"You've already received inquiries?"

"I get them all the time," Daphne exaggerated. "I even spoke to a woman this morning who hung up on me when she found out there was no fountain yet."

"Really?"

"I keep telling that know-it-all Candice we need to move quicker. But she just won't listen. We're losing sales because of her."

"Daphne, try to understand. Candice is a professional project manager who's worked on a lot of other developments. She knows exactly what needs to be done to get our condos built."

"I know just as much as she does about all that," Daphne declared.

"Oh come on, Daphne," Vincent replied. "She's got years of experience."

"So what? I bet I could do just as good a job as her."

"But there are so many little details."

"You mean like selecting an architect, approving the building plans, surveying the building site, hiring a civil engineer to plan county road access, obtain both village and state permits for the septic system, the electrical lines, the gas mains..." Daphne said with smug self-assurance. She continued rattling off details of the building project, including some things Vincent hadn't even considered. Although Daphne recited the memorized list almost perfectly, she had absolutely no clue what any of it meant.

Vincent was astonished. "How do you know all that?"

"We covered that sort of thing in college," Daphne bluffed. "And I've been doing a lot of research on the internet. Property development isn't rocket science, and there's a lot of information out there if you know where to look."

Vincent stroked his chin as he pondered this.

"I can send you a memo outlining all the details if you want," Daphne added.

Vincent's cogitation was interrupted when Louis Nickels shouted in his direction. "Hey!" he barked, snapping his fingers. "I don't have all day!"

As Vincent and Daphne turned, they noticed that Moon had taken up position in front of the bulldozer and was hamming it up as the reporter from the *Stirling Harbor Gazette* snapped pictures. The caterers had meanwhile festooned the area with red helium balloons and bunting and a few passing motorists that had stopped to check out the hoopla now helped themselves to the buffet.

Louis Nickels stepped towards Daphne. "Here you go, lady. Here's the bill for services rendered. I accept cash only."

"Hold on, mister," Vincent said. "We don't operate that way."

"But me and the blond girl had a deal."

"Excuse me! Excuse me!" the reporter from the *Stirling Harbor Gazette* interrupted. "Could I get everyone together for a group photo please?" As she spoke, she herded everyone into position with the bulldozer serving as backdrop.

"Don't worry," Vincent said as both men stood side by side facing the camera. "You're going to get paid. We just can't pay you in cash."

The reporter took a series of photos, moving people into different positions in an attempt to achieve the perfect shot. Two girls from the caterers' staff took up places on opposite ends of the group and stretched out a bright red ribbon between them.

"Why not?" Louis Nickels asked.

"Because it's all handled through our accounting department," Vincent replied. "You send us the bill, and we pay you by check at the end of the month. Understand?"

Louis Nickels grumbled something unintelligibly. "Well, OK," he relented. "Sign that invoice, lady, and give me the top copy." Daphne did as instructed and handed the bottom copy to Vincent. Louis Nickels looked down at the paper and scowled. "Alright, Moon," he said through gritted false teeth. "Let's get out of here."

"One moment, please," the reporter from the *Stirling Harbor Gazette* interjected. "It's time to cut the ribbon. Who's going to do the honors?" One of the girls from the caterers held forth a large pair of sheers which Moon accepted unabashedly. He looked towards the camera and smiled as the reporter snapped a picture of him cutting the red ribbon.

Thomas spent the better part of the morning drinking coffee with Jack. He looked forward to spending the afternoon at home working on his lecture for the archaeology club, and after picking up Roxanne's *Save the Bayview Woods* pamphlets, headed for home.

Thomas slowed as he passed the so-called Bayview Woods, his eyes drawn to a gaping hole in the tree line. Hitting the brakes hard, he swerved across the double yellow line onto the shoulder. Thomas sprung from his truck and sprinted along the freshly turned ground into a gouged and rutted clearing. Berms of uprooted trees and displaced earth surrounded the perimeter of a circular, flattened area about the size of a baseball infield. As Thomas looked around the nightmarish scene, his eyes were drawn to the far side of the clearing, where a fawn stood eating the green leaves of a toppled tree. Noticing Thomas, the beast came to startled attention before bounding deep into the woods.

Thomas swooned with anger. "Tremayne, you bastard," he grumbled aloud. "You were supposed to wait for a permit before doing this." Thomas spent some time inspecting the devastation, and as he did, his sense of anger gave way to feelings of profound sadness and loss. Having seen enough, he went directly home and reported the violation to the Stirling Harbor Police Department.

CHAPTER 7

Although the first meeting of the archaeology club was scheduled for seven o'clock, Thomas arrived a little early. He'd grown quite excited about meeting these people and hoped to make a good impression from the very start. Yet, in spite of his best efforts to prepare what he hoped would be a compelling inaugural lecture, Thomas had found it difficult to get any work done over the weekend on account of all the hubbub. He'd just have to wing it.

The club was scheduled to meet in the newly renovated conference room on the mezzanine level of the library. Thomas parked in his usual spot and walked the short distance across the quad. Sure enough, he was the first to arrive. Sitting himself down in the comfortable swivel chair at the head of the table, he closed his eyes and enjoyed a few moments of quiet solitude.

Thomas heard the chatter of people approaching in the hallway and felt a surge of excitement. A woman with turquoise earrings poked her head into the room. "Is this where the archaeology club is meeting?" she asked.

"Yes. Welcome," Thomas said rising to his feet. He introduced himself and gestured for everyone to take a seat.

"I'm Sibyl," the woman with the turquoise earrings said.

"Hello, Dr. McGrath. It's so good to meet you," a man with a graying beard said. "I'm Thor Svenson. We've been looking forward to our get-together for some time."

"So have I, Mr. Svenson," Thomas replied as he made a quick head count. "Are there only four of you? I was given to understand that the group was a little bit bigger. Should we wait for the others to arrive before we get started?"

"There are supposed to be a few more people," Sibyl said, "but, um… not everybody could make it this early."

"Ah," Thomas acknowledged. "Well, in any event, I'm glad we have this opportunity to get to know one another."

"So am I," a youthful woman with just a hint of gray in her pageboy haircut said. "My name is Chloe. I've been a big fan of yours for a long time."

Thomas was taken aback. "Really? Have we crossed paths before?"

"Not in person," Chloe replied. "I feel like I know you from the way you write. I've read all your work."

"No kidding?"

"So have I," the fourth person said. "We all have. Excellent stuff! By the way, my name is Casey."

"Thank you, Mr. Casey," Thomas replied with a self-deprecating bow. His anxiety about this first meeting had all but evaporated. "You might be interested to know I'm working on another book right now. I expect it to go to print by the end of the year."

"We know," Sibyl said. "We're very excited."

"We're really looking forward to reading it," Thor Svenson added. "You know, we specifically sought you out as our club leader."

"Yes, I was told you'd approached the college president about forming this club," Thomas replied. "It's nice to know other people have a genuine interest in archaeology."

"Yes. How true," Thor Svenson said. "But I think you miss my point. I met with the college president and specifically asked for *you*—by name—to be our club leader. We're very taken with your theoretical approach."

Thomas was intrigued, yet a bit confused, since Social Scientific theory was something that generally bored him. "I'm gratified, but I'm not really sure I understand."

"Your article on the Solutrean hypothesis was a *masterpiece*," Chloe purred. "Totally iconoclastic!"

"And your piece on the Kensington Runestone was… was…" Casey said, groping for words, "It was fantastic!"

"The Kensington Runestone paper? My God, I'd forgotten about that. That was a conference paper I delivered when I was in graduate school back in the '80s. I think I chaired a panel discussion on OOPArt."

"OOPArt?" Thor Svenson asked.

"Yes, OOPArt. It stands for *Out of Place Artifacts*," Thomas explained. "Every so often someone will discover an artifact that's seemingly out of place—like a wristwatch in an Egyptian tomb. Most of the time they're the result of site contamination by careless field workers. Often, though, these 'artifacts' turn out to be intentional hoaxes. But in a few instances the evidence is inconclusive and we're left with an archaeological anomaly."

"Interesting," Thor Svenson said.

"But your article about the possible discovery of Neolithic European projectile points in North America was much more recent," Chloe said with a smile. "I think your call for a reappraisal of the 'Beringia Only' migration model was *so* thought provoking."

"Well, that's very kind of you," Thomas said. "But I was only arguing that the anthropological community should wait for more evidence before dismissing the Solutrean hypothesis out of hand. I believe the current research is still inconclusive, though."

"But you *do* believe there was pre-Columbian contact across the Atlantic, don't you?" Thor Svenson asked.

"Of course," Thomas affirmed. "Without a doubt."

"So, you think the Kensington Runestone is genuine then?" Casey asked.

"Well, to be honest, I've never argued that the Kensington Runestone was proof of Norse migration deep into North America. The point I was making in that paper was that the traditionalists who argue for a 'Beringia Only' pre-Columbian migration route into the Americas need to let the evidence support the theory and not vice versa. Even if the Kensington Runestone proves a hoax, it's still necessary to examine it with the same curiosity one would show any newly discovered archaeological anomaly. You always have to entertain the possibility that a find might be genuine, even if its veracity threatens to overturn the assumptions of the status quo."

"So, what exactly *do* you believe about the Kensington Runestone?" Thor Svenson asked. "Could it be genuine?"

"It's possible," Thomas conceded. "I never followed up on it seriously, but I've read some journal articles here and there. From what I gather, the best evidence tends to demonstrate it's a hoax."

"But you're not sure," Sibyl observed. "You won't dismiss the possibility it might be real."

Thomas sighed. "You know, there's a part of me that really *wants* to believe it's real. This field has become too stodgy. It would be fun to shake things up with the discovery of something *revolutionary*."

"Agreed," Thor Svenson remarked. "It's that kind of thinking that brought us together. The reason we sought you out is because of your willingness to approach things like this with an open mind."

Thomas marveled. Things were turning out far better than he expected. Not only were these people well-read, but they were passionate and intellectually provocative. What a refuge this club would be from the workaday grind of teaching disinterested freshmen. "You folks are very kind."

"Well, Dr. McGrath," Thor Svenson said. "I believe we're off to an excellent start." The other three enthusiastically nodded in assent.

"I'm very pleased you think so," Thomas said. "However, I must admit, I've been somewhat derelict in my duties regarding this club."

"How so?" Thor Svenson asked.

"Well, I hoped to have an inaugural lecture prepared for our first meeting. Unfortunately, my department chair informed me about this club just a few days ago and I haven't had time…"

"That's not important, Dr. McGrath," Thor Svenson replied with a dismissive wave. "There'll be plenty of time for that kind of thing in the future. What we were really hoping for was something more akin to a roundtable discussion."

Thomas was relieved to be off the hook. "Great," he said.

"We thought you might moderate a little debate we've been having," Casey said. "We'd love to bounce a few ideas off you."

"I'd be delighted," Thomas replied with relaxed ease. "What's on your mind?"

"We've been discussing archaeoastronomy," Sibyl said.

"No kidding? That's an arcane subject, even for professional archaeologists."

"But the role astronomy played in shaping ancient cultures is just so fascinating, don't you think?" Chloe opined.

"I do," Thomas replied. "But it's important to keep in mind that many critics of the discipline argue that much of archaeoastronomy is mere speculation, given the lack of supporting textual evidence."

"But you're more receptive of the subject," Sibyl said.

"I would say so," Thomas agreed. "Remember that anthropologists specializing in American Indian civilizations work within an established cultural context. We know Indian peoples used certain monumental architecture and artifacts for astronomical purposes because the Spanish wrote about it shortly after the conquest. For instance, I've been researching the missionaries' accounts of South American sun worship and its relationship to regional planting and harvesting patterns. I'm particularly interested in the Inca use of solar observatories to…"

"…establish the seasonal agricultural cycle in the Lake Titicaca region," Sibyl said, nodding thoughtfully.

"Yes! Exactly!" Thomas exclaimed. "How did you know that?"

Sibyl shrugged and batted her eyes. "I'm clairvoyant," she said with a chuckle.

"Amazing," Thomas marveled. "Anyway, enough about my interests. What is it you folks wanted to discuss?"

"We were hoping to get your take on the Antikythera mechanism," Casey said. "What are you able to tell us about it?"

Thomas sat back and rubbed his chin thoughtfully. "Mediterranean archaeology isn't my field, but I'm familiar with the basic facts—it's an intricate bronze device with a clock-like mechanism and it was found about a hundred years ago by sponge divers on a shipwreck off the Greek island of Antikythera. I think the latest research indicates it functioned as some type of calculator that could correlate lunar and solar cycles and predicted eclipses."

"Yes. But *why*?" Thor Svenson asked.

"Eclipses were considered bad omens by some ancient peoples," Thomas replied. "Perhaps it was used to predict inauspicious events."

"That's one theory," Chloe said. "But I can tell you there's much more to it than that. Did you know that researchers have found twenty seven gears in the mechanism? They speculate there were probably even more gears and the device could accurately predict the motion of the planets."

"It's an impressive technological marvel," Thomas stated. "I'm sure it's going to keep researchers busy for years."

"Well, I have reason to believe the Antikythera mechanism also had the ability to accurately calculate polar precession," Sibyl remarked.

"You mean the complete revolution of the celestial North Pole?" Thomas asked. "That takes thousands of years, doesn't it?"

"Twenty five thousand, seven hundred and seventy two," Sibyl replied.

Thomas considered this. "That would seem like quite a difficult thing to do, given the size of the mechanism itself. Wouldn't there have to be a huge gear in it to calculate something over such a long time period?"

"Not if the Antikythera mechanism was only part of a much larger device," Chloe replied. "Maybe it's just a small piece of something much bigger, like a memory chip in a computer."

"I suppose that's possible," Thomas conceded. "But I couldn't say for certain. As I say, Mediterranean archaeology isn't my field. Even so, I've never seen evidence that the Greeks developed anything that sophisticated."

"What makes you think the Antikythera mechanism is Greek?" Casey asked.

Thomas was taken aback. "It has Greek lettering on it."

"Well that's another matter entirely," Casey remarked. "But getting back to the point—tell me, from your recent analysis of the solar alignment of the Mayan pyramid at Chichen Itza, wouldn't you agree that..."

"Whoa!" Thomas exclaimed. "How did you know I've been researching Chichen Itza? I haven't told anybody about that!"

"I'm clairvoyant too," Casey said, meeting Thomas' gaze directly. "Anyway, we know that the *Chilam Balam* prophesies state that the god Kukulkan is supposed to return during the winter solstice and there's compelling evidence from the Mayan Calendar that this was scheduled to occur in 2012. You do realize this correlates with a major transition point in the polar precession cycle, don't you?"

Thomas repressed a condescending smirk. *There's one in every crowd*, he thought. "Well, the Mayan Calendar is very interesting," Thomas said diplomatically. "But I think all that talk about the end of the world was debunked last year when the solstice passed without incident."

"That is precisely what we wanted to discuss with you, Dr. McGrath," Thor Svenson said. "We're hoping your insight might help us put some of these foolish assumptions about ancient astronomy to rest once and for all."

"Well, whatever the case, it's always important to keep an open mind," Thomas said, treading lightly so as to not trample on Casey's feelings. "Ancient mythology and archaeoastronomy are interrelated fields, but I never put much stock in doomsday prophesies. My interest in the solar observatory at Chichen Itza has to do with the study of ancient agricultural cycles—along the same lines of what I've been working on with the Incas."

"Oh come on, Dr. McGrath," Casey said. "You must have given some thought to the *Chilam Balam* prophesies. If you consider the Mayan long count calendar, all indications point to..."

"Please, Casey!" Sibyl said. "Dr. McGrath is clearly not interested in all that silly business. The Antikythera mechanism has nothing to do with Chichen Itza."

"I'm not the one making that claim," Casey fired back. "But we know without a doubt the Mayans accurately calculated the length of the polar precession cycle. And if you're right about the Antikythera mechanism having the same capability, the implications are mind-boggling!"

"We've been through this so many times," Sibyl said wearily. "This was supposed to be a serious discussion about..."

"Hold on," Thomas interrupted. "I don't understand what you're saying. Casey, are you arguing that the Antikythera mechanism might have come from Chichen Itza?"

"Don't be ridiculous!" Casey said with a hearty laugh. "What kind of nut do you take me for?"

"I just wanted to be clear," Thomas said with relief. "No offense, but you'd never believe the crackpot theories we have to deal with in this field."

Everyone around the table laughed. "Oh, I have no doubt, Dr. McGrath," Thor Svenson said mirthfully.

"That's just crazy!" Casey exclaimed. "The Antikythera mechanism couldn't possibly come from Chichen Itza."

"That's right," Thomas affirmed.

"It came from Palenque," Casey remarked. "It was part Lord Pakal's spaceship."

A pained groan went up among the others seated at the conference table. "Casey is fixated on the Maya," Chloe said.

Thomas was unsure about how he should respond to this obvious fallacy. It was not uncommon to come across folks with far out beliefs about ancient astronauts, and Thomas usually just laughed them off. But to do so in this instance brought with it a host of complications. Was it worth it to risk alienating a member of so small a group, especially during the club's first meeting? If Casey thought Thomas dismissed his beliefs out of hand, might he withdraw out of sour grapes? And what of the other members of the group? If Thomas failed to offer some correction, might he lose credibility as a serious scholar? He decided to play the diplomat as much as possible.

"You know, I've been to Palenque," Thomas remarked. "I did the field work for my doctoral dissertation in southern Mexico."

"Then you know what I'm talking about," Casey said.

"I've even gone down into the Temple of the Inscriptions to see Pakal's sarcophagus up close," Thomas explained. "I can certainly understand why some people might think the stone carvings look like a man in a space capsule."

"See!" Casey said to the others. "I told you he'd agree with me."

Thomas took a deep breath. "But there's a couple of problems with your theory, Casey, the most important of which is chronology. Pakal lived hundreds of years after the Antikythera mechanism was lost at sea. If he did have a space ship, the Antikythera mechanism couldn't have been on it."

"But you're leaving out the important capabilities of advanced technology," Casey contended. "The mechanism itself was the guidance system of a time travel machine."

Thomas glanced at the other members of the group and noticed that Sibyl shook her head in disgust. "Casey, when are you going to listen to reason?" she said. "What you're saying is just so bizarre."

"What makes you think your idea is any better?" Casey fired back.

"Well, for one thing it doesn't involve time travel," Sibyl replied. "Unlike you and your friends on the lunatic fringe, my conclusions are based on *reason*."

Thomas was relieved by Sibyl's level-headed response. It was better that a rebuttal of Casey's outlandish claims come from someone within his own circle of friends. "I take it you have a different opinion?" Thomas asked probingly.

"Of course," Sibyl replied. "The Antikythera mechanism was undoubtedly Greek—probably from the city of Syracuse."

"I think I read something about that," Thomas said. "Isn't there a theory kicking around that it might have been invented by Archimedes?"

"Yes," Sibyl replied. "But establishing provenance only solves part of the riddle. The question remains as to what its *purpose* was."

Thomas nodded. "That's going to be difficult without the ability to place it in a clear cultural context."

"Not at all," Sibyl contradicted. "We have enough evidence simply from the number and size of the gears to determine its purpose. It's really quite obvious."

Thomas pondered this. "I'm sorry. I don't follow."

Sibyl sighed with exasperation. "They found twenty seven gears in the device, right?" she asked impatiently.

"I think that's what Chloe said a little while ago," Thomas replied. "She would know better than me."

"Well, we know that each of those gears had an odd number of teeth," Sibyl explained. "But these are not just odd numbers, they're *prime* numbers to be precise. Nineteen, fifty-three, two twenty-three, and so on."

"OK," Thomas said tentatively. "I still don't see your point."

"Well, it's obvious then. There couldn't have been only twenty seven gears because twenty seven is not a prime number. It's simple math, for Pete's sake! If you take the ratio of the first seven gears starting with the smallest and divide each by *pi*, then multiply the results by the ratio of each successively larger gear, you still only wind up with a fractal of the largest gear which, as we've already established, is twenty seventh in the sequence, which is not a prime number…."

Thomas' eyes began to glaze over.

"This proves my point," Sibyl continued. "There had to be additional gears with exponentially larger ratios, each of which exactly corresponded to the total number of teeth within the entire mechanism, divided by the square root of *pi*, and multiplied to the power of seven. It's so simple even a child can see the implications!"

Thomas winced. "The total number of teeth in the mechanism?" he asked, utterly confused.

"Which can be determined algebraically, of course, by letting x stand for that number," Sibyl said matter-of-factly. "It's just a matter, then, of solving the equation backwards."

Chloe giggled mirthfully as she scratched out a series of equations on a notepad. "See?" she said, pushing the notepad towards Thomas.

"Marvelous," Thor Svenson muttered. "Simply marvelous."

Thomas glanced at the notepad. "I'm not a mathematician. I still don't get it."

"The number adds up to twenty five thousand, seven hundred and seventy two," Sibyl remarked. "The exact number of years to complete a cycle of polar precession. If you divide this by twelve you come up with two thousand, one hundred and forty seven point six years."

Thomas shrugged. "So?"

"So if we calculate the number of sidereal years in the last arch of precession," Sibyl explained, "it demonstrates that the Antikythera mechanism was used to predict the exact moment the new celestial age would begin. The calculations don't lie. As of December twenty first last year, we have entered the Age of Aquarius! The stars are finally in alignment!"

"Big deal!" Casey exclaimed. "I could have told you that."

"*La de da*," Sibyl taunted.

"Clearly, it all adds up," Chloe interjected, "but the Antikythera mechanism isn't from Syracuse."

"No?" Thomas asked.

"No. It's from Atlantis," Chloe declared.

"You're as crazy as he is!" Sibyl exclaimed, pointing to Casey.

"Folks, I'm sorry," Thomas said. "I applaud your enthusiasm, but I don't think I can contribute to this discussion. I'm an anthropologist, not a mystic."

"Don't be so modest, Dr. McGrath," Chloe said playfully.

"Listen," Thomas said. "I don't believe in any of this. Atlantis is a myth."

A gasp of shock simultaneously arose from those sitting around the table. "That's blasphemy!" Thor Svenson cried.

"I was born in Atlantis," Chloe declared. "I still have family there."

"Excuse me?" Thomas asked in wide-eyed disbelief. "Are we talking about the legendary continent that was swallowed by the sea?"

"That's a fairy tale," Chloe said. "Atlantis is located inside the Earth. Everyone knows the Earth is hollow."

Thomas checked his watch. "I think it's getting late."

Chloe smiled seductively at Thomas. "Don't be so coy, Dr. McGrath. You know as well as I do the Earth's crust is only two hundred miles thick. The inside surface is concave, with continents and oceans, just like the convex outside surface. That's where Atlantis is."

"And you were born there?" Thomas asked, playing along. "How did you wind up here?"

"The Antikythera mechanism," Chloe declared. "We Atlanteans use them to open inter-dimensional portals between the two worlds. You see, the harmonic convergence that occurs during certain astronomical alignments allows us to…"

As Chloe spoke, the sound of footsteps came from the hall. "I think the room is this way," an approaching voice said. A man poked his head into the room and frowned. "They're in here," he said, calling over his shoulder. "Sorry we're late. Wasn't the shuttle bus supposed to leave at 7:30?"

Sibyl rolled her eyes as the two men entered and helped themselves to vacant chairs. Thomas sensed a palpable tension as the other members of the archaeology club sat in awkward silence. "There must have been some misunderstanding," Thor Svenson said after an icy pause.

"Hello, Dr. McGrath," the first man said. "I'm Dr. Carl Schuyler. This is my research assistant, Gus Armstrong."

"Pleased to meet you," Thomas said, reaching to shake hands with the newcomers.

"Apparently you were in the middle of some discussion," Schuyler said with feigned good humor. "So sorry to interrupt. Please go on."

Chloe glanced up with a look of guilt mixed with fright. "It's not important, really. We were just getting ready to head back to *Von Däniken Village*."

"No. I insist," Schuyler said with an authoritative air. "Continue."

Chloe fidgeted and looked down at her hands. "I was just saying that during times of harmonic convergence, we use the Antikythera mechanism… you know… to travel back and forth…" Chloe looked up at Thomas with a furtive glance.

Schuyler drummed his fingers on the table. "To Atlantis?" he asked accusatorily.

"That's right!" Chloe cried, jutting her chin forward. "To Atlantis!"

Schuyler glared at her, letting the full weight of his silent indignation erode her defiance. At length, Chloe looked away. Schuyler looked from face to face before observing Thomas' weary countenance. "Am I right to understand," he asked in low, grave voice, "that you've been wasting Dr. McGrath's precious time with crackpot talk about Atlantis and the Antikythera mechanism?"

"We've been exchanging theories in an open forum," Thor Svenson explained. "After all, that's the purpose of this club."

"I'm sure Dr. McGrath thinks you're all a bunch of flakes," Schuyler exclaimed. His confederate, Gus, sat stone-faced.

"You may recall, *Doctor* Schuyler, that we sought out Dr. McGrath because of his open-mindedness," Casey said. "He is willing to consider a variety of opinions, unlike some other so-called scholars I could name."

"And may I remind *you* that Dr. McGrath is a *serious* anthropologist who is highly respected by the academic community?" Schuyler rhetorically asked. "And I for one find it disgraceful that you've subjected him to your brand of nonsense."

"We were having a very enlightening conversation until you arrived," Sibyl remarked. "And I'm sure Dr. McGrath would agree with me on that. Wouldn't you, doctor?"

"And *I'm* sure Dr. McGrath was just being polite," Schuyler replied. "If I were in his position, I would have walked out on you a long time ago."

The confrontation had reached such a pitch that Thomas thought it best to defuse things by changing the subject. "Dr. Schuyler, I take it from your title that you have an academic background. Are you an anthropologist?"

"No. My Ph.D.'s in Biology. I studied at Université Heuvelmans in Brussels."

"Ah," Thomas intoned noncommittally, knowing nothing of the institution. "What brings you to archaeology, then? Does it touch upon your professional interests somehow?"

"Indeed, it does," Schuyler replied, in a composed, collegial tone. "For the last ten years or thereabouts I've been researching the decline of the Neanderthals and the appearance of Cro-Magnon man in the Upper Paleolithic period."

"Interesting," Thomas said. "That's a hot topic among the physical anthropology crowd. Some of my colleagues who got their start on Upper Paleolithic digs have branched into DNA analysis and there's a pretty active debate right now about the degree to which Cro-Magnon hunter-gather communities absorbed the Neanderthals."

"That's putting it mildly," Schuyler said. "It's more of a *hatchet fight* than a debate. Where do you stand on the matter?"

"That's not my bailiwick," Thomas conceded. "As I was telling your friends a little while ago, my area is Amerindian archaeology. The furthest I go back is about 11,000 years to the Clovis culture of New Mexico."

"Well, surely you have to teach about the Neanderthals in your Anthropology 101 classes," Schuyler said. "How do you approach the subject?"

"I pretty much defer to the experts," Thomas said. "The generally accepted theory is that the Neanderthals died out about thirty five thousand years ago, but there's some evidence they might have survived a bit longer in Spain."

Gus, who to this point had been sitting silently, burst out laughing. Schuyler shook his head and chuckled condescendingly. "Just a bit longer in Spain, huh? What about other parts of the world?"

Thomas was taken aback by Schuyler's confrontational manner. "I don't follow the latest developments in Neanderthal research. I really couldn't say."

Gus leaned sideways and whispered something to Schuyler who listened in thoughtful consideration. After conferring for a few moments in hushed tones, the two men turned their attention back towards the group. "What would you say if I told you we have evidence of Neanderthal migration to North America?" Schuyler asked.

Thomas' temple began to throb. "I would say..." he began cautiously, "...that you are probably mistaken. Neanderthals never migrated to the New World."

Gus cast Schuyler a sidelong glance. "What if I told you we have incontrovertible evidence that colonies of their descendents still inhabit the continent?" Schuyler inquired.

Thomas scanned the faces of the other club members and found their expressions inscrutable, with the exception of Thor Svenson, who was beaming with delight. "I really wouldn't know what to say. I find the entire proposition incredible."

Gus drew a large manila envelope from his satchel and handed it to Schuyler.

"Oh yeah? Take a look at these," Schuyler commanded, withdrawing a stack of glossy, eight by ten photographs from the envelope. "Now what do you have to say?"

Thomas glanced at a blurry black and white photo but could discern no recognizable image. "What am I supposed to be looking at?"

"That, sir, is a photograph of an adolescent *Gigantopithecus canadensis*," Schuyler said with theatrical flourish. "That picture was taken last night in the Pine Barrens with an infrared camera, not more than three miles from this very spot."

Thomas buried his face in his hands.

"Spectacular!" Thor Svenson warbled. "Truly magnificent!"

"Let me see those," Casey demanded, snatching up the photos. He scrutinized the image as Chloe peered over his shoulder.

"Is this what I think it is?" Chloe asked in wide eyed wonder. "Could it really be?"

"There's no doubt about it," Schuyler replied. "That, my friends, is photographic proof of the existence of Sasquatch."

"Oh, God," Thomas moaned.

Casey frowned as he sifted through the stack of blurry black and white photos. "This proves nothing."

"Oh yeah?" Schuyler rejoined. "What do you think of this?" As he spoke, Gus withdrew a shoebox from his satchel and tossed its contents on the table. "Just look at that turd! From its form and size, it could only be the feces of an adolescent Mid-Atlantic Appalachian Sasquatch. I've collected a dozen specimens just like it from the surrounding forestland."

"Wow!" Chloe exclaimed. "That's amazing."

"Dr. McGrath," Schuyler declared, "I demand that you have the college laboratory run a full DNA analysis of this stool sample."

"You're all out of your minds," Sibyl said in disgust.

Casey tossed the photographs on the table. "This is nonsense. These photographs are useless and that poop proves nothing."

"How dare you!" Schuyler said, rising to his feet. Casey rose to face him eye to eye, as did Gus and Sibyl and a heated shouting match ensued. Chloe bent forward and poked through the feces with a pencil.

As Thomas slipped into a morose funk, Thor Svenson leaned over and tapped him on the shoulder. "Thank you so much, Dr. McGrath," he said in hushed tones as the argument raged overhead. "I believe we have accomplished so much during this first meeting of our club. I'm sure I speak for the others when I say how much we've enjoyed our discussion, and when I see the college president tomorrow, I'm going to suggest he make arrangements for our club to hold meetings here at least once a week."

CHAPTER 8

Most real estate insiders would agree that running an outfit as small as Country Squire was beneath the caliber of someone like Candice Brennan. She could've had her pick of jobs anywhere, yet, most other development projects were located closer to the city, in the congested suburbs she'd only recently fled. Since heading the Von Däniken development a while back, Candice grew fond of the rural east end lifestyle and had purchased a weekend house in the area. She always dreaded the Sunday evening return to the urban rat race, so when the offer came to head up Country Squire, she jumped at it. Now she had second thoughts.

Upon their very first meeting, Candice realized Daphne was an idiot. She'd met young trophy wives before and generally harbored no resentment towards them, but Daphne was a nuisance. Her impulsive indiscretions and eagerness to sell non-existent condominiums threatened to derail the entire Country Squire development project. That would be bad enough were it not for Vincent Tremayne's indifference. Worse still, Vincent himself really didn't seem that bright. Candice couldn't fault him for not understanding every intricacy of the commercial real estate business. After all, that's precisely why he hired her—to bring her expertise to the table. But for all he offered to pay her, Vincent seemed singularly unwilling to heed her advice, and if he didn't do something about Daphne soon, the ensuing chaos might torpedo the whole project. Fearing this, she gave serious thought to resigning rather than waste any more time on something doomed to fail.

With the permit hearing only two days away, Candice needed to complete some important paperwork. On her way to the office, Candice's route along the Main Road took her past the Country Squire project site. Traffic was light, but as she approached the woods, cars began backing up and traffic came to a slow crawl. As Candice rounded a bend, she observed two patrol cars and at least two dozen private vehicles on the shoulder adjacent to the Country Squire property. At first she feared a nasty pile-up. Drawing closer, she realized it was some sort of demonstration, with crowds of people waving signs that read *Save the Bayview Woods.* In the crowd, a woman with curly red hair chanted through a cheerleader's megaphone, "Permit hearing! Village Court! Thursday morning, nine a.m.!" As she surveyed the size of the crowd, her eyes were drawn to a bulldozed gap in the tree line, just behind the milling mob. She parked along the shoulder and got out to investigate.

Other motorists had stopped and the demonstrators busily handed out leaflets to the growing throng. Stepping through the tall grass towards the edge of the scarred woods, Candice noticed a small group of protesters in the clearing, snapping photos. As she tried to make sense of it all, a man saddled up beside her and pressed a pamphlet into her hand. "Hi, there," the man said. "Are you a local?"

"I live on Holland Point," Candice said. "What happened here?"

"It's a disgrace. They're planning to cut down the woods and put up condominiums. It's just unthinkable."

"But what exactly happened *here*?" she asked, gesturing to the circular clearing.

"It seems as though the builders are planning to install a fountain on this spot. They went ahead without the required permits and bulldozed this section of woods just yesterday. Just wait 'till the judge hears about it!"

"A fountain, huh? Are you sure?"

"I have a picture of it right here," the man said as he withdrew a dog-eared postcard from his pocket. "This came in the mail last Friday and my wife called the number on the flipside. She spoke with none other than the Senior Sales Agent who confirmed it."

Candice immediately recognized the postcard. "Oh, my God," she exclaimed.

"I know! It's horrible, isn't it? Listen—there's a hearing this Thursday at the Village Court and it would be great if we could pack the place. Do you think you could join us?"

"Excuse me," Candice said, ignoring the question. "I need to talk to the police."

"I already reported the incident," the man called as Candice brushed past. "The chief said they're conducting an investigation."

Candice made her way towards the patrol cars and found the policeman with the most gold braid on his hat. "Are you in charge here?" she asked.

"I'm Chief Latham, ma'am. What can I do for you?"

Candice pulled Chief Latham aside and introduced herself as president of the Country Squire Development Corporation. "We have a problem here, Chief," she said gravely.

"I should say so," Chief Latham agreed. "Who is it that authorized the illegal clearing of that patch of woods?"

"I assure you, Chief, I just found out about it myself and I plan to get to the bottom of it," Candice replied. She paused as she looked around at the swelling crowd of protesters and curious passersby. "But I think we have a more immediate public safety concern right now, don't you?"

"As you can see, I have three TCOs directing traffic and two uniformed patrolmen keeping people off the roadway. And there's a detective over there in the clearing talking with representatives of the coalition. I think we have things pretty well under control."

"Coalition?" Candice asked. "What coalition?"

"The *Save the Bayview Woods Coalition*," Chief Latham replied. "I think you folks are in for one hell of a court battle."

Candice swooned with anger but kept her composure. "That may be," she said perfunctorily. "But for now, may I remind you that these people are trespassing on private property?"

"Not if they're on the shoulder," Chief Latham replied. "That's part of the county right of way."

"I was referring to the people beyond the tree line, in the woods," she replied politely, but firmly. "On behalf of the land owner I request that you ask them to leave. It's for their own safety."

"Ms. Brennan, I don't know if you've ever been back in those woods, but they're crisscrossed with walking trails and deer traces. Those trails have been there longer than anyone can remember. Under the law, any continuously open trail or path, even though it passes through private land, is classified as a *public easement* and the usual laws of trespass don't apply."

"So you won't clear those people out?" Candice asked.

"I can't clear them out. Unless the land owner decides to fence in his property—which is entirely his right—those people are free to roam about the woods. Only after an attempt is made by the owner to seal off the easements and enclose the land do the laws of trespass come into effect."

"I see," Candice replied as she shook the chief's hand. "Thank you. I'll be sure to pass that information along."

Candice sped the rest of the way into Stirling Harbor and parked in front of the development office. Stepping from her car, she noticed the inconspicuous DBA CSDC placard had been taken down and replaced by a huge sign bearing an image of the *Fontana di Nettuno* underneath bold letters spelling out the company name in full. "That's it," she mumbled. "I'm out of here." She debated whether she should even go inside, but thought it advisable to retrieve a few personal items from the back office.

Inside, Candice was greeted by the sight of Rayette standing rigidly at attention with arms outstretched while Daphne stooped behind her, violently tugging on her skirt zipper. "Come on," Daphne urged. "Breath in!"

"It's too tight," Rayette whined. "I can't suck it in any more."

"Just a little more… There! Put your arms down now." Daphne stepped back to regard the makeover.

"Why do I have to wear a uniform?" Rayette asked. "I'm just a secretary, not a salesperson."

"Everyone in the company has to wear a uniform. It's a new policy," Daphne replied, as she turned to face Candice. "That goes for you too."

"Hi, Candice," Rayette said.

"Rayette, I'm going to be leaving," Candice stated, ignoring Daphne.

"Oh? Where are you going?" Rayette asked.

"I'm not sure yet. I wish I had something to offer you, but I don't right now. I'll keep in touch, OK?"

"OK," Rayette said sadly.

Candice brushed past Daphne on her way to the back office. "So what's that supposed to mean?" Daphne snapped. "Are you quitting?"

"That's right. I just need to get a few things. It'll only take a moment." Candice gathered up a few papers and made for the door. She lingered long enough to regard Rayette's ample form stuffed into the ill-fitting outfit. Candice reached out and took her hand. "You take care, Rayette."

"Bye," the secretary called as Candice departed.

Both Daphne and Rayette watched as Candice drove off.

"Good riddance!" Daphne exclaimed. "Finally we'll get something done around here."

Rayette slavishly affixed adhesive address labels to a stack of postcards bearing the image of the *Fontana di Nettuno* while Daphne considered carpet samples for the development office. She was trying to decide between the navy and the royal blue when her phone rang. From the caller ID she realized it was Vincent. "Country Squire. Senior Sales Agent Daphne speaking," she said playfully.

"I just got off the phone with Candice Brennan. She's quit. She's not coming back."

"Good! She was nothing but dead weight anyway."

"Yeah, but we've got problems. Candice said there's a bunch of protesters down by the building site. She thinks they might be planning some kind of sit-in."

"Then call the police. Have them arrested."

"Candice said the police won't do anything unless we enclose the land with a fence. That's going to cost a fortune!"

"Let *me* handle that," Daphne said confidently.

"It looks like you're going to have to handle *everything* on the list you sent me. Are you sure you're up to it?"

"Trust me. I can handle it."

"OK. Now listen—we need a fence right away, but we need to do it on the cheap, at least until our capital loan is approved. Understand?"

"Leave it to me," Daphne responded.

"We're also going to need to hire a real estate appraiser to file a tax reduction petition with the Village."

"Yeah, yeah, yeah! I'll take care of it. I'll talk to you later." Daphne left the carpet samples and approached Rayette. "Hey! Do you know anybody who can put up a fence?"

"No," Rayette replied. "Maybe you could check the phone book."

Daphne found the business directory and flipped through the alphabetized pages. *Cut costs and keep expenses low*, she thought as she scanned the fence company ads. Her eyes fell on one ad in particular. "Bingo!" she said, reaching for her phone.

Louis Nickels opened the window and popped his head out of the cupcake. "Hey Moon! Drop what you're doing and go get the post hole digger. We got a job."

Moon was on a step ladder hacking at a tree branch with a pole saw. "What kind of job?"

"Putting up a fence. Unload the scuba gear and the welding torch from the trailer. We've got to make room for the pipe cutter and the cement mixer. I'll meet you around back with the Edsel."

After rummaging around the office for a few minutes, Louis Nickels locked the door to the cupcake and went over to the car. He peeled off a magnetic placard from the driver's side door which read *Louis Nickels Cut-Rate Underwater Welding* and replaced it with one that read *Louis Nickels Cut-Rate Fencing.* He jumped behind the wheel and threw the car into reverse, backing around to meet Moon behind the cupcake.

CHAPTER 9

So many people turned out for the permit hearing that the proceedings had to be moved from their usual second floor conference room to the main courtroom on the first floor. At ten minutes to nine, Martin Farquhar waited on the Village Court steps amidst a murmuring throng of people wearing *Save the Bayview Woods* tee shirts, many of whom were trying to push past the bailiff into the overcrowded courtroom. From his perch, Martin watched with sympathy as an elderly woman, with great difficulty, was attempting to parallel park in front of the courthouse. She was making a third attempt to back into a space when suddenly a black Porsche rounded the corner and quickly slipped into the open spot. Vincent's grin betrayed a malevolent satisfaction as he alighted from the Porsche.

Vincent's demeanor changed as he approached Martin on the courthouse steps. "They can't all be here about Country Squire," he said with concern. "How many hearings are on the docket today?"

"Just yours," Martin replied. "Where's the Senior Sales Agent? Don't tell me she's too busy to attend the hearing."

"She's at yoga. My God, Martin, look at this crowd! What are we going to do?"

"Don't look so surprised. You brought this on yourself. By the way, I've heard Candice Brennan gave her notice."

"There was no notice. She up and quit—over the phone."

"I can't say I blame her. I've given serious thought to dropping you as a client too."

"How could you say that?" Vincent cried. "We're in this together."

"We're *not* in this together," Martin corrected. "I have no stake in Country Squire."

"But we've been friends for so long. You wouldn't just leave me hanging."

"I was friends with your father. You and I are business associates. I'm going to provide you with legal counsel as best I can, but not for free. You already owe the firm of Walsh, Farquhar and Dunn quite a bit of money."

"Good grief, Martin! What's gotten into you?"

"The way things are going, I have no confidence you'll remain solvent long enough to cover my fees."

"But Martin…" Vincent whined.

"It's almost nine o'clock," the lawyer interrupted. "We can't keep the judge waiting."

Martin and Vincent pressed through a jeering crowd as they made their way to the front of the courtroom. Once situated, Vincent glanced over at the leaders of *Save the Bayview Woods Coalition* seated across the aisle and noticed that the organization was headed by Doctor Roxanne McGrath. That idiot college professor husband of hers sat by her side, glaring at him.

"How could you do it, Tremayne?" Roxanne called across the aisle.

"Are you talking to me?" Vincent asked pugnaciously.

"How could you cut down the woods? It's your neighborhood too. Don't you care?"

"I don't know what you're talking about."

"If you cut down the woods you'll lose *your* barrier to the Main Road. Haven't you thought about how it will affect *your own* quality of life?" Roxanne asked.

Vincent chuckled. "I'm not staying in that house forever, Tex. I plan to flip that shoebox and be in something bigger by the end of the year."

"So, to hell with the rest of us then?" Thomas asked accusatorily.

Vincent thought to respond with some adolescent taunt when the bailiff stepped forward and cleared his throat. "All rise! The Village of Stirling Harbor Court is now in session, the Honorable Judge Alan Schulman presiding. All who have cause to plead draw near and be heard!"

Judge Schulman took his seat behind the bench and scowled. "This was supposed to be a simple permit hearing," he grumbled to the bailiff. "What the hell are all these people doing here?"

"There's a citizens' group here in opposition," the bailiff explained. "They request to be heard."

"This court's in session," Judge Schulman said, banging his gavel. No sooner had he spoke than the entire courtroom erupted in a cacophony of recriminations as each member of the *Save the Bayview Woods Coalition* hurled accusations at Vincent Tremayne. Judge Schulman slammed the gavel again with enough force to a drive tenpenny nail. "Everybody shut up while I review this paperwork," the judge shouted. He leisurely picked his nose in silence while looking over the Country Squire permit application. "I don't see what the problem is here," he said at length. "This application seems perfectly in order."

Vincent leered at the McGraths and smiled tauntingly as an agitated murmur rose in the courtroom. Roxanne shot to her feet. "But your honor, you haven't heard our side of things."

Judge Schulman squinted as he fixed his eyes upon her. "Who are you?"

"Roxanne McGrath. President of the *Save the Bayview Woods Coalition*."

"Alright. So what's your beef?"

"Well, that fella Tremayne over there is fixin' to cut down our woods! It just isn't right!"

"They're not your woods, Madam President. And you're going to have to present a better argument than that."

"But look at how many people oppose what he's trying to do. The whole community is up in arms over it."

"That doesn't change the fact that the land is Tremayne's private property. Unless you come up with a material reason why it's in the public interest to deny his permits, I see no reason to stand in the way of progress."

"Yes!" Vincent said, jabbing his fist in the air.

Someone in one of the back rows stood up. "There are endangered species in them woods."

"Like what?" Judge Schulman asked.

"Uh… Deer," the man replied.

"I don't think so," Judge Schulman said snidely. "Try again."

A woman three rows behind Vincent stood up. "Raccoon," she cried.

"No," Judge Schulman said.

"Blue jay," someone blurted out.

"No."

"Ground hog."

"No."

"Box turtle," an elderly woman warbled.

"Not even close," Judge Schulman said.

"Chiye-tanka," a man said with grave conviction.

"You're making that up," Judge Schulman remarked.

"Sasquatch."

"Alright, knock it off!" Judge Schulman barked. "I'm not here to play games. There's nothing endangered out there that couldn't slither to the other side of the road, and you people haven't given me one good reason why I should deny Mr. Tremayne his permits. Unless you come up with something pronto, I'm going to sign these permits and then go try to have a normal bowel movement."

"Your honor, before you do that, there's something important you should know," Thomas said, rising to his feet.

Judge Schulman peered at him suspiciously. "Haven't I seen you here before?"

"Well… yes. But that's beside the point. Your honor, are you aware that Mr. Tremayne has only just recently acquired the Bayview Woods from the Makanhassett Indian Tribe?"

Vincent shot Thomas an angry look. "So what? It was a legal transaction and I paid cash."

Judge Schulman peered down at the two men. "So, what's your point?" he asked Thomas.

Thomas looked at the crib notes Jack had prepared for him. "Your honor," he began. "If I may quote from the State Code, Article Eighteen, Section Eleven titled 'Parks, Recreation and Historic Preservation'…" Thomas proceeded to rattle through the whole section having to do with the protection of culturally significant tribal lands. "…and so, your honor, since Tremayne plans to build on what was indisputably Makanhassett tribal land, I request that you order an official Cultural Impact Survey prior to the issuance of any permits."

Some of the more vocal members of the *Save the Bayview Woods Coalition* loudly seconded the motion. Vincent turned to Martin Farquhar. "What does he want?"

"He wants a State archaeologist to conduct a field survey to see if there's anything of cultural value on your property."

"Anything of value? You mean like gold?"

"Shhh," Martin chided. "Pay attention."

"You seem to have some knowledge of the law," Judge Schulman said to Thomas. "Are you an attorney, Mr…?"

"It's Doctor. Dr. Thomas McGrath. I'm an anthropology professor."

"Egghead idiot," Vincent muttered just loud enough for Thomas to hear.

Judge Schulman frowned as he glanced at the permit application. "Mr. Tremayne, there's no denying that this was once Indian land."

"Yeah, but I bought it fair and square. I don't know what McGrath is driving at."

"There's one more thing, your honor," Thomas interjected. "I believe you have a police report attesting to the fact that Tremayne went ahead without first securing the proper permits and cleared a portion of the Bayview Woods."

"That was just a little mistake," Vincent said dismissively. "And besides, that land is going to be cleared sooner or later." Vincent turned to Martin. "Why are they making such a big deal about this?"

"Shut up and listen," Martin advised.

Judge Schulman reclined. "This puts things in a different light."

Thomas sensed it was time to press his point. "Your honor, in my opinion, the Bayview Woods may sit atop an area of incalculable cultural value."

Something of incalculable value?, Vincent thought. *What's McGrath driving at?*

"But do you have tangible cause to think so, Dr. McGrath?" Judge Schulman asked. "Have you ever found hard evidence of anything valuable back in those woods?"

"Your honor, all I can say is that I've walked those trails hundreds of times and my training leads me to believe that the Bayview Woods most likely contains a treasure trove of archaeological data," Thomas bluffed. He wondered if he was laying it on too thick. "Material evidence from other local sites demonstrates that…"

A treasure trove? Vincent mused. *Has that bastard been poking around my woods looking for treasure?* "Is he talking about a pirate treasure?" he whispered to Martin. "You know, Captain Kidd supposedly landed somewhere around here. Wait—maybe it was Bluebeard."

"You mean Blackbeard," Martin replied in a hushed voice. "Bluebeard was a serial killer."

"Blackbeard then. You think Blackbeard's treasure is buried on my land?"

"For God's sake, shut up."

"…and so you see, your honor," Thomas concluded, "in Mr. Tremayne's haste to illegally clear that land, he may have damaged one of the richest undiscovered archaeological sites on the eastern seaboard. Only a Cultural Impact Survey can determine this."

Judge Schulman thought for a moment. "Dr. McGrath, I'm forced to agree with you. I'm going to grant your request and order the commencement of a Cultural Impact Survey as soon as practicable."

The members of the *Save the Bayview Woods Coalition* erupted in boisterous cheers. Roxanne threw her arms around Thomas and squeezed him joyously.

"Wait a minute!" Vincent cried. "What does this mean? Martin, say something."

"It means we've just shut you down!" Roxanne jeered across the aisle.

"Relax," Martin Farquhar whispered. "It's just a delaying tactic. All they've done is buy a little time." The lawyer cleared his throat. "Your honor, may I suggest a compromise?"

"What kind of compromise?" Judge Schulman inquired.

"Your honor, my client will wait for the results of a Cultural Impact Survey before resubmitting a permit application. In the meantime, we request that Country Squire Development Corporation be allow to go forward with certain 'non-invasive' work while the Cultural Impact Survey is underway."

"Like what?" Judge Schulman asked.

"Well, the footprint of the building site still needs to be surveyed. The Village Assessor has also agreed to readjust my client's property taxes upon submission of a real estate appraiser's property value report. This means the appraiser is going to need to make a site inspection. My client would like to go forward with little things like that."

"That seems reasonable," Judge Schulman opined. "I'm going to rule that Country Squire Development Corporation can go forward with any 'non-invasive' work—and by that I mean nothing that breaks ground in any way—until the Cultural Impact Survey is completed. Fair enough?"

"And then what?" Roxanne asked cautiously.

"That depends on what the Cultural Impact Survey turns up," the judge replied. "It's premature to speculate about that right now."

A delaying tactic? Vincent thought. *Buying time for what?*

"What about a fence?" Thomas queried. "You know he's trying to fence us out of woods? He's got two guys working on it right now."

"He's within his right to put up a fence," Judge Schulman advised. "But just around the perimeter of the property, mind you."

"But now we can't use the trails."

"It *is* private property, Dr. McGrath. You're getting your Cultural Impact Survey and he's getting a fence. Be happy with that."

The fence! He's pissed off about the fence, Vincent mused. *Now I get it. That egghead knows about a buried treasure somewhere on my land and he's probably been trying to find it for years. That chiseler knows we're going to dig it up once we break ground and then he'll have missed his chance. All this so-called Cultural Impact Survey means to do is buy him more time so he can find the treasure before it's too late. No wonder he's so worried about getting fenced out.*

"Thank you, your honor," Martin Farquhar said.

"You're welcome," the judge replied. "Now there's just one small matter before we adjourn. Mr. Tremayne, I'm levying a fine against Country Squire Development Corporation for five hundred dollars."

"What?" Vincent shrieked. "Five hundred dollars? What for?"

"For illegally bulldozing that patch of woods mentioned in this police report. You can square up with the clerk on your way out."

"But… But…" Vincent whined.

"Adjourned," Judge Schulman said, banging down the gavel.

"Five hundred dollars!" Vincent gasped.

"Just pay the fine," Martin Farquhar sneered.

CHAPTER 10

The State Office of Cultural and Historic Preservation had very few professional archaeologists on its full-time staff. For this reason, whenever local jurisdictions submitted requests for Cultural Impact Surveys, the State office would farm out the job to certified archaeologists, many of whom were just doctoral students or adjunct professors looking to supplement their income with temporary State employment. Assignments were made from a rotating list and there was no way to predict which archaeologist would get any particular assignment. It was entirely the luck of the draw, then, that the Bayview Woods Survey had been assigned to Thomas' friend and former student, Lisa Tavolaro-Hennessey.

Lisa had been a student at Peconic Community College more than a decade earlier, where as an entering freshman, she was more or less forced to take anthropology with Professor McGrath. At first disinterested, to her surprise she grew to love Anthropology, and over the next two years signed up for everything Dr. McGrath taught. Lisa decided to make a career of archaeology, and acting upon Dr. McGrath's advice, transferred to one of the more prestigious upstate universities where she earned both a bachelor's and master's degree. Now back on the island, she was in the Ph.D. program at the State University. To build her resume, Lisa worked as an adjunct professor at the university, teaching mostly night classes. Like all graduate students, though, money was tight, and Lisa found it necessary to supplement her income with non-academic jobs like bartending on the weekends. She was always looking for ways to make a buck—all the better in ways that might hone her craft—so when the call came from the State about this Cultural Impact Survey, she took the assignment without hesitation.

Thomas contacted Lisa, who was thrilled to reconnect with her old mentor and the two arranged to meet the next day for coffee at Silvio's Café. Thomas arrived early, and taking his regular seat on the patio, waited for her arrival.

"Dr. McGrath, as I live and breath!" Lisa exclaimed as she came up behind him.

Thomas rose and greeted her with a fatherly embrace. "My God, Lisa, look at you—all grown up and almost a doctor. We have so much to talk about. How've you been?"

People came and went as Lisa and Thomas spent the next half hour discussing her anthropological research, occasionally digressing to commiserate over the joys and miseries of academic life. Over a second round of coffee, Lisa confided that she still loved anthropology, but found teaching a disappointment on account of students' ennui. She found field work fascinating, but funding for archaeological expeditions was hard to come by. In short, a professional anthropologist could do little else except teach, and even at that, full-time tenured positions were as rare as hen's teeth.

"I know," Thomas confided. "I complain about my students all the time, but I'm really very lucky just to have a job."

"Damn straight!" Lisa said in her forthright manner. "And you live in such a beautiful area too. Your gig at Peconic Community College would be a dream-come-true for me—away from the rat race up west, I mean."

Thomas felt guilty every time he caught himself commiserating about his job with an underemployed adjunct. This was compounded when he considered that under the best of circumstances, even his full-time colleagues didn't have it as good as he did—living in an old farmhouse along a private road, peacefully nestled between the woods and the bay. *The woods*, he thought as his guilt gave way to a sense of urgency. Enough beating around the bush. He needed to come to the point with Lisa about the Cultural Impact Survey.

"Yes," Thomas agreed. "You're right. It is a beautiful area. That's part of the reason I contacted you. You can't imagine how happy I was to learn that you'd be the archaeologist conducting the Cultural Impact Survey."

"I thought your email was more than just coincidence. You mentioned in class years ago that you and your wife lived next to a tract of undeveloped woodland. So that's where they're planning to build this condominium complex?"

"Unfortunately, yes. It would really be a shame to lose the Bayview Woods."

"Is that what they're called? I really know very little about the North Fork."

"That's what we've taken to calling them," Thomas replied. He explained the entire circumstance as best he knew about how Tremayne purchased the land from the Makanhassetts for the purpose of building condominiums, and of how his wife, Roxanne, had formed the *Save the Bayview Woods Coalition* in opposition to the project. He admitted the Cultural Impact Survey had been his idea, but held back any suggestion that Lisa drag out the survey as a way of wearing down Tremayne's resolve. It had been a long time since they'd last spoken, and he had no idea how receptive Lisa might be to this ploy.

"So, you believe the Makanhassetts might have left behind something of archaeological significance in those woods," Lisa surmised. "Do you know how long it's been since the area was occupied?"

"I'm not sure. Not recently though, I can tell you that." As Thomas spoke, Lisa noticed a man and a woman at a nearby table curiously staring in their direction.

"What do you suspect?" Lisa inquired. "Colonial era? Contact period?"

"It's hard to say. Somewhere in between, I would guess."

Disconcerted, Lisa couldn't help but glance over Thomas' shoulder at the couple who continued staring at them. "Well, what do you suspect might be out there?" she asked. "A burial ground, maybe?"

"Possibly," Thomas demurred. "You need to make a thorough search of the area to be sure."

"It's an awfully big tract of land," Lisa said with mild frustration. "It might help if you gave me some indication of what I'm looking for so I can narrow my search." She shot a look at the two sitting behind Thomas and decided she'd had enough. "Do you have any idea who those people are—the ones staring at us, I mean?"

Thomas nonchalantly turned around to investigate and came face to face with Chloe and Casey. As soon as Thomas made eye contact, Chloe started waiving vigorously. "Hi, Dr. McGrath! We thought that was you sitting there."

Thomas smiled and waved. "Crap," he muttered below his breath.

"Friends of yours?" Lisa inquired.

"Not exactly."

"Mind if we join you?" Casey asked as he and Chloe buffaloed into two vacant chairs beside Thomas and Lisa. Before Thomas could object, Casey introduced himself and Chloe to Lisa.

"Are you Mrs. McGrath?" Chloe asked.

"Ah, no," Lisa said with an embarrassed chuckle. "Dr. McGrath and I are old friends. I was actually one of his students years ago."

"So, what line of work are you in?" Casey asked.

Thomas winced. He didn't want to be rude, but Chloe and Casey were the last people he wanted to talk to, especially with Lisa around. "Lisa and I are in the middle of discussing some… uh… sensitive business," Thomas said awkwardly.

"I'm an archaeologist," Lisa replied. "Dr. McGrath and I were discussing a field survey I'll be conducting for the State Office of Cultural and Historic Preservation."

"No kidding?" Casey exclaimed. "We love archaeology."

"Does it have anything to do with the Cultural Impact Survey that's been ordered for the Bayview Woods?" Chloe asked.

"Yes, as a matter of fact," Lisa replied.

"Jeez! News travels fast," Thomas observed. "How did you find out about the court order?"

"Schuyler told us," Casey replied. "He and Gus were at the hearing."

Thomas was perplexed. "Why would *they* go to the hearing? You folks from *Von Däniken Village* aren't really locals."

"They went in support of the *Save the Bayview Woods Coalition*," Chloe explained. "They're concerned about the shrinking habitat of the Chiye-tanka."

"Oh, no," Thomas muttered.

"The Chiye-tanka?" Lisa asked. "What's that?"

"Personally, I think the two of them are crazy," Casey remarked. "But Chiye-tanka is the Lakota Sioux name for…"

"Folks, please," Thomas interjected. "Professor Tavolaro-Hennessey and I were in the middle of discussing something very important."

"Something about the Bayview Woods?" Chloe asked.

Oh, no, Thomas thought.

"Schuyler told us you were the one who requested the Cultural Impact Survey," Casey said. "What's the scoop?"

"There's no scoop," Thomas said. "It's just routine."

"Come on, Dr. McGrath," Chloe chided. "You can't fool us."

"There's nothing routine about a Cultural Impact Survey," Casey said. "You wouldn't have requested one unless you thought something was out there."

"I bet it's magical," Chloe speculated. "I can sense the energy."

"There's nothing out there!" Thomas cried.

"Then why am I wasting my time?" Lisa asked.

"No, wait," Thomas backtracked. "Of course there's something out there. It's just…"

"Tell us, then," Casey demanded. "We have a right to know what it is."

Lisa glanced between the three suspiciously.

"You can't hide it from us forever, Dr. McGrath," Chloe cautioned.

"I'm not hiding anything," Thomas replied. "This is just a routine survey to make sure nothing of significance gets damaged or destroyed. It's just precautionary."

Chloe and Casey gave one another a knowing look. "Do you take us for fools, Dr. McGrath?" Casey asked. "We know they're putting up a fence around the woods."

"And now the government's getting involved," Chloe said, gesturing towards Lisa.

"I smell a cover-up!" Casey said, slamming his fist on the table. "It's like Area 51 all over again."

"Or Rozwell," Chloe added.

"Or the Philadelphia Experiment," Casey threw in for good measure. "We've seen the *X Files*, you know."

"Excuse me," Lisa interjected. "May I ask how you all know one another?"

"Dr. McGrath is our leader," Chloe warbled with starry-eyed admiration.

Thomas' temple began to throb. "Don't get the wrong idea," he pleaded. "We've got this archaeology club, see, and…"

"Hey! I have an idea," Casey said. "Why don't you let us help you with the survey? It could be a club activity—like a field trip."

"Thanks," Lisa replied, "but it's against regulations. I couldn't let you assist even if I wanted to."

"Why not?" Chloe asked.

"Because only employees of the State Cultural and Historic Preservation Office may participate in these surveys," Lisa said. "I have to prepare an official report that's admissible in court. You have to be certified to do this kind of work."

"Are you certified, Dr. McGrath?" Casey asked.

"Well, no," Thomas conceded. "My work is more academic in nature."

"But here you are, by your own admission, talking about 'important business' with the State archaeologist," Chloe taunted playfully. "Since you're the one who requested the Cultural Impact

Survey, I find it hard to believe you two aren't in collusion somehow."

"That counts as *participation* in my book," Casey opined.

"Now hold on a minute," Thomas demanded.

"Dr. McGrath, I really should be going," Lisa said.

"Please, Lisa," Thomas begged. "We really need to talk."

"Oh, don't let us interrupt you," Chloe said.

"Please, go right ahead, Dr. McGrath," Casey urged. "We'll just sit here quietly."

Thomas groped for words. "I… I…" he stammered.

"Go on," Chloe said. "Pretend we're not here."

"I'd like to speak to Professor Tavolaro-Hennessey in private," Thomas stated.

"See!" Casey said. "I knew it. There's something out there and the government is trying to cover it up."

"Just like they did in *Close Encounters of the Third Kind*," Chloe remarked.

"And *Hanger 18*," Casey added.

"Dr. McGrath," Lisa said. "I really should…"

"There you are," a familiar voice called from the patio door. "They told us we'd find you here."

Everyone looked up to observe Schuyler stepping onto the patio followed by Gus, who was wearing a tee shirt emblazoned with the words *I'm Squatchin' You!*

"Oh, brother," Casey growled.

"Good work in court the other day, Dr. McGrath," Schuyler said as he and Gus pulled chairs up to the table. "I don't think the judge even read our *amicus curiae* brief, but if he refuses to consider the endangered species argument, at least you were able pin him down on the cultural impact angle."

"They're putting up a fence, you know," Chloe advised.

Schuyler and Gus gasped. "That's unacceptable!" Schuyler bellowed. "The Mid-Atlantic *G. canadensis* is migratory, especially during rutting season. A fence could disrupt its entire reproductive cycle."

"There's an endangered species in the Bayview Woods?" Lisa asked.

"That's right," Schuyler replied. "Not the entire species, actually, just the Mid-Atlantic Appalachian variety. Its Rocky Mountain cousin is far more numerous."

"I'm not familiar with *G. canadensis*," Lisa conceded.

Schuyler gave Lisa a concerned looking-over. "I don't think we've met," he said.

"Lisa is a colleague of mine," Thomas said, checking his watch. "Gosh, Lisa. Look at the time. Didn't you say you had to get going?"

"Colleague?" Schuyler queried. "Are you an anthropologist?"

"Yes," Lisa replied. "I'm working on my Ph.D. in archaeology."

"She's the State archaeologist conducting the Cultural Impact Survey in the Bayview Woods," Chloe chimed in.

"Well, then, since we'll be working together, allow me to introduce myself," Schuyler said jovially. "I'm Dr. Carl Schuyler and this in my research assistant, Gus Armstrong."

Lisa looked perplexed. "Working together?"

"In the Bayview Woods," Schuyler replied. "I'm really looking forward to our collaboration on the field survey. When do you plan on getting started?"

"Hold on a second!" Thomas exclaimed. "Lisa is conducting a court-ordered investigation. You can't barge your way into official State business."

"I propose nothing of the sort," Schuyler said with a measure of effrontery. "I'm only suggesting that we all share our research findings. If Gus and I come across anything Lisa should know about, we'll pass the information along to her. Out of professional courtesy I'm sure she'll do the same."

"Of course," Lisa said. "But I'm still confused. Dr. Schuyler, are you tracking an endangered species for the Department of Environmental Conservation?"

"The State DEC?" Schuyler gasped. "Good heavens, no! We're working under a private research grant."

"For what institution?" Lisa asked.

"The Université Heuvelmans in Brussels, Belgium," Schuyler replied.

"It's a diploma mill," Casey scoffed.

Schuyler shot Casey an angry look. "I see you've met our paranoid friend. By now I'm sure you've gathered Casey's as credible as a three dollar bill."

"Dr. Schuyler, I'd be happy to pass along any useful information," Lisa confided. "But I still don't know what it is you're looking for."

"Gus has a specimen here in his bag," Schuyler said, motioning to his assistant.

"Don't you have somewhere to be, Lisa?" Thomas urged.

"This will only take a moment," Schuyler affirmed as Gus handed him a Mason jar filled with damp soil. "Obtaining hair samples during the summer is almost impossible, but we're in the middle of rutting season. The male *G. canadensis* is throwing off pheromones like crazy right now so our best evidence for their presence is their scent." Schuyler uncapped the jar and thrust it under Lisa's nose. "Smell that," he directed.

Lisa recoiled in disgust and started gagging. "What the hell is that?"

"Sasquatch urine," Schuyler replied. "Can you discern the rich undertones of musk?"

Lisa rose and pushed past Gus and Chloe as she bolted for the patio door.

"Lisa, wait!" Thomas said, following her through the café. "We still need to talk."

Lisa waived Thomas off as she ran out the front door onto the street.

"I'll call you," Thomas cried as she departed.

CHAPTER 11

Vincent sat in his office, brooding alone in silence. Summer was normally a slow time for the oil business, but even factoring in seasonal fluctuations, business was way down. Construction of Country Squire was on indefinite hold, yet bills from the development corporation kept pouring in. Soon, property taxes would be due, and adding insult to injury, Vincent was out five hundred bucks on account of that puny patch of woods. Not long ago, he considered cash like that mere pocket change. Now, money was tight and by all outward appearances, everything was going to hell.

Oh, how Vincent hated the McGraths! That hick cowgirl Roxanne came off as such a smart-ass, but at least she was a real doctor. She could be trouble enough on her own, but that idiot college professor husband of hers really irked him. Archaeology—what a laugh! That guy never worked a day in his life! How deadbeats like Thomas McGrath came to suck off the public teat he'd never understand. Yet, here he was, not just slinging the bull in front of a bunch of college kids, but fobbing himself off before the judge as some kind of expert. Cultural Impact Survey—what nonsense! But there has to be something behind it. McGrath kept blabbing about a treasure. He's some kind of archaeologist and isn't digging up treasure what archaeologists do? That freeloader's probably been poking around those woods for years trying to find whatever's out there. After all, there *were* pirates on the North Fork back in colonial times. McGrath must know something about a secret pirate hoard. Maybe he's got an old map or a captain's log. Then again, it could be Indian treasure. The *History Channel* is always running shows about Aztec gold and crap like that. Maybe it isn't crap after all. Maybe those Aztecs buried their gold somewhere around here and McGrath has insider knowledge of it. Too late now, buddy! No matter who buried that treasure, it's on private property now, so McGrath can go piss up a rope.

Vincent's secretary broke his reverie when she entered the inner office. "There's some bills here you need to take care of," she advised.

"Send them to Accounting," Vincent said coldly. "Let them handle it."

"I did, but Accounting sent them back with a note. It seems these are bills from Country Squire and our people can only sign off on oil company business. They say you need to either pay these bills yourself or send them to the accounting office at Country Squire and have them handle it."

Vincent sighed. "Alright. Give them to me."

"Here you go," the secretary said, placing the papers before him. "This one is the property tax bill for the Bayview Woods, and the other is…"

"Stop calling it that!" Vincent barked.

"I'm sorry? Stop calling it what?"

"'The 'Bayview Woods.' Stop calling it that. That's a name invented by that pain in the ass, Roxanne McGrath. We call it the 'Country Squire property.' Got it?"

The secretary rolled her eyes. "Yeah, I got it. The second one is an invoice from the contractor who bulldozed that section of the Bayview… er, the Country Squire property."

"Just leave them and get out."

Alone once again, Vincent sullenly snatched up the property tax bill and winced when he looked at the bottom line. *Goddammit!* he thought, considering the payment due date. *I got to get the taxable property value reappraised downward right away.* Vincent tossed the tax bill aside and took up the other one. "Louis Nickels Cut-Rate Excavations," he mumbled as he read the invoice heading. Having passed this bill on to Accounting once before without really scrutinizing it, Vincent's eyes popped out when, for the first time, he noticed the charges. He was still trying to overcome the shock when the intercom buzzed.

"The Senior Sales Agent from Country Squire is on line one again," the secretary advised.

"Get rid of her," Vincent replied.

"It's the third time she's called this morning. She knows you're here."

"Tell her I've gone to lunch."

"It's only 10:00 o'clock. And I'm getting sick of lying."

"Yeah, yeah. I'll be right with her." Vincent looked over Louis Nickels' hand-written bill one more time and realized it didn't specifically mention for whom he'd rendered excavation services. *This might not even be the right bill,* Vincent rationalized. *Maybe this bill was meant for some other client.* Vincent looked at Daphne's chicken scratch signature and knew for certain the bill was correct. *Well, no one could make out that signature*, he thought. After a moment's equivocation, Vincent crumpled up Louis Nickels' bill. "Screw him," he mumbled as he tossed the wad of paper in the garbage.

The intercom buzzed again. "Your wife is still on line one," the secretary reminded.

"Alright, already," Vincent grumbled as he picked up the phone. "Yeah? What is it now?"

"Vincent! I've been trying to reach you all morning. I need money right away."

Vincent frowned in disgust. "Is your credit card maxed out again?"

"It's not for me," Daphne replied. "It's for Country Squire. The fence company has run out of chain link and needs to buy more."

"How much more?" Vincent inquired. Although Daphne muffled the mouthpiece at her end, he could hear her relaying the question to someone standing nearby.

"About two thousand feet more," she responded. "Give or take a hundred feet."

Vincent cursed below his breath. "Can't they bill us?"

"Maybe. I'll find out."

"Great," Vincent said with indifference. "Listen, Daphne. I need you to get on with hiring a real estate appraiser."

"A real estate appraiser? That's—like—number five on my list of things to do."

"Make it priority number one."

"Why?"

"Because the Country Squire property tax bill is coming due and we really need to get the taxable property value lowered as soon as possible. The only way we can do that is if we submit a tax reduction petition to the Village Assessor along with an independent real estate appraiser's report."

Daphne was feverishly scribbling notes as Vincent spoke. "Of course. I know all that. I just wanted to know why we're skipping all the other jobs."

"We're not skipping them. We're just shuffling the order a little."

"Fine. Now what about the *Fontana di Nettuno*? After hiring a real estate appraiser we need to move that up to priority number two, don't you think?"

"I already told you you're going to have to wait on that!" Vincent exclaimed. "Everything depends on the results of that stupid Cultural Impact Survey."

"Well, when are they going to get that done?" Daphne demanded. "Didn't you tell them to hurry up?"

Vincent muttered more curse words. "Look at the time," he said, fishing for an excuse. "I… uh… I got to go to a meeting," he lied as he hung up. He picked up the tax bill again and cursed when he considered how much he owed.

The job of enclosing the Country Squire property came to a standstill when Louis Nickels and Moon ran out of chain link. So far, they hadn't seen a dime from Tremayne and Louis Nickels was getting pissed off. He wasn't about to lay out any money if he could get the blond girl to cough up some cash, so rather than head to the fence wholesaler, he and Moon drove to the Country Squire Development Corporation office on the far side of town.

At first thinking them prospective customers, Daphne looked up with excitement upon their arrival, only to sigh disappointedly when she recognized them. "Are you done yet?" she asked.

"We ran out of fence," Louis Nickels informed. "You've got to come across with some loot to buy more."

"Don't you people have an account somewhere? Just get some more and put it on our bill."

"Money don't grow on trees, girlie! Do you think I'm a bottomless pit? Unless you people loosen the sluice pretty soon, Moon and I are headed for the poor farm."

"Alright," Daphne relented. "Let me make a phone call."

As Daphne busied herself dialing, Louis Nickels looked around the Country Squire office with a measure of suspicion. Moon, in the meantime, had sauntered over to Rayette's work station. He hiked up a leg and half sat along the edge of her desk, looking down with a roguish grin. Rayette caught his eye and blushed. "Would you like a donut?" she giggled, proffering a box of crullers.

"To be thankful for," Moon replied as he took a donut and chomped into it. "I long with passion of good tasting," he added as he stuffed the rest of the donut into his mouth.

"Oh," Rayette said with a broad smile. "Please, have another." Moon accepted without protest.

Louis Nickels stood close to Daphne and listened as she ran matters past Vincent. When all was said and done, she hung up the phone and looked down at her scribbled notes, trying to overcome the sense of confusion she felt on account of this change in plans.

"Hey!" Louis Nickels exclaimed, breaking her withdrawn cogitation.

"Huh?" Daphne uttered, looking up. "Oh, right, the fence. Is it possible for you to just bill us?"

"Forget that for now," Louis Nickels advised. "What's all this talk about hiring an appraiser?"

Daphne blinked. "Yes. We need to hire a real estate appraiser right away. Do you know anyone who does that sort of thing?"

"Yeah," Louis Nickels replied. "What do you want appraised?"

"The Country Squire property," Daphne replied, consulting her notes. "The tax bill is coming due soon and…"

"Yeah, I know all about it. You people are looking to dodge a big tax bill so you want to get that land devalued. It's an old scam."

"And we need to do it right away. Do you know anyone who can do it?"

"Yeah," Louis Nickels said after some consideration. He fished around his pockets looking for the right business card. Coming up short, he removed his Homburg and withdrew a card from the interior hat band and handed it to Daphne.

"*Louis Nickels Cut-Rate Real Estate Appraisals*," she read. "Wow! So, can you do the appraisal right away?"

"Hold on a minute," Louis Nickels demanded. "Let's talk about the fee schedule first."

"Fee schedule? Can't you wait until the end of the month to get paid?"

"That's not what I'm talking about," Louis Nickels replied. "The fee schedule is based on a sliding scale. Basically, you agree to pay us a fifty percent commission of the money we save you in the first year. Understand?"

Daphne stared him blankly.. "No," she said.

Louis Nickels scowled. "Pay attention! If we submit a lowball appraisal and the Village Assessor agrees to knock a few hundred grand off the taxable value of your land, that means you'll save a bundle on taxes this year, right?"

"Right," Daphne acknowledged.

"So, whatever amount you save between the old and the new tax bill, we get half."

"That sounds OK. How much can you save us?"

"It depends on how much we lowball the property value. If you want to save more money, then we tell the Village Assessor the property ain't worth much. They tax you at a lower rate and you save a bundle."

"Well then, tell them the land is worth nothing," Daphne advised. "That way we won't have to pay any taxes at all."

"It don't work that way," Louis Nickels said. "The government is on to that trick. We can pitch the Village Assessor a lowball, but the appraisal's got to be somewhere in the zone. The best you're going to get is a reduction in taxable value of a few hundred thousand 'Gs.' Do you see what I'm saying?"

"I think so," Daphne replied. "Can you do it right away?"

"Keep your shirt on!" Louis Nickels snapped. "This ain't like reappraising some rinky-dink house. That's a big chunk of land out there and we need to put all our ducks in a row before filing any paperwork with the Village."

"OK. So now what?"

"First off, what did your old man pay for that land?"

"I don't know," Daphne confided. "I'll find out."

"We also need a copy of the survey."

"The Cultural Impact Survey? They're doing that now."

"No! Not that. The property line survey!"

"Oh. I don't think we have one of those."

"Well then, who put up all them pink ribbons along the property line?" Louis Nickels asked through gritted teeth. "We're sinking fence posts along those markers, so someone must have done a survey recently."

Daphne glanced around the sparse office. "I... I don't know where..." she stammered. Her eyes fell upon Rayette, who at that moment was using a pair of tweezers to pluck hairs out of the space between Moon's eyebrows.

"Hey, you!" Daphne called. "Where's the property line survey?"

Rayette looked up. "I don't know," she said with perplexed concern. "Candice probably has it somewhere. Do you want me to call her and ask?"

"No!"

"Well, we need a property line survey to do the job," Louis Nickels remarked.

"Can't you rely on the pink ribbons?" Daphne asked.

"You can't send pink ribbons to the Village Assessor. They want paperwork. We need a few other bits and pieces too to finish this job."

"Like what?" Daphne asked as Rayette and Moon looked on.

"Like the results of the aquifer test—and the actuary's report on potential flood damage."

Daphne looked at Rayette. "Well? Where are they?"

"Candice would know," Rayette replied. "Are you sure you don't want me to call her?"

"Forget Candice!" Daphne exclaimed. "We'll get our *own* survey. The same goes for those other two things."

Moon whistled with amused incredulity.

"Yeah, well we need them things right away if you expect us to submit an appraisal to the Assessor before tax day," Louis Nickels said.

"Do you know anyone in that line of work?" Daphne asked.

"Yeah," Louis Nickels replied. "Moon and I can handle that for you."

"Great! Let me know when it's all finished. OK?"

"Hold on!" Louis Nickels demanded. "No more hand-shake agreements, see? We want signed contracts up front from now on."

"OK," Daphne replied.

"And the same goes for the appraisal. We want you to agree to the payment terms in writing. If we bring in a devalued appraisal and the Village Assessor signs on, we get half the tax savings. Agreed?"

"Definitely! If you have a contract, I'll sign it right now."

Louis Nickels noticed that Moon had pulled a chair up next to Rayette and was intently pouring over a large scrapbook. "That's a picture of my grandmother," Rayette explained. "Her name was Rayette too. My grandpa was named Robert, but everyone called him Bobby. He worked on oil rigs but they say he could have been a concert pianist."

"Hey, Moon," Louis Nickels said. "Get the valise out of the Edsel. We got another job." As Moon slipped out to the parking lot Louis Nickels turned towards Daphne. "Now what about the fence?"

"Can't you finish that later?"

"Yeah, but we need to get paid. We already laid out half a mile of chain link and we still need to buy more."

Moon approached with an alligator-skinned briefcase. "Behold," he said, handing it over.

"We'd like you to bill us for the fence," Daphne said. "Is that OK?

Louis Nickels grumbled a string of incomprehensible obscenities as he tore through the document bag. "Yeah," he replied at length, pulling out a sheaf of forms. After filling in the pertinent information on each document he handed the pile to Daphne. "Here you go. Sign these."

Daphne did as instructed and handed everything back. Louis Nickels tore the top copies off and stuffed them in the valise before handing the bottom copies to Daphne.

"What am I supposed to do with these?" Daphne asked.

"Don't you have an accounting department?"

"Of course," Daphne replied as she thrust the pile of papers at Rayette. "Do something with these," she ordered.

"Should I file them under *accounts payable*?" Rayette asked.

"Whatever!"

Moon winked seductively at Rayette as she passed on her way to the file cabinet.

"Alright, Moon," Louis Nickels said. "Let's head back to the cupcake. We need to get the theodolite."

CHAPTER 12

Thomas watched Lisa jump into her jeep and speed off. He looked back at the group on the patio. Noticing that Schuyler and Casey were embroiled in a heated argument, he took advantage of the tumult and beat out unnoticed.

Things certainly had not gone as Thomas planned during his reunion with Lisa. In spite of their having drifted apart, he'd hoped to enlist her as a confederate in his conflict with Tremayne. Still, he remained unsure as to how far she'd be willing to go to help him. It was unlikely that Lisa would drag things out, since the State paid her a flat commission, and any extra time spent on the survey translated into less time devoted to more lucrative employment, like bartending. Could he persuade her to falsify the report and claim to have discovered something culturally significant that didn't really exist? Perhaps, but that would be perjury, and asking her to commit a crime was simply out of the question. Thomas understood that in all likelihood, Lisa's survey would turn up nothing. In that case, there'd be nothing left to do except watch as contractors bulldozed the Bayview Woods to make way for those hellish condominiums. He felt a twinge of panic as the reality of this set in.

Thomas turned off the Main Road onto the private dirt track that doglegged around the backside of the Bayview Woods before reaching his waterfront home. He grew alarmed as he bumped along, considering the progress of the fence installation in the short time he'd been away that morning. At this rate, it would only be a day or two before the entire tract of land was cordoned off.

Once home, Thomas found two messages on his answering machine. "What kind of factory rejects are you hooked up with?" Lisa's message began. "I almost puked when your friend stuck that jar of rat piss under my nose! Listen, I know we were in the middle of discussing the Cultural Impact Survey, and I think you were about to tell me something important, but there's no way in hell I'm coming back to Café Bizarro. I'll be working at the Salty Dog Restaurant tonight, but I'm planning on getting an early start on the Cultural Impact Survey tomorrow. Give me a call later if you remember what you were going to tell me. Bye!"

The machine skipped to the second message. "Hey, Thomas. I just thought you'd like to know the college president called this morning," Roz squawked in a gravelly voice. "It seems you've made a big hit with the NonTrads from *Von Däniken Village* and he wanted me to tell you how happy he is you've agreed to chair the weekly meetings of the archaeology club. In the end, it's going to be a win-win situation for everyone involved—if you catch my drift. I told you running the archaeology club would be worth your while, smartass!"

Thomas silently mouthed obscenities as he listened to Roz's message. Now he'd never be rid of those nuts. Hoping to take his mind off things, he figured he'd do a little work on his book.

As Thomas reached to turn on his laptop, he noticed the box of bogus projectile points sitting on the corner of his desk. Placing the box in his lap, he selected one particularly well made Clovis point replica, and turning the palm-sized blade over in his hand, imagined what it must have been like millennia ago, when nomadic hunters survived by stalking game across the boundless wilderness. He chuckled, recalling Roz's suggestion he try selling his replicas on Ebay. Someone with a trained eye would peg them for fakes even though most laymen might mistake them for the genuine article. *Not bad stone knapping, even for a modern guy*, Thomas thought, putting the box aside.

As the computer booted up, Thomas glanced again at the box of bogus artifacts. In a flash, he leapt to his feet and snatched up the fake Clovis point. Holding it up to the light, he examined the pristine edge. It was almost too perfect. He put the object back in the box and turned away from his desk. "No, no, no!" he shouted as a wave of felonious temptation flooded his soul. He paced into the kitchen. "Absolutely not!" he exclaimed with dying conviction. Thomas went back to his desk and took up the fake Clovis point again. *It would be so unethical*, he thought. *Unethical? Isn't cutting down the woods far more unethical? If the Cultural Impact Survey yields nothing, then it's time to kiss the Bayview Woods goodbye.* Since Lisa planned to commence the survey the next day, he had no time to waste. Thomas put the fake artifact in his pocket and left the house through the kitchen door. He thought he'd take a stroll in the woods.

Walking across the fallow farmyard, Thomas could faintly hear the rhythmic *thud-thud-thud* of what sounded like a hammer pounding on metal. He crossed the dirt road and entered the Bayview Woods along a walking path not yet blocked by the encroaching fence. As Thomas made his way, the intermittent *thud-thud-thud* grew louder. Approaching the bulldozed clearing, he spied two men unloading four-foot sections of galvanized pipe from a box trailer towed by an antique automobile. Thomas watched as the older man threaded a section of pipe into place, whereupon the younger fellow set to work with a sledgehammer, driving the pipe into the ground. Drawing closer, Thomas noticed a magnetic sign affixed to the car door which read *Louis Nickels Cut-Rate Hydrology*.

Startled by Thomas' sudden appearance, the older man turned and peered at him from underneath the brim of a black felt hat. "You got something on your mind, bub?" the skeletal old man growled.

"What's going on here?" Thomas asked.

"What's it look like, Sherlock? We're doing an aquifer test."

"Aren't you the guys I saw putting up the fence?"

"What's it to you?"

"Well, nothing, but… what about the court order? I thought you weren't allowed to do anything invasive until after the Cultural Impact Survey."

"How do you expect us to test the water without driving a well first?

"But… you're not supposed to do any work that involves digging."

"Take that up with the property owner, pal," the old man said. "Now if you don't mind, we've got a job to do."

As Thomas retreated, he felt for the Clovis point in his pocket. He toyed with the idea of calling the police to report this violation of the court order, but realized all the ensuing hubbub might foil his plans. He thought it best to ignore this infraction until he'd accomplished his anthropological subterfuge.

Back at the house, Thomas formulated a plan to return to the woods that night and plant the bogus artifact somewhere close to the test well those workmen were drilling. Having a clear landmark as a guide, Thomas could then suggest to Lisa that she narrow her search to that area. The fake Clovis point might not fool Lisa for long, but it would induce her to file a report suggesting that a more extensive study of the site was advisable. Hopefully, such a costly delay might persuade Tremayne to abandon the project entirely. It wasn't a great plan, but under the circumstances, Thomas thought it offered the best chance of saving the woods. Yet, there was one factor that gave Thomas pause—and that was the fear of getting caught. It wasn't the police or even Tremayne he feared—it was Roxanne. If Roxy found out about this he'd be in the doghouse forever. But how could he manage to slip out that night and plant the fake artifact? Roxanne would be home before sundown and his plan called for a stealthy foray into the woods under the cover of darkness. It wasn't like him to just 'go out' at night alone. He'd need to offer her a reason—some purpose that required him to be away from home a few hours after dinner. Racking his brain, he hit upon a plausible excuse—he'd tell Roxanne he had a meeting with the archaeology club. The new club's meeting schedule was still so tentative that she'd never realize it was all just a cover story. He'd have a nice dinner waiting for her by the time she got home, and, as usual, she'd probably turn in early. He'd admonish her not to wait up, and then leave—ostensibly for a meeting with the *Von Däniken Village* wackos. In reality, he'd sneak into the woods and plant the artifact, then kill a few hours driving around. There'd be no reason for Roxy to suspect anything.

Thomas did as planned. He'd grilled some chicken and set a cheerful table on their deck overlooking the bay. Everything was in place by the time Roxanne's boat hove into view, and, over dinner, Thomas explained how he'd gotten his wires crossed about the archaeology club's meeting schedule. Shrugging the matter off, Roxanne said she'd probably be asleep by the time he returned. As evening fell, Roxanne curled up on the couch with a book. Thomas checked his watch and thought it a plausible time to leave.

It would have been far easier just to walk across the private dirt road into the woods, but that would have roused Roxanne's suspicion. Maintaining the pretense that he was actually headed to the college, Thomas started his pickup truck and bounced off down the dirt road before turning westward on the Main Road.

Having traveled about a hundred yards, he parked on the shoulder and darted back on foot towards the Bayview Woods. He was walking in the tall grass towards the bulldozed clearing when a vehicle approaching from the opposite direction flashed its high beams. Hoping to avoid detection, Thomas quickly dove for cover beyond the tree line.

Vincent Tremayne had a rotten day and was looking forward to getting home and jumping in the hot tub. He down-shifted the Porsche as he approached the turn off for the private dirt road when something moving on the shoulder caught his attention. Fearing that a deer was about to jump in front of him, he flashed on his high beams. It wasn't a deer, but rather, a pedestrian. The person was visible for only a few seconds before cutting into the woods, but there was no mistaking it—it was that rat bastard McGrath! Vincent slowed to see if he could make out what that idiot college professor was up to, but McGrath had retreated too far into the woods. *He has to be after the treasure,* Vincent thought. *He knows he doesn't have much time now that the fence is nearly finished.* Vincent considered pursuing McGrath on foot, but instead made a U-turn and doubled back on the dirt road. He turned off the Porsche and waited in the darkness, hoping to catch that sneaky rat McGrath as he returned home.

Crouching in the trees as the car passed, Thomas wondered if he'd been observed. It didn't really matter. He wasn't breaking any laws and he had every right to take an evening stroll in the woods. Even so, Thomas hoped to avoid the hassle of having to explain himself to a nosey neighbor and breathed a sigh of relief when the car moved on.

Thomas found the spot in the bulldozed clearing where the two men had sunk the test well earlier that day. The final section of galvanized pipe had been capped off, and the area marked by a blue plastic flag staked into the ground. The light of the moon was bright enough for Thomas to find his way around the clearing. He located a patch of soft, sandy soil about ten feet due south of the test well, which he thought a suitable spot to plant the bogus Clovis point. Not wishing to make things too obvious, he placed the faux artifact on the ground and scooped a handful of pebbly dirt over it, leaving about six inches of sharp edge exposed and plainly visible to a vigilant passerby. Satisfied he'd staged a plausible scene, Thomas made his way out of the woods.

It was still too soon to go home if he hoped to maintain his cover story with Roxanne. What to do with himself for the next few hours? He realized he still needed to make contact with Lisa, and remembered from her phone message that she'd be tending bar that evening at the Salty Dog Restaurant. Perhaps he should nonchalantly drop in for a drink.

The bar at the Salty Dog Restaurant was decorated with a mixture of major league sports memorabilia interspersed among photographs and trophies attesting to the establishment's longstanding tradition as a hangout for big game fishermen. Patrons clustered at opposite ends of the bar watching baseball on the large screen televisions that hung nearby. In spite of the crowd, Thomas found an open stool towards the middle of the bar, and, after waiting a few minutes, caught Lisa's eye.

"What are you doing here?" she asked, swabbing the bar with a towel.

"I was hoping to have a quick word," Thomas replied. "We never got to finish our conversation at the café."

"Those friends of yours are too much! What are you drinking?"

"Just a ginger ale," Thomas said, squinting to read the bar menu. "I'll take a plate of the zucchini sticks too."

Lisa placed the food order and came back with Thomas' drink. "So, what's on your mind?"

Lisa's attention was divided on account of the bar crowd and Thomas knew he'd need to keep the conversation short and to the point. "You know, Lisa, I've been walking around those woods for years and never really found anything. But after they bulldozed that area other day, I took a look around and began to find some interesting things."

"Like what?" Lisa asked as she poured a pint of beer for another patron.

"Like stone flakes in the upturned soil."

"That's no big deal. They could have resulted from the bulldozer breaking up rocks close to the surface."

"No," Thomas replied. "These were flint flakes from deliberate stone knapping."

"Flint? Are you sure they were flint flakes?"

"I'm sure. And you know as well as I that flint is not a local stone. You realize what this means, don't you?"

"Of course," Lisa replied. "It means that whoever left those flakes had to obtain a block of flint from somewhere off the island."

"That's right," Thomas affirmed. "Flint is easier to knap than most local varieties of stone, and the island tribes could only obtain it through trade with mainland Indian communities. Those trade networks could be pretty extensive, as you know."

A steady turnover of customers came and went, calling Lisa away to fill other drink orders. When she returned, Thomas could tell from her pensive expression that her wheels were turning. "Where did you say you found those flakes?" she asked.

Thomas explained how he stumbled upon workmen driving a test well earlier that day and claimed he'd found the flakes just a few yards south of the capped galvanized pipe. He explained that the area was easy to find on account of the blue plastic flag that marked the spot.

"I'd really like to gather more evidence about just how extensive these trade networks were," Lisa said with earnest determination. "I didn't get a chance to explain earlier, but believe it or not, this is exactly what I've been researching for my doctoral dissertation." A bell rang somewhere in the distance. "Those are your zucchini sticks," she said. "I'll be right back."

A thunderclap of guilt shook Thomas' conscience. *Oh, my God!* he thought. *Is my fake artifact somehow going to screw up Lisa's doctoral research? Maybe I've gone too far? Maybe I should…*

Thomas was so absorbed in thought he paid little attention when someone took the bar stool next to him. "Hi, Dr. McGrath! Come here often?" a woman to his left chirped. Recognizing the voice, Thomas felt a shudder of dread as he turned to face Chloe, who stared back at him with a broad grin.

"Oh, no," Thomas moaned.

"So, did you find anything unusual in the woods today, Dr. McGrath?" a man to Thomas' right inquired. He turned and saw it was Casey, who had pulled his bar stool so close that the two men practically touched.

Thomas, flustered by Chloe and Casey's sudden appearance, was momentarily at a loss for words. "Hi, guys," he finally said awkwardly.

"We didn't get as chance to say goodbye when you left the café this morning," Chloe remarked.

"Yeah, well…" Thomas muttered. "I, uh… Wait a second. How did you know I took a walk in the woods earlier today?"

"Don't you remember? We're both clairvoyant," Chloe replied.

Lisa returned with Thomas' zucchini sticks. "The plate is hot," she said, sliding it into place in front of him. "Do you want another ginger ale?"

"Well isn't this a coincidence?" Casey observed with mock incredulity. "The abstemious professor just happens to run into the moonlighting State archaeologist—*in a bar*. What are the chances of that?"

"You've got it all wrong!" Thomas shouted. "Now listen…"

"No, all of you nut-jobs listen!" Lisa barked as she slammed her open palm on the bar. "I've had enough of you people for one day. You'd all better behave yourselves or I'll boot you the hell out of here. And God help you if I catch you monkeying around with any jars of piss!"

Thomas quickly pulled out his wallet and withdrew a twenty dollar bill. "This should cover everything," he said, tossing the note on the bar. "I've got to go."

"Aren't you going to eat your zucchini sticks?" Casey asked.

"You have 'em. I've lost my appetite."

"Don't forget the archaeology club meeting on Monday," Chloe called as Thomas made for the door. "We'll see you then, if not sooner."

CHAPTER 13

Thomas spent the weekend agonizing over whether or not he'd done the right thing by planting the fake Clovis point. Fearing that his unethical act might inadvertently serve to skew Lisa's doctoral research, he seriously considered removing the fake artifact before its discovery. Yet, he equivocated when he realized that the Cultural Impact Survey might yield nothing, thus allowing the Country Squire project to go forward. *I'm damned if I do and damned if I don't*, he thought.

Returning home from their outings late Sunday afternoon, the McGraths found a message on their answering machine. "Hey, Dr. McGrath," Lisa began with unconcealed exuberance. "I'm so excited I don't know where to begin. I looked in the area you suggested and all I can tell you it that I found something—and I mean something *BIG*! State protocol requires I present my findings to the judge before going public, but I can tell you right now this is revolutionary. I'm not kidding! We're going to have to revise everything we thought we knew about pre-Columbian North America if what I've found turns out to be the real thing. Anyway, I'm planning a press conference right after the hearing on Tuesday. I've already alerted a friend who works for the local newspaper as well as some people I know at *Scientific American* and *National Geographic*. You've got to be there too. I'm telling you, Dr. McGrath, you're not going to believe…" The message came to an abrupt end when the machine cut off.

"Wow," Roxanne said. "What do you make of all that?"

Thomas shrugged. "I don't know what to make of it," he said guardedly.

"She sounds pretty excited. By the way, what's that she mentioned about you suggesting a place where she should look?"

"Oh, that's was nothing really. I thought I saw some stone flakes indicative of tool knapping in the bulldozed clearing the other day. I suggested she might begin her search in that area."

Roxanne looked at him skeptically. "You didn't search the area yourself?"

"I thought it best to leave that for Lisa. After all, it wouldn't really do us any good if I went poking around and uncovered something before she did. Whatever might be out there properly belongs in Lisa's official report."

"I guess you're right. I wonder what she's found. Do you think you should give her a call?"

Thomas pretended to give the matter some thought. "I don't think so. I don't think she'd tell me anyway. After all, protocol dictates she present her findings to the judge first. It would be bad form for me to ask her to break protocol."

Roxanne gave a derisive snort. "Bad form? When in the world did you ever give a hoot for proper form *or* protocol? I'm surprised you're not coming out of your skin trying to find out what she's discovered."

"All in good time," Thomas said with measured composure. "We'll find out soon enough. You *are* taking off from work on Tuesday for the hearing, aren't you?"

"I wouldn't miss it for the world," Roxanne replied, studying him with suspicion. "You are an odd duck, Professor McGrath. I would have expected a more emotional reaction out of you, given the circumstances. You do realize this might put a permanent halt to the development project, don't you?"

"I prefer not to count my chickens before they hatch. If I've learned anything during my career it's to not overestimate the importance of any preliminary archaeological find. Whatever Lisa found is going to be analyzed and studied by other archaeologists to determine its importance. She might have come across something significant—but remember—every young archaeologist wants to rewrite the books. But not everyone can be another Howard Carter or Hiram Bingham, you know."

"I don't know who those people are, doll," Roxanne said. "But I think I get your point. Maybe her enthusiasm has gotten the better of her judgment and she's seeing things through rose colored glasses."

"Maybe," Thomas agreed. "Then again, maybe she's really found something important. Either way we'll find out on Tuesday."

The archaeology club had its second official meeting that Monday evening. Roxanne couldn't understand why the club met with such frequency, but grudgingly bought Thomas' lie that a regular weekly schedule was still in the formative stage.

Arriving at the college shortly before seven, Thomas found the second floor conference room already packed, as the membership of the club had at least tripled since their first meeting. The founding members were all in place along with Schuyler and Gus, the latter of whom sat holding a manila folder.

"Good evening, Dr. McGrath," Thor Svenson said as he politely rose. "We've saved you a seat at the head of the table."

"Thanks." Thomas marveled at the size of the group. "I see we have some new members."

"Yes," Thor Svenson remarked. "And more are on the way. The shuttle bus is not big enough to bring everyone at once."

"Great," Thomas said with affected enthusiasm. "Shall we wait for them?"

"No. Let's get down to business," Sibyl said coldly. A hush fell over the room as Thomas felt every eye on him. "Dr. McGrath, we want you to inform us exactly what the State archaeologist found in the Bayview Woods."

"Yes. Please, tell us," one of the new members said as others around the table seconded the request.

Thomas drew a deep breath and exhaled wearily. "Folks… I have no idea what she found."

Thomas' claim of ignorance was met with angry murmurs.

"Come on!" Casey exclaimed. "You expect us to believe that?"

"The State archaeologist was a student of yours," Sibyl said. "In fact, you were her mentor. We know the two of you talk."

"Of course we talk," Thomas admitted. "But not about her recent find. That would be a breach of protocol."

"But you *did* suggest where she should look," Chloe remarked. "What's so special about that particular spot?"

"Nothing," Thomas said defensively. "I just suggested she take a look in the bulldozed clearing."

"You mean the area you were scouting around," Casey said. "Just south of the capped test well, right?"

Thomas grew flustered. "How did you… Did Lisa—I mean Professor Tavolaro-Hennessey—tell you that?"

"Of course not," Chloe replied. "She works for the State."

"She's part of the cover-up," Casey added.

"There is no cover-up!" Thomas exclaimed. A number of people around the table grumbled in disbelief.

"Then why not just tell us what's so special about that area near the test well?" Chloe asked.

"I don't know what you're talking about," Thomas replied angrily.

"Come on, Dr. McGrath," Casey urged. "We know you were there."

Thomas arched an eyebrow. "Have you been following me?"

The room erupted in mocking guffaws. "Really, Dr. McGrath!" Sibyl exclaimed. "Don't act so paranoid."

"Please, Dr. McGrath," Thor Svenson interjected. "Everyone here is very excited by the possibility that a major archaeological discovery has been found. Surely you must understand our desire to learn as much as we can about it." As Thor Svenson spoke, a group of late arrivals from *Von Däniken Village* filed into the conference room and silently took the overflow seats aligned against the back wall.

Thomas sighed. "I understand your curiosity. After all, archaeology is my life's passion. Believe me, I want to know about this new find as much as you do. But as a professional, I know that field researchers can get a bit carried away with enthusiasm regarding their own discoveries."

"So, you think the State archaeologist is making a mountain out of a molehill?" Casey asked.

Thomas weighed his words. "Listen. I was eleven years old when I found my first arrowhead. I was convinced I'd come across something as valuable as the crown jewels until my grandmother took me to the museum where the curator showed me cases full of arrowheads and spear points. There were thousands of them—many of them better than the one I'd stumbled across. Even so, I still thought my arrowhead was the best. You know why?"

"Tell us," Thor Svenson urged.

"Because *I* found it!" Thomas said emphatically. "Lisa Tavolaro-Hennessey is a good archaeologist and I have no doubt she's found something interesting. All I'm saying is that her enthusiasm might be disproportionate to the find's actual significance. Let's just wait for her report before we jump to any conclusions."

Everyone around the table pondered this while Sibyl studied Thomas skeptically. "You're still holding something back," she said with firm self-assurance. "You know a lot more than you're letting on."

Thomas threw up his hands in frustration. "Well then, what do *you* think is out there?"

"I believe your friend has uncovered the remnants of an alien ship," Casey said to rousing applause.

"Which probably indicates the presence of an inter-dimensional portal somewhere nearby," Chloe added to even greater applause.

Thomas rubbed his furrowed brow. "Here we go again," he grumbled.

Clearing his throat with theatrical effect, Schuyler stood to his feet. "Dr. McGrath, if you would allow me…" he said with collegial good manners. "Friends, I can explain with *scientific certainty* what's out there."

Casey rolled his eyes. "This ought to be good."

Schuyler motioned to Gus who produced a stack of grainy black and white photographs. "These were taken shortly after dark this past Friday," Schuyler explained as the photos were passed around. "Gus and I had just arrived in the Bayview Woods and were setting up our observation post when we noticed movement across the clearing."

Thomas' eye began to twitch.

"So, now you can see in the dark?" Casey challenged.

"Gus was wearing night vision goggles," Casey replied. "Our best equipment hadn't been unpacked yet and as you can see, we were too far away for our hand-held infra-red camera to capture images at a higher resolution. But in these photos you can clearly make out the form of a bipedal humanoid in the clearing."

Thomas held his breath as he glanced at the photos. To his relief, he observed that the fuzzy images revealed no identifiable facial features.

"These are all blurry," Casey said dismissively. "There's nothing 'clear' about them."

"Hear, hear!" someone concurred.

"The preponderance of evidence suggests only one thing," Schuyler continued, ignoring the skeptics. "Given its diminutive size and erratic behavior, I believe we are looking at a female Sasquatch, most likely in heat."

Hoots of derision rose among the skeptics while others scrutinized the photos with renewed interest. Soon, everyone squabbled with the person next to him over Schuyler's assertion.

"This might be a major breakthrough," Thor Svenson opined.

Thomas had had enough. "Folks," he began, rising to his feet. "I refuse to speculate about what Professor Tavolaro-Hennessey's report may contain."

"Why should you speculate if you already know?" Chloe quipped.

"We will all find out tomorrow after she presents her report to the judge," he continued, ignoring Chloe's remark. "And with that, I bid you all a good night. I'm going home."

By 9:30 the following morning, the Stirling Harbor Village Courthouse was packed. In addition to the *Save the Bayview Woods Coalition*, many residents of *Von Däniken Village* were on hand, waiting for Lisa's big announcement. Thomas and Roxanne sat near the judge's bench, awaiting ten o'clock for the proceedings to commence.

"I wonder where your friend Lisa is," Roxanne said in hushed tones.

"I suspect she's in the judge's chamber right now, presenting her findings," Thomas stated. "If I recall, protocol dictates she present a summary report to the judge before making any public announcement."

At five minutes to ten Vincent Tremayne and Martin Farquhar entered, making their way toward the front of the courtroom. "Hey, McGrath," Vincent called across the aisle. "What were you doing in the woods the other night? That's private property, you know."

Thomas felt a rush of fear. "I don't know what you're talking about."

"I saw you trespassing on the Country Squire property Friday evening," Vincent challenged. "What were you doing in there?"

Roxanne glanced at Thomas. "What's he talking about?" she whispered.

"I haven't a clue," Thomas lied. "He must be crazy."

"I know it was you McGrath," Vincent affirmed. "I waited by your driveway for half an hour hoping to catch you when you returned. What were you doing in there for so long?"

"Thomas," Roxanne whispered, "is there something going on that I don't know about?"

"No," Thomas emphatically replied.

"I'm going to catch you, McGrath," Vincent vowed before Martin Farquhar told him to keep quiet.

Thomas was about to reply when the bailiff entered the courtroom. In expectation of the judge's entry, at least half the people rose. "Hold on a minute, folks," the bailiff announced. "There's going to be a slight delay." Whispered speculation circulated amongst the spectators as the bailiff approached the people seated in the front row. "Judge Schulman would like to see you folks in his chamber," he said to Roxanne and Thomas. "That includes you too," he said to Vincent and Martin Farquhar. "Please follow me."

The bailiff ushered the four into the wood paneled chamber where Lisa and Judge Schulman waited. "Please sit," Judge Schulman said, motioning to a row of leather chairs arranged before his expansive desk. A court stenographer sat to the judge's right. "After hearing the preliminary findings of the State archaeologist, I have decided to hold this phase of the permit hearing *in-camera*," the judge began. He wrapped his knuckles on the desk. "This court's officially in session. Let the record show that in addition to the State archaeologist, Country Squire Development Corporation is represented by Vincent Tremayne and Martin Farquhar, Esquire, and the *Save the Bayview Woods Coalition* by Drs. Roxanne and Thomas McGrath." Judge Schulman squinted at his brief. "So, you're both anthropologists?"

"No, I'm a physician," Roxanne replied. "My husband is the anthropology professor."

"Yes sir," Thomas affirmed. "More specifically, I'm an archaeologist."

"So, that's how you knew to ask for a Cultural Impact Survey," the judge observed. "Very interesting."

"Hey! Isn't that unfair?" Vincent interjected. "It seems kind of like insider trading to me. How can he get away with that?"

"Well, it might be a very good thing Dr. McGrath thought to request a Cultural Impact Survey," Judge Schulman opined. "Wait 'till you hear what Professor Tavolaro-Hennessey has to say."

"Oh, great," Vincent said under his breath. "Another egghead."

"What was that?" Judge Schulman asked, his eyes widening in anger.

"Your honor, my client apologizes and we ask that his remarks be stricken from the record," Martin Farquhar stated. He pulled Vincent close. "Behave yourself," he whispered through gritted teeth.

Assuaged, Judge Schulman turned the floor over to Lisa, who distributed copies of her preliminary report, along with a file folder of supporting photographs. "Before I begin, perhaps you'd like to take a minute and look these papers over."

Vincent and Martin Farquhar glanced through their copies of the report. Roxanne looked on as Thomas read intently. "Oh, my God," he said gravely, flipping to the next page. "Oh, my God," he repeated in astonishment.

"Professor Tavolaro-Hennessey, you're going to have to help us by explaining all this," Martin Farquhar advised.

"By all means," Lisa replied. "Let me cut through all the technical jargon. After an initial surface survey in the bulldozed area on Saturday, I noticed a certain discoloration of the soil indicative of partially decomposed organic matter. I observed what I thought were linear patterns in the soil discoloration, suggesting that a man-made object, most likely made of wood, had been buried in that location. I never would have found it had the area not been bulldozed, thereby exposing the substrata."

"I knew it!" Vincent exclaimed. "You found a treasure chest on *my* land. What do you think of that, McGrath? She beat you to it, and it *all* belongs to me!"

"I'm sorry to disappoint you, but it's not a treasure chest," Lisa corrected. "It's something much bigger."

"I can't believe it," Thomas muttered as he flipped through the photographs. "I just can't believe it."

Martin Farquhar frowned. "Please, young lady. Continue."

"When I realized the size and general shape of the discoloration, I thought it best to take some overhead photographs, so I ran up to the hardware store and returned with a twelve foot step ladder. From that perspective, the shape of the buried object is clear."

Martin Farquhar examined the eight by ten glossy photographs from different angles. "It looks like a boat. Kind of like a canoe."

"They buried my treasure in a canoe?" Vincent asked.

"It's not a canoe," Lisa replied. "The dimensions and the construction material are inconsistent with any known pre-Columbian aboriginal boat design."

"Pre-Columbian?" Martin Farquhar asked. "Are you sure?"

"Oh, yes," Lisa replied coolly. "It predates Columbus by about five hundred years."

"This is the most amazing thing I've ever seen," Thomas remarked, transfixed on the photograph. "It's simply unbelievable."

"What in the world is it?" Roxanne asked.

"I'm going to have to call in experts in this field of archaeology to verify it," Lisa remarked. "But I believe we are looking at the remains of a clinker-built boat constructed of oak, with an approximate length of twenty meters and a beam of five meters."

"So what's the big deal?" Vincent asked angrily. "Some idiot buried a boat."

As Thomas came to grips with the implications of the discovery, he remembered the bogus Clovis point he'd buried nearby. "Where exactly is this boat located," he asked, masking his dread.

"Exactly where you suggested I should look," Lisa replied. "The center of the boat is approximately ten feet south of the test well."

"Wait a minute!" Vincent demanded. "Do you mean to say that McGrath told you what to look for? Your honor, these two are in cahoots!"

"Get a hold of yourself, Mr. Tremayne," Judge Schulman advised.

"Did you excavate?" Thomas asked guardedly.

"Good heavens, no," Lisa replied. "Apart from a six inch sounding I made to obtain a wood sample, I've left the site entirely undisturbed. Whatever human remains and grave goods are most likely buried at the center of the site must be excavated by experts. I've already made contact with the right people in Oslo and Stockholm."

"What the hell are you people talking about?" Vincent demanded. "You mean to tell me that some dead guy is actually buried in a boat—*on my land*?"

"That's exactly what I'm suggesting," Lisa replied. "We won't be certain until we've conducted a more detailed excavation of the site."

"Your honor, this is crazy!" Vincent barked. "Who in the world would bury somebody in a boat?"

"The Vikings," Thomas said with reverent awe.

"Now hold on a moment," Martin Farquhar said. "Your honor, with all due respect to Professor Tavolaro-Hennessey, this seems a bit farfetched. We have no evidence the Vikings ever made it this far across the ocean."

"You mean no evidence until now," Judge Schulman replied.

"It's not as far-fetched as you might think," Lisa stated. "The Norse sagas tell of how the Vikings visited a place called Vineland somewhere to the southwest of Greenland, and we know for certain the Norse reached L'Anse aux Meadows in Newfoundland around the year 1000. Their continued exploration could have brought them this far south."

"Exploration is one thing," Martin Farquhar conceded. "But a ship burial is another thing altogether. Wouldn't a burial site of that nature indicate the presence of a significant Viking colony in this area? If the Vikings settled here, how come we haven't we found evidence of it before now?"

"I don't know," Lisa replied. "All I can tell you is that my preliminary findings demonstrate that this site bears a striking similarity to ship burials excavated in Scandinavia, the Baltic, and the British Isles. This may be the first discovery of its kind in North America. If further investigation substantiates this, we're going to have to rethink everything we thought we knew about pre-Columbian trans-Atlantic contact."

"Let's cut to the chase," Vincent said. "How long is it going to take to wrap up your little investigation so we can finally bulldoze the rest of the woods and start building condos?"

"Build condos?" Lisa cried. "Mr. Tremayne, I don't think you understand. We may have discovered the first confirmed Viking burial site in North America."

"So, why can't we just dig the dead guy up and bury him someplace else where he won't be in anyone's way?" Vincent demanded.

Lisa's jaw fell open. "I've made my recommendation to Judge Schulman," she said after a stunned pause. "What happens next is up to him."

"Your honor, I'll offer to buy the dead guy a brand new coffin and a nice gravestone if we can just bury him someplace else," Vincent said. "Hell, I'll even throw in a new suit so the mortician can spruce him up for the wake."

Martin Farquhar sighed. "Your honor…" he began.

Judge Schulman held up a hand. "I've already made my decision," the judge advised. "This court finds there is sufficient preliminary evidence that the Country Squire property may contain one of the most significant archaeological discoveries in recent history. Until a more thorough study of the site is conducted, the Country Squire development project is on indefinite hold. In the meantime, so as not to disturb the integrity of the site, the property shall remain off limits to everyone except the research team designated by the State Office of Cultural and Historic Preservation."

"How long is that going to take?" Vincent demanded.

"I don't know," Lisa replied. "I can tell you that our Norwegian colleagues are very eager to get a look at the site, and, once the Swedes are on board, I'm sure we'll begin working in a few weeks."

Thomas thought of the bogus Clovis point and made a mental calculation. He didn't have much time.

"A few weeks?" Vincent moaned. "Do you realize how much this delay is costing me?"

"Investing in real estate is full of risks, Mr. Tremayne," Judge Schulman replied. "You're just going to have to wait."

Vincent shook his head in disbelief. "I just don't get it," he said. "What's so important about a dead guy and some old boat?"

"Mr. Tremayne, try to understand," Lisa urged. "This could be one of the greatest archaeological treasures of all time."

Vincent was about to protest but held his tongue. *The treasure! It's all about the treasure!* he thought. *This is a set up. McGrath... this archaeologist girl... maybe even the judge too. They're conspiring to steal a buried treasure on my land right out from under me.*

"Were you about to say something Mr. Tremayne?" Judge Schulman asked.

"No, your honor," Vincent said, red with anger.

"Good," the judge remarked. "There are just two more items before we adjourn. First, I'm imposing an injunction on the public release of anything having to do with this Cultural Impact Survey. No announcement is to be made to the press until the

State Office of Cultural and Historic Preservation has secured the site and begun a more extensive study."

"Why?" Lisa said, betraying an air of disappointment. "I've already called a press conference to announce the find."

"Cancel it," Judge Schulman ordered. "I realize you're eager to capture the headlines, but if you go public at this time, every looter with a metal detector and a shovel will be hopping the fence at night looking for buried treasure."

Damn! Vincent thought. *Is he able to read my mind?*

"I see your point," Lisa admitted dejectedly.

"Don't worry," he added. "You'll get to announce your find soon enough." Judge Schulman next summoned the bailiff and directed he announce to the courtroom spectators the indefinite suspension of the Country Squire building project. With that, everyone in the judge's chamber rose to leave. "Hold on," the judge demanded. "There's one last thing. Mr. Tremayne, this court is imposing on you a fine of five hundred dollars."

"Another five hundred!" Vincent squawked shrilly. "What for?"

"The test well," Judge Schulman replied. "It's in clear violation of my last order prohibiting any invasive work. By disregarding my explicit order you could have damaged something priceless."

"Your honor, please," Martin Farquhar implored. "My client is not in direct supervision of the daily operations of the Country Squire Development Corporation. I assure you, the test well was commissioned by mistake, not in defiance of your orders."

Judge Schulman pondered the matter. "Alright," he said congenially. "Mr. Tremayne, I'm suspending the fine, but I'm letting you off with a warning. If I catch you in violation of my orders again I'll throw the book at you. Nobody—and I mean *nobody*—is allowed on that land unless they are there on official business at the behest of the State Office of Cultural and Historic Preservation. If I learn that any portion of the land had been tampered with or damaged in any way due to your negligence, I will hold you in contempt of court and you may face serious criminal charges. Am I making myself clear, Mr. Tremayne?"

Martin Farquhar spoke before Vincent had the chance to put his foot in his mouth. "My client thanks you for your leniency and is eager to comply in every way."

"Very well," Judge Schulman said. "*Now* we are adjourned."

CHAPTER 14

The courtroom spectators had grown restless to the point of rowdiness, yet everyone fell silent when the bailiff emerged from the judge's chamber. "Can I have your attention please," the bailiff announced. "Judge Schulman has ruled that the Country Squire development project is on indefinite hold pending further investigation of the building site by the State Office of Cultural and Historic Preservation. There will be no public hearing today. That is all."

Cheers erupted in the courtroom when Roxanne and Thomas emerged from the judge's chamber. After a round of handshakes and back-slapping with the members of the *Save the Bayview Woods Coalition*, the McGraths escaped by slipping out a side door. Outside on the courthouse steps, a throng from *Von Däniken Village* pressed around Lisa, expecting a press conference.

"Ladies and gentlemen, I'm sorry," Lisa began. "By order of the judge, the preliminary findings of the Cultural Impact Survey are sealed for the time being. There will be no press conference today."

"No press conference?" someone shouted. "What's going on here?"

"You people were supposed to tell us what's been discovered," another person cried.

Lisa held up her hands in an attempt to quell the angry protests. "Please! Please! Try to understand. I would love to discuss this with you, but the judge has ordered the findings sealed until a more extensive study of the site is made. I urge you to be patient."

Casey pushed his way to the front of the crowd. "What are you people hiding? The public has a right to know what's out there."

"We're not hiding anything. It's just that the judge believes the public's best interest is served by not disclosing what's been discovered."

"So, you *have* discovered something," Sibyl observed. Every eye fell on Lisa and the crowd grew silent, awaiting an explanation.

Lisa drew a deep breath and thought for a moment. "No comment," she said at length.

"This is a cover up!" a man shouted.

"They're sending government agents in to remove the evidence!" a woman cried.

"No! No!" Lisa protested. "It's nothing like that."

"I bet they've found evidence of extraterrestrial life!" Casey shouted to rising cheers.

"I think they've cornered Sasquatch!" Schuyler declared.

"They must have opened a portal to another dimension!" Chloe warbled ecstatically.

"Please! Be reasonable!" Lisa urged.

"This could be what we've all been waiting for!" Thor Svenson exclaimed as the hysteria mounted.

"It's the Age of Aquarius!" Sibyl proclaimed with uplifted hands.

"Everybody, please listen!" Lisa cried to no avail as the tumult rose to a frenzy.

"If they won't tell us what's in the woods," a man shouted, "let's find out for ourselves!" With that, the crowd turned and rushed towards the *Von Däniken Village* shuttle bus parked by the curb. Dozens more climbed into private vehicles and raced off in the direction of the Bayview Woods.

Lisa watched in stunned disbelief as the crowd disbursed. Realizing the danger, she rushed back into the courtroom to find the bailiff. "Call the police!" she cried. "Those old nuts are headed for the archaeological site!"

"Yeeeeeeeeeeeehaaaaaaaaaa!" Roxanne howled as Thomas pulled out of the courthouse parking lot. "Them woods ain't goin' nowhere!" she declared in her most raucous West Texas accent. "Boy, it's time to celebrate. I'm goin' to buy you a beer!"

"Great," Thomas said dryly. "But it's not even 11:00 o'clock yet."

"Who cares? Let's go crazy! Good news like this doesn't come along very often."

"Alright," Thomas said with a hint of melancholia. "Where would you like to go?"

Roxanne shot Thomas a quizzical look. "Thomas, what's wrong with you? This is a time for rejoicing. Why aren't you happy?"

"I'm happy. This is a most agreeable outcome."

"A most agreeable outcome? That's got to be the understatement of the century. When did you turn into Mr. Spock?"

"What do you mean?"

"Good God in heaven! The Bayview Woods are saved! *And* there's a Viking grave about a quarter mile from our back door. A Viking grave, Thomas! Even *I* know that's about the biggest deal ever in the archaeology world. You should be doing cartwheels. Why aren't you excited?"

"I am excited. As Lisa said, if this find turns out to be genuine, it's going to force us to rethink everything. But it's also going to piss off a lot of people."

"But why?" Roxanne asked. "I'd think everyone would be really thrilled about this discovery. It gives the scholarly world a whole new perspective on what actually happened before Columbus. Just think of the implications."

"And that's exactly why I'm restraining my enthusiasm. Roxy, don't you realize the incredible firestorm this find is going to generate?"

"Why do you have to put it in such a negative light?"

"Listen. A few mavericks have spent their careers arguing that the Bering Land Bridge wasn't the only route of migration into the New World. They argue that Neolithic hunter-gatherer groups from Europe also made the journey, moving westward along the pack ice."

"Well, then, doesn't this prove their argument?" Roxanne asked.

"Not exactly," Thomas replied. "Viking contact with the New World took place significantly later than the Neolithic period. But you are correct in saying that proof of Viking colonization of North America puts the lie to the impossibility of a pre-Columbian trans-Atlantic migration."

"But that's a good thing. Isn't it?"

"Yes, but don't forget—most mainstream anthropologists have dismissed these theories as nonsense. If Lisa's discovery turns out to be genuine, there's going to be a lot of academics who'll be forced to eat crow. Rather than suffer the humiliation of having to admit they were wrong, you know what they're going to do?"

Roxanne look puzzled. "Well... No. What?"

"They're going to go on the attack," Thomas replied. "They're going to nitpick. They're going to look for any inconsistency... any anomaly... any archaeological outlier... anything at all that they can latch onto to discredit this discovery and brand it a hoax. Because the very existence of this site will challenge the 'Beringia Only' theory, they will pull out all the stops and go to war against it."

"OK," Roxanne said. "But isn't a healthy dose of skepticism a good thing? After all, if archaeologists didn't critically analyze all the evidence, what's preventing some disreputable huckster from coming along and cooking up an archaeological hoax by littering the field with counterfeit artifacts? That kind of thing must happen from time to time, doesn't it?"

Thomas thought of his undiscovered fake Clovis point, poised to contaminate one of the greatest archaeological discoveries of all time. "Yeah," he said. "It does."

Gianna Fox, senior reporter for the *Sterling Harbor Gazette*, mingled in the crowd on the steps of the courthouse. She was grateful that Lisa had given her a couple of days notice about this press conference, allowing her enough time to formulate pertinent questions around which to flesh out an interesting article. She was disappointed by it's abrupt cancellation, yet the very fact that this was by order of the judge piqued her interest, and the crowd's angry reaction only added to her curiosity that perhaps something really newsworthy had taken place. A cutesy local interest story might fill space, but an exposé about a court-ordered cover-up would make the front page headline.

Gianna jumped in her car and took off in pursuit of the *Von Däniken Village* shuttle bus. Before reaching the outskirts of town, Gianna's police scanner crackled to life. "All available units—10-34 in progress, in the vicinity of Main Road and Private Road 6," the dispatcher announced. "All units proceed with caution."

Wow! Gianna thought. *A 10-34—that's the code for an active riot.* Knowing that other news agencies monitored the police frequencies, she realized it was only a matter of time before other reporters came poaching on her beat. Determined to get the scoop, she stood on the gas and shot past the shuttle bus on her way to the Bayview Woods.

Vincent stormed past his secretary towards his office and slammed the door behind him. Snatching up the phone, he punched in Daphne's cell number.

"Country Squire Condominiums," Daphne answered. "Senior Sales Agent Daph..."

"Yeah, enough with that already," Vincent snapped. "What's going on with the appraisal of the Country Squire property?"

"They're working on it, as far as I know. As soon as they're done I'm planning to move ahead with the fountain installation. By the way, did you get a chance to look at the color swatches I left…"

"I can't be bothered with any of that right now!" Vincent shouted. "We're facing a huge tax bill and we need to get the new appraisal to the Assessor's office immediately. When the hell are you going to submit the paperwork?"

"Well, aren't you Mr. Grumpy! If you think you can handle things any better, why don't you take care of it yourself?"

"Daphne, I don't have time for this. Just get it done. I want the appraiser's report submitted to the Assessor by the end of the week, do you understand? Do whatever it takes!"

"Fine, Grouchy!" Daphne fired back. "Now about those paint swatches…"

Vincent noticed the blinking light on his phone. "I've got another call," he said as he hit line two. "Vincent Tremayne here."

"Mr. Tremayne, this is Chief Latham of the Stirling Harbor Police Department. I'm calling to inform you of a little incident we're dealing with right now out at the Bayview Woods…"

Louis Nickels and Moon arrived unexpectedly at the Country Squire Development Corporation office. "Where's the blond girl?" Louis Nickels asked as he entered.

"I think she's on the phone in the back office," Rayette replied. She glanced at Moon and smiled. "Oh, hello," she said, blushing.

"Expulsions are opportunity best for luncheon," he said, handing her a cardboard box containing six chilidogs. "Vending truck makes of worthy stopping—with chips and soda, of course."

"Ooo…" Rayette cooed admiringly as Moon pulled up a chair.

Daphne poked her head out of the back office. "Hey! Are you guys finished with the appraisal yet?"

"No," Louis Nickels replied. "The cops bounced us off when all those weirdoes showed up and started poking around."

"Were they customers? Was anyone asking about the *Fontana di Nettuno*?"

"That's none of my business. All I know is that we can't submit an appraisal to the Village Assessor without first completing the actuary's report."

"How long is that going to take?"

"Open your ears! I just told you the cops threw us out. How do you expect us to estimate potential flood damage if we're not allowed on the property?"

"Well, isn't there any other way?" Daphne asked.

"Yeah," Louis Nickels replied. "But it ain't going to be cheap."

"What do you…" Daphne's inquiry was interrupted when her cell phone rang. "Hold on," she said, taking the call.

"I just got off the phone with the Chief of Police!" Vincent bellowed. "There are people swarming all over the Country Squire property!"

"Which is exactly why we need the fountain, smarty pants," Daphne rejoined. "Those are all customers with refined taste. I can't just hand out brochures to people like that."

Daphne could hear Vincent's heavy breathing. "What we need is a fence. Why the hell haven't they finished putting it up?"

"All you do is complain!" Daphne shrieked. "And I'm sick and tired of it. I'm the Senior Sales Agent, not the complaint department!"

Vincent fought hard to suppress his rage. "You're right," he replied softly with great effort. "I'm sorry. Do you think you might be able to give a call to the fence company and suggest they finish the job soon?"

"One day it's the appraisal, the next day it's the fence. You keep nagging me with all these little jobs. Stop flip-flopping and get your priorities straight!"

Vincent balled his fists and drew a deep breath. "OK," he said cheerily. "The fence, then. Is that alright?"

"I'll handle it," Daphne replied. "Now *I* have to go. *I* have a meeting," she added with unconcealed satisfaction as she hung up on him.

Louis Nickels stood nearby, scowling. "So what's it going to be? I haven't got all day."

"Can you finish the fence today?" Daphne asked.

"Yeah. But what about the actuary's report?"

"Can you get everything to the Village Assessor by Friday?"

"Yeah," Louis Nickels said. "But I told you, it ain't going to be cheap."

"Do whatever it takes, then."

"Not without a contract."

"Fine," Daphne said. "Just get the paperwork to the Assessor by Friday."

Louis Nickels turned to observe Moon cutting into a cannoli the size of a pipe bomb. "I can only eat half," Rayette giggled.

"Moon, go out to the Edsel and get the valise," Louis Nickels directed. "We got another job."

CHAPTER 15

Laura Croft did a back flip across a chasm of boiling tar. "Come on, baby!" Lance Fairchild cried. "Do it! Do it! That's it!" He felt his abdomen tighten as his true love crouched to avoid the snapping maws of a lunging Hydra. "Damn!" he exclaimed as the enraged monster smashed the last remaining causeway to bits of rubble. "Now! Now!" Lance urged as Laura Croft leapt to a lower ledge. "Damn you!" he cursed as the Hydra's molten venom ignited a rope bridge. "Come on, baby!" he repeated.

Bix Fairchild stormed into the Makanhassett Tribal Council chamber. "Quick!" he said. "Turn on News 12."

Lance put the game on pause. "Huh?" he murmured, looking up from the recliner.

"Right. OK," Bix said into his cell phone. He snapped his fingers at Lance. "Come on! News 12, right now!"

Lance rolled forward and hit the remote, switching back to TV mode. Bix hung up and flopped into the neighboring chair. "Who was that on the phone?" Lance asked.

"Cousin Sol," Bix replied. "Shut up and let me watch this."

"*...disturbance began yesterday after Village Justice Alan Schulman placed an indefinite hold on all building permits sought by the Country Squire*

Development Corporation. The controversial project involving a parcel of wooded land along the Main Road just west of the business district has been…" a television reporter explained.

"Hey!" Lance interrupted. "Isn't that the land we sold to Tremayne?"

"Yeah," Bix said. "Shut up, will ya?"

"… *adding to the controversy, Judge Schulman caused quite a stir with the sudden imposition of a gag order restraining the State archaeologist from disclosing her findings. A press conference scheduled for after the hearing was abruptly cancelled, fueling speculation among some of an official cover-up,*" the reporter continued. "*We spoke with one woman who identified herself only as 'Crystal'…*"

"Come on, Bix," Lance said. "This sucks. Let me go back to playing *Tomb Raider.*"

"Would you shut up?" the chief chided. "This is important."

The news report cut away to recorded footage of a middle aged woman in an iridescent body suit standing in front of a high chain link fence. "*It's just not right, man,*" Crystal said, staring wide-eyed into the camera. "*Somebody from the government obviously found something very important here, but they won't tell us what it is. This land belonged to the Native Americans long before any of us were born and they were very spiritual with a cosmic consciousness that transcends anything we can remotely comprehend to the point of communing with extraterrestrial life as pure energy in quantum fields of light where space and infinity merge as wholeness. Do you see what I'm saying, man?*"

"*So, you believe this is a deliberate cover-up?*" the reporter asked.

"*Oh yeah, man!*" Crystal replied. "*I mean, it's like they're totally trying to hide something! You can feel it here, man. This place has such energy! That's why they fenced us out, man. Do you see what I'm saying? Right on this spot the Indians, or the Native Americans or whatever name they called themselves, spoke with extraterrestrials that they called gods, or God, or the divine force or the Unmoved Mover like the ancient Greeks called him or her or them, whatever, man, the Big Bigness that fills the void. This is why the government killed off the Indians or the Native Americans or whatever they called themselves because the government doesn't want people to learn how to transcend like they used to and that's why they outlawed mescaline, man. Do you see what I'm saying?*"

The news report cut back to the reporter standing in front of a Village of Stirling Harbor patrol car. "*When asked to comment, all Judge Schulman would say is that eventual disclosure of all preliminary findings will follow a more thorough archaeological study of the site,*" the reporter explained. "*Sources tell News 12 that the State Office of Cultural and Historic Preservation has assembled an international team of experts and that a second site survey will begin in the next few days. In the meantime, the site has been sealed and the police are keeping the curious at bay. In other local news…*" Bix grabbed the remote and hit the mute button.

"Can I go back to my game now?" Lance asked.

"No," Bix said. "We're having an emergency meeting of the tribal council. Sol is on his way over and Ralph went to get Old Earl."

Twenty minutes later all the members of the Makanhassett Tribal Council sat around the conference table in the council chamber. As chief, Bix Fairchild called the meeting to order. "In case you haven't heard the news, let me bring you all up to speed. Last month we unloaded that bug-infested patch of marshland on the North Fork to Vincent Tremayne, the oil man."

Everyone around the table chuckled. "How much did we beat him out of?" Old Earl asked.

"Eight hundred thousand," Bix replied.

Old Earl nodded. "Not bad. We probably could have pressed him for eight fifty."

"Probably," Bix conceded. "I was sick of haggling with him, though."

"We still took him for a ride at eight hundred grand," Old Earl remarked.

Bix nodded silently in consideration.

"I can't stand that guy," Lance said.

"Me neither," Ralph added. "The diesel he sells us is crap. Three of our trawlers have been out of service at one time or another this summer with fouled fuel lines."

"We all agree Tremayne's a bastard," Bix said. "But I'm having second thoughts about whether we should have sold off that parcel of land."

"I don't think we could have gotten a better deal," Ralph stated. "You've got to remember, Bix, that half that land turns to swamp with the spring rains. It's a rotten place to build anything."

"Still, in light of recent developments, I think we should try to get it back," Bix said.

"Get it back?" Old Earl cried. "What on earth for? We made a killing on it."

"I know," Bix said. "But Sol and I think there's an opportunity here for us to really clean up."

The members of the tribal council looked at the chief with suspicion. "How?" Lance asked.

Sol Pharaoh held up a copy of the *Stirling Harbor Gazette*. "Have you guys seen this story?" he asked, pointing to the front page headline. "Tremayne's building plans are on hold because an archaeological survey turned up something 'culturally significant' on the land."

"So?" Old Earl said. "What's that to us? Let Tremayne deal with it."

"Let me explain," Sol replied. "This whole story became front page news when the judge over in Stirling Harbor sealed the findings of the State archaeologist. Now there's a lot of people convinced this is some kind of government cover-up."

"I still don't see why this concerns us," Old Earl said.

"According to this story, some odd-ball theories are floating around that the government is covering up something like a UFO landing site," Sol explained. "There are other crackpot theories too. One woman speculates that some kind of magnetic anomaly might link the site to the Bermuda Triangle. And check this out," he said pointing to a particular paragraph. "Here's a guy who thinks the State archaeologist uncovered evidence of Big Foot."

"Wait a second," Lance said. "What if they *did* find Big Foot?"

"Don't be ridiculous!" Sol exclaimed. "These people are a bunch of kooks. We get nuts like this all the time at the Visitor's Center."

"And that brings us to the main point," Bix said. "Since we're not running a casino, people always assume we must be really *spiritual*."

"What do you mean?" Lance asked.

Bix turned to his cousin. "Tell us, Sol. As Public Relations Chairman, how often do you get inquiries about when we're having the next 'Sweat Lodge'?"

"At least ten times a day," Sol replied. "You should also see the emails I get from people who want one of us to guide them on a 'Vision Quest'."

"Our ancestors gave up the Sweat Lodge thing way back," Ralph interjected. "And our people were *never* into the Vision Quest. That's something Indians do out West."

"But none of that matters," Bix said. "People *believe* we're into all that stuff."

"In fact," Sol added, "most people are pretty disappointed when I explain the way it really is with us Makanhassetts."

"I still don't see what you boys are driving at?" Old Earl commented.

"Yesterday afternoon I got a call from Gianna Fox, the reporter who broke this story," Sol explained. "She wanted me to offer some explanation about what the archaeologist might have found, since the land used to belong to the tribe."

"What did you tell her?" Ralph asked.

"I told her I hadn't a clue what the archaeologist found," Sol replied. "At first she didn't believe me, but I told her I really didn't know. She kept pressing me though, figuring the State archaeologist or the judge must have contacted us about the discovery."

Old Earl looked puzzled. "Why would she think they'd contact us?"

It was Sol's turn to look perplexed. "Isn't it obvious? A mysterious archaeological discovery is made on land that once belonged to the Makanhassett Tribe. You'd think the State archaeologist would've had the courtesy to tell us what it is."

"But why?" Old Earl asked.

"Because whatever it is, chances are it was made by our ancestors," Sol replied. "Hell, it could even *be* one of our ancestors for all we know. Anyway, she told me off the record that there's a buzz going around Stirling Harbor Village Hall that what they found is so serious, Tremayne is *never* going to get his building permits."

"Screw the greedy bastard then!" Ralph interjected. "It serves him right for selling us crappy diesel."

"Hold on a second," Old Earl said. "Getting back to what you were saying about trying to get the land back—if Tremayne can't get his permits, what possible value would that land be to us?"

Bix and Sol smiled conspiratorially. "We were thinking of turning it into a theme park," Bix explained.

"Cool!" Lance cried. "Are we going to have a rollercoaster?"

"Not that kind of theme park," Bix replied. "A *spiritual* theme park."

"What in the world are you fellas getting at?" Ralph inquired.

"Didn't you see that report on News 12?" Sol asked. "There had to be at least a hundred nut cases trying to gain access to that land—all because it has something on it they think is spiritually significant. If we can get that land back and make a big deal over whatever they've found, we can cash in on it."

"A rollercoaster sounds much more fun," Lance opined.

"You're missing the point," Bix explained. "There's already a big market for anything involving Indian spirituality—dreamcatchers… kachina dolls… you name it."

"But that's Chippewa and Hopi stuff from out West," Ralph protested.

"Right," Bix conceded. "But whatever turned up on Tremayne's land is from *our* culture. Why don't we try to get that land back and take advantage of all this free publicity?"

"Wait a second," Ralph said. "I think I see what you're getting at. You're suggesting we stoke the flames of this conspiracy theory nonsense and get people really jazzed up over whatever's out there."

"That's step one," Bix said.

"And then once everyone is convinced it's the most sacred thing in the Makanhassett universe, we charge folks an entrance fee just to get close to it so they can soak up the spirituality," Ralph concluded.

"Exactly," Bix remarked. "And in the process, we soak them. Since that land is worthless to Tremayne without a building permit, I bet he'll sell it back to us really cheap."

"That's an interesting scheme," Old Earl remarked. "But you boys are overlooking an important detail."

"What's that?" Bix asked.

"The tribe only acquired that land in 1953," Old Earl said. "I haven't a clue what they found on it, but it almost certainly has nothing to do with us."

A stunned silence fell. "No way!" Sol Pharaoh finally exclaimed. "Are you sure about that?"

"I'm certain of it," Old Earl replied. "I can remember exactly when we bought it. It was right after I got back from Korea. Everyone in the country was buying automobiles and we were all hepped up on the idea of building a drive-in movie theater. Stirling Harbor was just beginning to take off as a summer tourist destination, so we figured a location along the Main Road just west of town couldn't lose."

"You mean that's not our ancestral land?" Bix asked in amazement.

"I'm afraid not," Old Earl replied. "We acquired that land from an outfit called the *Peconic Rod and Gun Club*. Before they had it, it had been a part of the old Hancock estate going back to colonial times."

"But what ever happened to the drive in theater?" Sol asked.

"We never built it," Old Earl replied. "Half the property is marshland and it's loaded with mosquitoes too. Once we weighed the construction costs against operating expenses, we figured it just wasn't worth it. Anyway, we didn't pay much for the land, so it was no big deal. We figured we'd just sit on it until a buyer came along."

"Well, I guess that plan's out the window," Lance said. "We could still buy it back and put up a rollercoaster, though."

Bix sighed. "I'm sorry I dragged you guys here for nothing."

"It was a pretty good plan, though," Ralph opined.

"It still is a good plan," Old Earl said. "I don't think you boys should throw in the towel just yet."

"What do you mean?" Sol asked. "I thought you said the thing they found out there couldn't be from our ancestors."

"Well, maybe it is, maybe it isn't," Old Earl said. "Don't forget, there were Indians here for thousands of years, even if they weren't Makanhassetts. In any case, it doesn't really matter what they've found, just so long as we *claim* it's ours."

Everyone pondered this. "But what if they found something that turns out to be stupid," Sol asked. "Like an old washing machine or a rusted bicycle."

"It doesn't matter," Old Earl replied. "You guys said it yourselves—people already believe there's something out there that the government's trying to hide. If what the State archaeologist found turns out to be important, then we can claim it's ours and make a big deal out of it. If the find turns out to be something dull, we'll just make something up anyway and tell everyone the government was trying to hide it from the public."

"Make something up?" Ralph asked. "Like what, for example?"

"Oh, I don't know," Old Earl conceded. "Didn't you say someone thought maybe they found evidence of extraterrestrials or a UFO or something?"

"Yeah," Sol said. "That seems to be a common speculation."

"Well then, if we get the land back, we can make up some wacky story that our ancestors used to commune with the sky gods on that spot," Old Earl explained. "We'll make up some crazy *ancient* folktale that our shamans used to meet there during the full moon with the Sky Spirits who came from another world in a flying machine."

"Do you think anyone would really fall for it?" Bix asked. "Can we draw in enough people to make it worth our while?"

Old Earl chuckled. "Listen. I was discharged out of Camp Pendleton after I got back from Korea. One of my buddies had a car, so a bunch of us chipped in for gas and we all drove back east together. You should have seen Route 66 in those days! There were roadside attractions everywhere. Giant corn cobs, concrete teepees, you name it. But the Queen Mother of them all was the *Mystic Spot*."

"The *Mystic Spot*?" Lance marveled. "Where was that?"

"Tucumcari, New Mexico," Old Earl replied. "We started seeing billboards for the *Mystic Spot* hundreds of miles before we got there. Every sign was more intriguing than the one before it. I remember one sign had a spinning spiral surrounded by bouncing question marks. *Don't Miss the Mystic Spot! You Will Be Amazed!* Anyway, by the time we got to Tucumcari we were in such a lather to see it. We pulled off the highway, and I'm telling you—you wouldn't believe your eyes! A line of cars backed up half a mile just to get into the parking lot."

"What did you do?" Lance asked.

"We waited, just like everyone else," Old Earl explained. "I'll never forget it—while we waited on line, this old timer came rolling along, pedaling a bicycle vending cart. When he came up alongside us, we couldn't help noticing that the old boy had no legs! The whole thing was worked with hand cranks. 'Lost my gams at Belleau Wood,' he said. Well, we'd be damned if we were going to let a fellow Letherneck pass by without buying something."

"So what'd you buy," Sol queried.

"Just about every damn thing he had," Old Earl replied. "I think we drank half a case of coke before we even made it to the parking lot. That was the first time I ate tamales, too. Well, we eventually found a parking spot and then stood in line for half an hour to buy tickets to go through the gates—into the *Mystic Spot.* Guess how much it cost."

"Tell us," Ralph begged.

"A whole buck!" Old Earl replied. "That was serious money back in those days. But we were happy to pay it just to get a chance to finally see the *Mystic Spot.* Do you boys catch my drift?"

Bix and Sol nodded silently while Ralph sat stone-faced. Lance was on the edge of his seat in eager expectation. "No," he said.

"He means those people in New Mexico were making a fortune from suckers who would've paid a buck just to watch paint dry," Ralph explained.

"Was the old Marine in on it?" Bix asked.

"Who knows?" Old Earl replied. "Either way, we bought a cartload of his tamales."

"You think we could pull off something like that nowadays?" Sol asked.

"Well, isn't it essentially the same business plan you boys are thinking about?" Old Earl replied. "It doesn't matter what's on the land. All that matters is that people *think* it's a big deal. According to those news reports, you guys already have a large clientele. All you need to do now is give them what they want."

Bix nodded. "So, that puts us back on track," he said. "If you guys are in agreement, I'll contact Tremayne and make him an offer."

"For how much?" Old Earl asked.

"Four hundred grand," Bix said. "That's half of what he paid."

"Good!" Old Earl said. "But not one cent more. Play hardball with him. If he agrees to four hundred, you have my vote."

"Me too," Ralph added. "I vote 'yes' if we get him down to four hundred grand."

"What do you say, Lance?" Bix asked. "Are you with us?"

"Yeah, but what if he balks?"

Everyone considered this. "If he balks, we'll threaten to go to the press," Old Earl said. "Sol, did that reporter from the paper leave you her number?"

"Got it right here," Sol replied. "And her email address too."

"Good. If Tremayne holds out, we'll threaten to go to the press with the *whole truth* about how that land was sacred to our ancestors. Tell Tremayne we'll raise such a stink that he'll never find another buyer for that land, much less get a permit to build on it. That should bring him to his senses."

"Wow!" Ralph exclaimed. "If we pull this off, we'll still be up four hundred thousand bucks."

"And don't forget the money we stand to make with the Great Spirit theme park," Bix added.

"So what's the next step?" Ralph asked.

Bix checked his watch. "If we're all agreed, I think it's time to give Tremayne a call."

"Hold on," Lance cried. "I have one more question."

"Shoot!" Bix said.

"What exactly was the *Mystic Spot*? I'm dying to find out."

Old Earl stroked his chin. "It's hard to say exactly," he replied after giving it some thought. "It was unlike anything I've ever seen before or since."

"But.. but…" Lance stammered. "What *was* it?"

"I don't really know, to tell you the truth. It was unique, I can tell you that."

"Was it worth a buck, though?" Sol asked. "Was it really worth waiting in line for?"

"It was worth every penny," Old Earl replied. "And if I had it to do over again, I'd wait in a line twice as long."

"You're not joking, are you?" Ralph asked.

"Good heavens, no," Old Earl affirmed.

"You really liked it?" Sol queried.

"The *Mystic Spot* was one of the most amazing things I've ever seen," Old Earl responded. "It was truly marvelous."

"And you didn't feel cheated?" Bix asked.

"Are you kidding?" Old Earl rejoined. "The whole experience changed my life."

CHAPTER 16

"Mr. Tremayne, you have a call on line one," the secretary said through the intercom.

"Who is it?"

"Bix Fairchild, of the Makanhassett Tribal…"

"Yeah, yeah. I know who he is," Vincent interrupted. He picked up the phone and pressed the button. "Vincent Tremayne here," he said unceremoniously.

"Vincent, old buddy! How are you doing?" Bix said cheerily.

"You didn't call to find out how I'm doing. What do you want?"

"Well, we couldn't help but notice you've run into some trouble getting your building permits. That's really unfortunate. All of us on the tribal council wanted to express how sorry we are about that."

Vincent immediately grew suspicious. "Thanks," he said guardedly, followed by an awkward silence.

Bix cleared his throat. "Well, we were wondering what you're planning to do now—in light of these recent setbacks, I mean."

"Quit beating around the bush. Tell me why you really called."

"Alright," Bix replied with a restrained chuckle. "The tribal council would like to help you out of your predicament and buy the land back from you."

Everyone's after my treasure, Vincent thought. *I wonder how high they'll be willing to go.* "That's great," Vincent remarked. "I'm ready to make a deal."

"Super!" Bix responded.

"Two million," Vincent said.

"I beg your pardon?"

"I'll sell the land back to you for two million dollars."

The audacity of Vincent's price left Bix momentarily speechless. "Two million? You do realize the tribal council is offering to do you a favor, don't you?"

"Listen, I'm very busy. You can have it for two million. Take it or leave it."

"You're never going to get a building permit for that land, Tremayne. And no other buyer will touch it in light of recent events. It's worthless as a building site."

"Then why do you want to buy it back?"

Bix thought a moment before answering. "We would like to reclaim our cultural heritage."

"I don't know what that means," Vincent remarked.

"The land has sentimental value to us," Bix bluffed. "We want to reclaim it to honor our ancestors."

"You can reclaim it for two million bucks."

"Be serious, Tremayne. We'll give you three hundred grand for it."

"Go to hell," Vincent said coldly.

"I strongly advise you to reconsider."

"That almost sounds like a threat."

"There's no threat. I'm just trying to impress upon you the reality of the situation. Once word gets out about how sacred that land is to the Makanhassett people, you're going to find yourself in an even more awkward situation. Why not sell now and recoup some money while you still can?"

"If that land is so sacred to the Makanhassett people, why did you sell it off in the first place?"

Lacking a credible answer, Bix ignored the question. "Listen Tremayne. I really think you should…"

"You know what *I* think?" Vincent challenged. "I think that hick cowgirl who works for you tipped you off about the treasure on *my* land. Now that you've realized your mistake, you're working in cahoots with the McGraths to chisel in on *my* treasure."

What treasure? Could he be serious? "Listen. That's our cultural heritage," Bix bluffed. "When the public finds out that you cheated a bunch of poor Indians, do you realize what's going to happen?"

"That sounds like another threat," Vincent said.

"OK, Tremayne," Bix said in a conciliatory tone. "Let's not argue. We'll up our offer to three fifty. What do you say?"

"I say 'up yours,' Chief!" Vincent barked as he slammed down the phone.

Bix Fairchild calmly hung up. The members of the tribal council silently studied his countenance. "What'd he say?" Lance asked.

"He won't budge," Bix replied. "But he did say something *very* interesting. He thinks we're in on some kind of conspiracy with Roxanne and Thomas McGrath to get at a *treasure*."

"A treasure?" Lance asked. "Like—*a pirate chest full of doubloons*—kind of treasure?"

"I don't know," Bix replied. "But I *do* know Tommy McGrath was the one who requested the Cultural Impact Survey in the first place."

"Do you think maybe Tommy is really on to something?" Lance asked. "He *is* an archaeologist, after all—just like Indiana Jones. Isn't that what they do—dig up treasure, I mean?"

"I'll drop by the clinic later and ask Roxy if she knows anything," Bix stated. "In any event, Tremayne's convinced there's something really valuable on that land."

"So what do we do now?" Ralph asked.

"We switch to Plan B," Bix replied.

"OK," Sol said. "I'll give Gianna Fox a call."

"You do that," Bix directed. "Invite her over here and we'll give her the old razzle-dazzle. One of us is going to have to play the part of the wise medicine man, though."

The members of the tribal council looked back and forth amongst themselves. "I volunteer," Old Earl said. "Leave that part to me."

Gianna Fox was on the prowl for another scoop, so when Sol Pharaoh called offering a lead, she jumped at it. "So, what's this new information you mentioned," she asked as Sol ushered her into the council chamber.

"There's been a big screw up," Sol explained. "You know that land over on the North Fork?"

"You mean the parcel you sold to Tremayne?"

"Yeah, that one. The old folks around here are very upset about what the tribal council did."

"What do you mean?" Gianna asked.

"We didn't really have the right to sell that land," Sol said. "I, uh… I don't know how to put this…"

Gianna looked puzzled. "But doesn't the council exercise fiduciary responsibility over all tribal property?"

"Yes, but…" Sol hesitated. "There's much more to it than that."

"I don't follow."

Sol appeared to grope for words. "This is a very sensitive matter. It involves the sacred beliefs of our ancestors. I could get in a lot of trouble with our shaman if I said too much."

"Your shaman? I didn't know the Makanhassetts had a shaman."

"Oh, yes," Sol remarked. "We try not to bandy it about since our ancient ways are normally hidden from outsiders—so as not to profane the sacred rites."

"Wow!" Gianna exclaimed. "If you tell me what's going on I promise I'll be discreet."

"I don't know," Sol said skeptically. "Maybe it would be better if you spoke with our shaman directly."

"That would be great! Can we arrange that?"

Sol bit his lip pensively. "I'm not sure he'll go for it. He's very old and *very* suspicious of outsiders."

"Please! I promise to be respectful. Could you ask him if he'll talk to me?"

Sol considered the matter. "Well, it couldn't hurt to ask. Let me see if he's done with his ablutions."

Gianna waited in reverent silence after Sol slipped out of the council chamber. Five minutes later the door creaked open and Sol poked his head into the room. "Please rise out of respect."

Gianna shot to her feet and watched as Sol led Old Earl into the room. Bedecked in wampum beads and a feather headdress, Old Earl stepped haltingly and grasped for a chair back to steady his gait.

"Sit here, grandfather," Sol said as he deferentially pulled out a chair. Old Earl lowered himself down with considerable effort. He sat silently for a moment with eyes closed, affecting a look of stoic grief.

"Please sit, young lady," Old Earl croaked in a barely audible voice.

Gianna pulled her chair close. "May I record this?" she asked, producing a mini recorder. The shaman had not yet opened his eyes and Gianna surmised he grappled with some deep inner turmoil. At length, Old Earl offered a slow and deliberate nod.

"Sir, I hear that the elders of your community are upset about the sale of some tribal land. Can you explain why?"

Old Earl's eyes fluttered open and he cleared his throat. "These young ones have forgotten our ancient ways," he said, pointing towards Sol. "That land was sacred to our ancestors."

"I'm sorry, grandfather," Sol said as he bowed his head.

"Sacred?" Gianna asked. "In what way?"

"The young ones mock us!" Old Earl exclaimed, deflecting the question. "They said the prophesies were just silly superstitions. But the ancient gods have revealed themselves once again, just as the prophesies foretold."

"We were foolish, grandfather," Sol said contritely. "Please forgive us."

"Does this have anything to do with that recent discovery by the State archaeologist?" Gianna asked.

Old Earl nodded with a frown. "Oh how my heart grieves! Who among our people will be on hand to greet the Sky Gods when they return?"

"The return of the Sky Gods?" Gianna gasped. "Please explain these prophesies to me."

Old Earl fixed his eyes on her with disdain. "You are an outsider. How could you understand?"

"Please!" Gianna replied. "I wish to learn. Tell me about the Sky Gods and why that land is sacred to your people."

Old Earl sighed dolorously. "Very well, young lady. Listen closely and I will explain…"

CHAPTER 17

Thomas maneuvered his pickup truck along the private dirt track on his way to Silvio's Café. As he approached the Main Road, he noticed that traffic heading towards Stirling Harbor was at a near standstill. Unable to go any further, he pulled to the side of the dirt road and got out to investigate.

Proceeding on foot, Thomas marveled at the hundreds of abandoned cars haphazardly scattered along the shoulder of the Main Road. As he walked, scores of pedestrians hustled past in a state of nervous agitation. He caught one older fellow by the arm, who regarded Thomas with a look of wide-eyed panic.

"What's going on?" Thomas asked.

"The return of the Sky Gods, man!" the older fellow replied as he shook off Thomas' hold. He scooted away before Thomas could get any more information.

As he rounded a slight bend along the Main Road, Thomas observed thousands of people thronging the shoulder, pressed up against the chain link fence near the bulldozed clearing. People continued arriving from both directions and the growing crowd began spilling into the roadway. Thomas jumped with a start when someone ran past wearing a silver space suit. A moment later, an elderly woman with a walker hobbled past, decked in an Egyptian headdress. As Thomas approached the fenced-in clearing, he was momentarily startled when a line of saffron-robed monks trotted past, spinning prayer wheels. "What in the world is going on?" he called to them.

"The return of the Sky Gods," a monk said over his shoulder.

As Thomas wended his way through the crowd, he spotted a circle of Dervishes whirling with outstretched arms around a stationary patrol car. Drawing closer, Thomas could see Chief Latham leaning casually against the hood, surveying the scene.

"Hey, Chief," Thomas called as he slipped between the rapidly whirling dancers. "Do you have any idea what's going on?"

Chief Latham reached into the patrol car and pulled out a copy of the *Stirling Harbor Gazette.* "Haven't you seen today's paper?"

Thomas took the newspaper and scanned the headline. "ANCIENT ASTRONAUTS VISITED NORTH FORK: SHAMAN PROPHYSIES IMMINENT RETURN," he read aloud. "Good Lord! What shaman?"

"Look at the picture," Chief Latham advised, pointing to the black and white photograph below the fold.

Thomas squinted as he scrutinized the image. "Oh, for crying out loud! That's no shaman. That's Old Earl. What kind of scam is this?"

"I don't know. But I'll bet the farm Bix Fairchild is behind it."

Thomas looked around with dismay. "My God, Chief. Just look at all these people."

"I've got a little problem here," the chief confided. "Right now, I've got two TCOs directing traffic and four patrolmen walking the perimeter just to keep these nuts from scaling the fence. If things start getting ugly I don't have the manpower to do much else."

"What are you going to do?"

"I've got a call out to the State Police. Hopefully they'll be able to provide some backup. In the meantime, I'm taking a non-confrontational stance."

The loud hiss of air breaks startled Thomas and Chief Latham as a coach bus emblazoned with the words '*Von Däniken Village*' lurched to a stop next to the patrol car. They watched as the bus door slid open and a stream of chattering passengers disembarked, making straight for the fence line.

"…a striking resemblance to the Mayan prophesies," Casey said as he stepped down from the bus. "You know, the *Popol Vuh* says…" he remarked over his shoulder to Chloe, who followed close behind.

Thomas quickly turned away and covered his face with the newspaper. "Friends of yours?" Chief Latham asked.

Before Thomas could explain, the sound of approaching sirens distracted them. "That must be the State Police," Thomas opined.

The intermittent sirens grew louder as two police motorcycles followed by a black SUV wove deftly through the traffic and came to a stop behind Chief Latham's patrol car. "That's not the State Police," the chief said, examining the striped blue and orange uniforms of the motorcyclists. "Who are you guys?" the chief asked as the motorcyclists removed their helmets.

One of the motorcyclists flipped open a leather folder and flashed an identity card. "SGI," the man said.

"SGI?" Chief Latham questioned. "What's that?"

"Swiss Guard International," the motorcyclist affirmed with a wink. "We're escorting a VIP."

Thomas gasped with reverent awe as he glanced at the SUV. "Is that..? Is that the Holy Father?"

One of the motorcyclists stepped forward with an intimidating glare. "Keep your voice down, damn it!" he said with the trace of a foreign accent. "What are you trying to do, start a riot?"

Thomas tried to make out the figure ensconced behind the tinted windows. "It isn't really him, is it?"

"Clam up, for God's sake!" the other motorcyclist growled. "It ain't the Pope, OK?"

"Who is it then?" Chief Latham asked.

"It's the Papal Nuncio to the UN," the first motorcyclist replied. "Are you happy now?"

"But what's he doing *here*?" Thomas asked.

"You're kidding, right?" the other motorcyclist asked snidely. "Haven't you read the paper?"

"Yes," Thomas replied. "But what's all that got to do with the Church?" As Thomas spoke, the backseat window of the SUV rolled halfway down and an elderly man in sunglasses and a purple cap leaned forward and snapped a series of digital pictures.

"You need to wise up," the first motorcyclist said. "We *always* keep tabs on the competition."

Both motorcyclists snapped to attention as the Papal Nuncio sharply wrapped his ring against the glass. "*Andiamo!*" he called, limply waving the motorcyclists on with the back of his hand.

The motorcyclists hurriedly mounted up. "Don't go getting any ideas," the first motorcyclist said as he slipped on his helmet. "This Indian Sky God thing is a complete hoax."

"I know," Thomas replied. "I don't believe any of it."

"Then what are you doing poking around here?" the second motorcyclist challenged.

"I was just curious…"

"Curious?" the motorcyclist scoffed. "That's how it always begins. Listen! Knock off this apostasy and get your ass back to church! Got it?"

With sirens blaring, the motorcyclists led the SUV into a tight U-turn across two lanes of traffic. Thomas and Chief Latham watched as the motorcade sped off in the other direction. "I'm speechless," the chief remarked. "I don't think things could get any weirder."

"Oh yeah?" Thomas rejoined. "Take a look at that."

Near the fence line, a large group of people began taking off their clothes. In their midst stood the elderly woman with the walker Thomas had seen earlier, who now, with the exception of the Egyptian headdress and a pair of orthopedic sneakers, was otherwise naked.

"*Ankh Nudi Ra Tut Ammon Tuti!*" the naked geriatric proclaimed. "I am the reincarnation of Queen Hatshepsut! Can you dig it?"

"*Tuti Ammon Ankh Nudi!*" the crowd of naked devotees cried in unison.

"Step forward and receive the Sign of Life!" Queen Hatshepsut exclaimed, brandishing a paintbrush. One by one the devotees approached, whereupon the reincarnated monarch painted a large Ankh on each person's torso.

"That can't be legal," Thomas remarked. "Shouldn't you do something?"

"I didn't see anything," Chief Latham replied as he turned away.

Thomas slowly wandered through the crowd, observing the unfolding spectacle. He spotted dozens of people milling about in *Star Trek* uniforms—one even sporting an expertly attached prosthetic Klingon forehead. He watched with mild interest as a bearded swami lay prostrate on a bed of nails. Scores of people pranced about, waiving sticks of incense and banging tambourines. He even found one loincloth-clad mystic entirely painted blue, save for an unblinking third eye tattooed above the bridge of his nose. Backing up to give a snake charmer a wide birth, Thomas absentmindedly stepped into a pentagram marked on the ground.

"Get off, you burke!" a fellow growled as he pushed Thomas' shoulder from behind.

"Huh?" Thomas uttered as he turned.

"Get off, I said!" the man repeated, gesturing to the chalky glyph beneath with a hazel wand. Thomas noticed a golden diadem encircled the man's evenly parted hair.

"Sorry," Thomas mumbled as he moved on.

Thomas wandered close enough to the fence to observe that the perimeter of the Bayview Woods had not been breached. He was so absorbed in thought he didn't notice the two men approaching. "Just look at all these weirdoes," a familiar voice remarked, breaking Thomas' reverie. He turned and saw Schuyler and Gus standing beside him. "What a disgrace," Schuyler added.

"At least the fence is doing a good job at keeping them out," Thomas opined.

"That fence is a catastrophe!" Schuyler exclaimed.

Thomas paid little attention to Schuyler as he pondered his own predicament. How, he wondered, with all this ruckus was he going to retrieve the ersatz artifact.

"A complete and utter catastrophe," Schuyler repeated. "And this gaggle of fools isn't helping matters either. The Sasquatch is a reclusive free-range hominid. This intrusion could disrupt its entire reproductive cycle."

"Really?" Thomas mumbled distractedly.

"We can't let this happen, can we?" Schuyler remarked.

"What do you mean?" Thomas asked, casting a sidelong glance.

Schuyler encouragingly grasped Thomas by the shoulders. "We are men of Science, you and I," he declared with enthusiasm. "We have a duty to act."

"I don't understand."

Schuyler was about to explain when he caught sight of Casey in the distance. "Would you look at that lunatic," he said, pointing.

Casey was gesticulating in the demonstrative manner of a symphony conductor. Although barely audible from that distance, Thomas thought he heard Casey singing. There were no words, but he recognized the tune as others joined in.

"LA DI DA… DUM DA…" the swelling chorus repeated over and over. "*LA DI DA… DUM DA… LA DI DA… DUM DA…*"

"Oh, brother!" Schuyler exclaimed in disgust. "The *Close Encounters* theme? How corny can you get?"

Soon, nearly everyone along the edge of the Bayview Woods joined in the collective mantra, the rising din showing no sign of stopping. Thomas found himself mesmerized by the transcendent melody when suddenly, his attention was drawn to a shadowy object in the sky beyond the tree line.

WHAP WHAP WHAP WHAP WHAP WHAP WHAP

"Look!" someone in the crowd exclaimed.

The flying object swept back and forth over the Bayview Woods just above the treetops. *WHAP WHAP WHAP WHAP WHAP WHAP WHAP WHAP WHAP WHAP WHAP WHAP WHAP WHAP WHAP WHAP*

"They're here! They're here!" another person cried.

"The Sky Gods have returned!" a man wearing a Yoda tee shirt screamed.

The unidentified flying object maneuvered into full view fifty feet above the clearing. *WHAP WHAP WHAP WHAP WHAP WHAP WHAP WHAP WHAP WHAP WHAP WHAP WHAP WHAP WHAP WHAP WHAP WHAP WHAP WHAP WHAP WHAP WHAP WHAP WHAP WHAP WHAP WHAP*

"Good God! What is that?" Schuyler marveled.

"It's a gyrocopter," Thomas replied. The flying machine made a low pass against the mid-morning sun, and Thomas discerned the silhouette of two figures seated in the open cockpit. The one at the controls appeared to be wearing a Homburg.

Hundreds dropped to their knees as the device swept over the crowd. "They're here! They're here!" people shouted joyously. "The Sky Gods have returned!"

Casey took off running beneath the flight path of the gyrocopter. "It's Lord Pakal! Take me with you! Lord Pakal, take me with you!"

As the flying machine turned to make another pass, Thomas observed the man next to the pilot leaning precariously out of the cockpit, apparently snapping pictures of the ground. Casey continued to trot along beneath the flight path, waving his arms, pleading not to be left behind. At length, the pilot broke off and slowly began flying westward along the Main Road.

"Take me with you! Take me with you!" the cry went up as thousands joined Casey in hot pursuit.

The tumult subsided as the frenzied crowd withdrew. Schuyler turned to Gus who suddenly drew two pairs of bolt cutters out of his satchel. "Dr. McGrath, we men of Science must stick together," Schuyler declared.

"I beg your pardon?"

"Cover us!" Schuyler commanded as he and Gus hustled towards the fence line.

"Cover you? What's that supposed to mean?"

"Distract the cops while we go to work," Schuyler said as he and Gus dropped to a crouch. Thomas watched nervously as the two began snipping at the base of the chain link.

"Wait!" Thomas demanded. "What the hell are you doing?"

Gus and Schuyler deftly managed to cut away just enough fence to scurry underneath. "We've got to cut some holes in this fence," Schuyler explained. "For the sake of the Sasquatch."

"That's so illegal!" Thomas gasped. "Do you have any idea what'll happen if you get caught?"

"Listen! We're all in this together, brother," Schuyler said from inside the fence. "If everyone does his part, we'll come through this OK."

"Wait a second," Thomas urged. "I'm not…"

"It's too late for cold feet," Schuyler warned. "You'd best get going."

Before Thomas could protest, Schuyler and Gus darted across the clearing and into the trees. Thomas quickly surveyed the area and realized their incursion into the Bayview Woods hadn't been observed by anyone else. Wishing not to attract suspicion, he nonchalantly walked away from the breach and headed home.

CHAPTER 18

That afternoon, Thomas returned to the Main Road on foot and observed a few hundred die-hards still milling about near the bulldozed clearing. Although intent on retrieving his fake Clovis point, he understood there was no way he could accomplish this in daylight without being spotted. The fence also posed a problem, as it restricted his access to the Bayview Woods.

Ambling home along the private dirt road, Thomas noticed something amiss behind a thicket of scrub pine. Venturing into the brambles, he observed a section of fence that had been cut and rolled back far enough to allow an adult to pass through. *This must be Schuyler's doing,* he thought. *I wonder if he managed to cut other holes.*

As Thomas mulled things over, he hatched a plan to recover the fake Clovis point that night. Taking advantage of Schuyler's hole, he'd venture into the Bayview Woods after dark and return to the spot where he planted the fake artifact. He couldn't use a flashlight in case any kooks might still be staked out near the fence line, but even so, he was sure he could locate the fake by moonlight. Thomas recalled he had some old hunting camouflage in the attic that probably still fit. *That should make me nearly invisible at night,* he thought. The big problem now was coming up with a believable story to tell Roxy about why he needed to go out after dark. The fib about meeting with the archaeology club worked once before and lacking a more plausible excuse, he figured he try it one more time.

Thomas dropped the story on Roxanne over dinner and, as before, she fell for it. Heading out shortly after dark, he drove his pickup truck about a quarter mile westward on the Main Road and parked along the shoulder. After awkwardly slipping on the hunting garb he'd stashed in the truck, he was ready to go.

Thomas crossed the Main Road on foot and made his way back to the private dirt track, intent on slipping into the Bayview Woods through the breach he'd discovered earlier that day. As Thomas approached the hole, a vehicle suddenly turned off the Main Road onto the dirt track. He took off running and managed to slip inside the woods before the car caught up with him. Once abeam the hole, however, the car stopped. Thomas dropped to his belly as the driver switched on a high beam searchlight and began panning back and forth amidst the trees and undergrowth. *Crap!* he thought. *It must be the cops.* He held his breath and hugged the ground as the beam passed just above him. Suddenly—the searchlight clicked off. Thomas' heart throbbed as he listened for approaching lawmen. To his relief, the car began slowly rolling away. He raised his head just enough to see that the vehicle had stopped again and he instinctively ducked as the searchlight passed over a section of woods twenty yards away. Thomas exhaled in relief when the light went out and the vehicle continued on its way.

Time to get going, Thomas thought as he hurriedly withdrew deeper into the woods.

"McGrath, yon son of a bitch," Vincent growled as he tossed the searchlight aside. He proceeded home and parked the Porsche before doubling back down the dirt road on foot. Vincent found the hole in the fence and cursed. "This damn fence is useless," he grumbled as he easily wiggled through the breach.

Thomas found his way to the edge of the bulldozed clearing. After pausing to survey the area, he dropped to a crouch and advanced slowly, stopping every few yards to double-check that the coast was clear. Using the capped test well as a landmark, he began searching the area where he'd left the fake artifact. Thomas' frustration mounted as every clod of earth he turned yielded only dust. "It's got to be right around here," he murmured. He squatted on his haunches and sifted the fresh soil with his fingers. "It's simply got to be here…" Suddenly, he felt something sharp embedded in the dirt. Thomas traced the object's outline with his fingers with growing excitement. "Wait a second… I think… this might be… Eureka!" he exclaimed in a low voice. "I've found it!"

The next thing he knew, Thomas found himself sprawled face-down in the dirt with a dull pain in his back.

Vincent stealthily approached the crouching figure when he suddenly heard McGrath's triumphant cry. *The treasure!* Vincent exulted. *He's found the treasure!* Seizing the moment, Vincent took a running leap and pounced, knocking McGrath to the ground.

Regaining his senses, Thomas sprightly sprang to his feet. He tried to make a break for it when his assailant pummeled him from behind again, driving him to his knees. Arching sideways, Thomas blindly landed a punch in his attacker's groin, who let out a high pitched squeal and fell backwards. Taking advantage of the lucky blow, Thomas scrambled to his feet and darted for the tree line without looking back.

Vincent rolled on the ground, clutching his testicles as he fought to catch his breath. With some effort, he rose to his feet and staggered forward in vain pursuit. "Arrrrgh!" he howled as McGrath slipped from view beyond the trees. Realizing the hopelessness of giving chase, with great effort Vincent haltingly walked towards the path that led back to the hole in the fence.

Thomas squirmed through the hole and jogged all the way back to his pickup truck. "Oh, hell," he grumbled. In spite of his best efforts, he'd failed to retrieve the fake artifact. The whole effort had been for naught.

Thomas shifted into gear and drove aimlessly as he gathered his thoughts. *Who the hell was that?* he wondered. *What if it was a cop? What if he's waiting for me at home? What if Roxy finds out about this?* "Roxy!" he gasped aloud. *Good heavens! She'd kill me if she knew!* Thinking it unwise to go home right away, Thomas decided to drive around a while.

Roxanne was preparing for bed when the phone rang. As was her habit, she let the answering machine screen the call. "Hello, Dr. McGrath. This is Thor Svenson from the archaeology club. I wanted to let you know about a change in plan…"

Roxanne pressed the button on the hand set to take the call. "Hello, Mr. Svenson. This is Roxanne McGrath."

"Ah, good evening," Thor Svenson replied pleasantly. "I hope I'm not disturbing you, but I wanted to alert Dr. McGrath about a change in venue for our meeting next Monday. That UFO sighting at the Bayview Woods earlier today has generated quite a bit of interest in our club, so we're going to need a much bigger room."

"I don't know anything about a UFO sighting, but I'm sure Thomas can make arrangements with the college for a larger meeting space."

"That would be wonderful."

"Why don't you suggest it to him yourself?" Roxanne asked after an awkward pause.

"Certainly. May I speak with him?"

"Uh… Aren't you going to see him tonight at the college?"

"No. Why would I see Dr. McGrath this evening?"

"Don't you folks have an archaeology club meeting tonight?"

"No. There's no meeting tonight. I'm afraid there must be some confusion."

"I see," Roxanne remarked.

"Would you please give him this message?" Thor Svenson asked. "Please let him know I called."

"Oh, Mr. Svenson, you can count on that."

Thomas quietly entered through the kitchen and was startled to find Roxanne sitting at the breakfast table, leafing through a magazine.

"Oh," he said nervously. "You're still awake."

"How was the meeting?" Roxanne asked without looking up.

"Great," Thomas said with feigned enthusiasm. "Everyone had a good time."

"What did you talk about?"

"Oh, you know. Archaeological stuff."

"Like what?"

"Uh………"

Roxanne looked up with an icy glare. "Where were you, Thomas? And why are you dressed up like Rambo?"

"Well, you see Roxy…"

Roxanne leapt from her seat and jabbed a finger within an inch of Thomas' face. "Don't you lie to me, boy! Before you dig yourself in deeper, let me remind you that God is listening!"

Thomas exhaled deeply. "Alright," he said, resigned to his fate. "Just sit down and I'll explain everything…"

Schuyler and Gus huddled around the computer monitor. "See if you can sharpen the image a little more," Schuyler urged. Gus made a series of keyboard entries and a digitally enhanced infrared image reappeared on the screen. "I guess that's the best we're going to get," Schuyler said. "Go ahead and run the video."

Transfixed, both men watched the grainy video of a semi-erect hominid advancing into the bulldozed clearing. "Wow!" Schuyler exclaimed. "That must be the female. Observe now as the male Sasquatch attempts to mount her from behind." Gus and Schuyler watched the fuzzy green video with wide-eyed awe. "That's amazing," Schuyler remarked. "She punches the male as he attempts penetration. I never imagined a female in heat would put up such resistance."

Gus nodded in silent acknowledgement as he replayed the video clip from the beginning.

"You know, that's the exact same location where we took the still photographs last week," Schuyler observed.

Gus turned towards Schuyler and arched an eyebrow.

"I know it's taking a risk," Schuyler remarked. "But next time we're going to have to get closer."

"Oh, Thomas, how could you?" Roxanne cried. "How could you *ever* think planting a fake artifact was a good idea?"

"Come on, Roxy. Don't be mad," Thomas protested. "I did it for us. They were going to cut down the woods, for crying out loud!"

"But it's so unethical. That fake spear point could sabotage one of the most significant archaeological discoveries of all time."

"I know," Thomas said sheepishly.

"Not to mention ruin everything for Lisa just as her career is getting started."

"Yes, I realize that, too. And I feel awful about it. That's why I tried to get the damn thing back."

"But you didn't. And all you've done is pile deception on top of deceit. And what do you have to show for it?"

"I'm sorry, Roxy," Thomas mumbled. "Do you think I should go back and try again?"

"Are you crazy?" Roxanne cried. "You almost got yourself thrown in jail."

"I don't know what else to do. I guess the only other option is to forget about it and hope for the best."

"Or you could come clean."

"What do you mean?" Thomas asked.

"Why not tell Lisa the whole story?" Roxanne suggested. "Maybe you can go back to the woods under her supervision and recover the fake."

Thomas considered the idea for a moment. "I don't know, Roxy. She might become really angry when she realizes I tried to trick her."

"I would too if I were her. But telling her what you did may be your only way out of this mess."

Thomas hung his head in self-reproach. "Maybe you're right. I need to think about it."

"OK, but don't think too long. Those foreign archaeologists are going to be here real soon."

CHAPTER 19

Louis Nickels stormed through the office door carrying a sheaf of papers. "Where's the blond girl?" he demanded.

Rayette inclined her head towards the back office. Moon traipsed in afterwards with an air of cool machismo. Turning towards Rayette, with pursed lips, he looked down with eyes half closed. Moon's steadfast gaze and self-assured swagger sent chills through Rayette, who returned his stare with mouth agape. At length, he silently produced a whole pineapple and winked as he handed it to her with a deliberate flourish.

Daphne emerged from the back office and approached Rayette with nervous urgency. "Did they send the fax yet?"

"Not yet," Rayette said distractedly, holding the pineapple like a bouquet.

"Damn it!" Daphne responded, pacing nervously. "Let me know as soon as it arrives. Understand?"

"OK," Rayette said, admiring the fruit.

"I'm so excited!" Daphne gushed as she turned towards the back office. "I really should call Vincent."

"Hey!" Louis Nickels shouted.

Daphne turned back with a start. "Oh. When did you get here?"

"Enough of the small talk. Let's get down to business. I got a copy of the completed appraisal right here."

"Great! When can you get it to the Village Assessor?"

"I already did," Louis Nickels affirmed through gritted teeth. "I hand delivered it yesterday right after Moon and I took these aerial photographs. You should be getting a new tax bill once the paperwork clears."

"When will that be?"

"What do I look like—a fortune teller? Probably sometime next week."

"Awesome," Daphne said with indifference. She glanced at Rayette, who giggled as Moon filled her palm with candy from a Buzz Lightyear Pez dispenser. "Hey! Are you sure that fax machine is even turned on?"

Rayette scooped the handful of candy into her mouth. "Yesh," she replied.

"Ahem…" Louis Nickels interrupted as he theatrically cleared his throat. "Listen! It's time we got down to brass tacks. What does a guy got to do to get paid around here?"

Daphne looked puzzled. "I don't know what you mean."

"Me and Moon have been breaking our backs to get this appraisal done and we still haven't seen one thin dime from you people. Do you have any idea how much a gallon of aviation fuel costs?"

Daphne gave Rayette an inquisitive scowl. "I've sent everything to the accounting office at Tremayne Fuels, just like you said," Rayette remarked defensively.

Daphne was about to speak when the fax machine buzzed to life. As the device began spitting out papers, Daphne gleefully jumped up and down as if she'd hit the jackpot on a slot machine. Rayette retrieved the papers and looked at the coversheet. "It's a shipment confirmation from *Giambologna and Sons*, in Vicenza, Italy."

Daphne gyrated and wiggled across the office. "Rooooo—Cooo—Coooooo!" she howled triumphantly.

Rayette looked the papers over soberly. "It says here 'all parts are guaranteed to fit but a qualified stonemason should make final assembly'."

Daphne quickly regained her composure. "A stonemason? Don't they mean *plumber*?"

"It says 'stonemason'," Rayette confirmed.

"I don't even know what that is. Where am I going to find a stonemason?"

"Oh, hell!" Louis Nickels exclaimed. "You cheapskates offer steady work but want everything done on credit!"

Daphne stared at the older man quizzically. "I'm not sure what you mean, but can you help me find a stonemason?"

Louis Nickels removed his Homburg, drew a business card from the inside hat band and handed it to Daphne.

"*Louis Nickels Cut-Rate Stonemasonry*," she read aloud. "Wow! Can you assemble the *Fontana di Nettuno*?"

"Yeah," Louis Nickels said with an air of misgiving. "But we need dough, just like the next guy. When are you people going to come across with some gelt?"

Daphne considered the matter. "Let me make a phone call," she said, withdrawing to the back office.

"Mr. Tremayne, the Vice President of Accounting is on line one," the secretary called through the intercom.

Vincent took the call on speaker phone. "What's up?" he said, reclining in his office chair.

"Mr. Tremayne, I've got a stack of bills here I don't know what to do with."

"Can't you just pay them?"

"They're not ours. We keep getting bills for work done on behalf of Country Squire. I know you own both companies, but it's going to really screw things up if we start paying Country Squire's bills out of the Tremayne Fuels account. The oil company's operating margin is pretty thin right now, too."

Vincent gave this some thought. "What kind of money are we talking about?"

"A few thousand here and a few thousand there. Taken together, they add up to quite a chunk of change, though."

Vincent considered the matter further. "Are there any individual bills that qualify for recovery in Small Claims Court?"

"No. There's too much money involved to bring a small claims action."

"Are any of those bills so big that someone would think it worth his while to sue?"

"I'm not sure what you mean," the accountant conceded.

"Let me put it this way," Vincent replied. "If somebody were to sue Country Squire Development Corporation to collect on any of those bills, would they spend more money in lawyer's fees than they would actually recover in court?"

"Mr. Tremayne, by themselves, each of these bills might not be worth suing over. But someone is expecting to be paid for services rendered, and it's unethical to screw with people the way you're suggesting."

"I didn't ask for an ethics lesson," Vincent snapped.

The accounting executive sighed. "What do you want me to do with these bills, then?"

Vincent thought for a moment. "Send them back to Country Squire."

"As you wish."

Vincent hung up and reclined in his chair. *Screw 'em*, he thought with arrogant satisfaction. *Let them chase me. I've got more important things to deal with.*

The buzzing intercom interrupted Vincent's avaricious reflection. "Mr. Tremayne, call on line one. It's your wife."

Vincent shifted in his swivel chair and picked up the phone. "Yeah?"

"Vincent, I have a big surprise!" Daphne declared.

"What is it?"

"I can't tell you now. It's a surprise. You're taking me out tonight to celebrate."

Vincent's thoughts turned to the treasure. "No, we can't. I've got to go out tonight."

Daphne frowned. "You went out last night. In fact, you've been out every night of the week."

"You know I go to the gym after work."

"That stupid gym! What about me? You never take me out anymore. When do I get to have any fun?"

Vincent's testicles ached on account of the previous night's ruckus. "I need to unwind after a day in the office. It's the same as you going to yoga every morning."

"I have to go to yoga in the morning because you sleep late."

"Look, Daphne. I can't take you out tonight. I've got something important to do."

"It's always about you!" Daphne cried. "You are *so* egotistical! Do you ever think about my needs?"

Vincent massaged his aching temple. "Daphne, please…"

"I never see you anymore!" she shrieked. "Sometimes I think you put me in charge of Country Squire just to get me out of your hair."

Vincent gritted his teeth as he restrained his rage. "That's not true," he said soothingly. "I put you in charge because you are the only person who can make Country Squire a success."

"You're just saying that. You're trying to get me off the phone."

"No, that's not true. You're doing a great job. In fact, I've been meaning to take you out to celebrate your big success with getting that fence put up around the Country Squire property." He thought of the hole he'd discovered the night before and angrily balled his fists.

"That's a pretty big deal, you know. Not just anybody could have managed that."

"I know," Vincent said admiringly. "And I really want to take you out to celebrate, just not tonight. How about tomorrow night?"

"Well, I guess so. Do you promise?"

"Yes. Tomorrow night. You can tell me your big surprise over dinner and champagne."

"Oooo…" Daphne cooed. "It's a date!"

"OK," Vincent said. "So I'll talk to you later, then…"

"Wait! I almost forgot…"

Vincent winced. "What now?"

"The workmen want to know when they're going to get paid. What should I tell them?"

Vincent felt a rush of satisfaction and smiled. "Tell them… tell them after Labor Day. Don't be any more specific than that."

"OK," Daphne replied. "Ooooo! I'm so excited! I can't wait to tell you the big surprise!"

"I'm looking forward to it," Vincent lied. "Now listen. I've really got to go," he said and hung up.

Vincent checked his watch and thought about the treasure. *Just a few hours to kill before sundown*, he mused.

Vincent made his way along the private dirt road in the dark with a shovel in one hand and a pick-ax in the other. Slipping through the hole in the fence, he made his way to the spot where he'd overheard McGrath the night before chortling over his discovery. There was enough moonlight for Vincent to make out features on the ground, but nothing significant grabbed his attention. *What now?* he thought as he dropped the tools. *I thought X was supposed to mark the spot. I don't see any X around here.* "What got McGrath so excited?" Vincent mumbled as he tried to locate some clue. He tried to recall everything he'd seen the night before. Like McGrath had done, Vincent dropped to a crouch and ran his fingers through the soil. *McGrath was definitely excited about something he found right around here*, he thought. Vincent continued sifting through the dirt until his fingers ran along something rough and sharp. "What's this?" he mumbled as he turned the object over in his hand.

Zzzzzzzz

Vincent looked up with a start, trying to make sense of the faint buzzing sound when in rapid-fire succession, two piercingly bright flashes left him momentarily blinded. *Pop—pop—pop—pop* the strobe light continued as the tripod-mounted camera captured digital images of Vincent holding the fake Clovis point in his open palm.

"We've got him, Gus!" a man shouted somewhere to Vincent's right. "Don't let him get away! Hurry!"

Vincent began running blindly and tripped over the camera tripod. Still unable to see, he heard the footfall of people approaching.

"Get the net over it, Gus!" the man urged. "I'll slip the lasso around its ankles."

As Vincent struggled to his feet, he found himself entangled in a nylon web. "Arrrggg!" he howled, trying to break free.

"Take him down, Gus!" the man cried as he clutched Vincent around the waist. "Use the tranquilizer gun if you have to!"

"Get the hell off me!" Vincent shouted as he vainly struggled to break free.

From just beyond the fence-line, headlights swung into view and illuminated the three men in the clearing. "This is the police," an amplified voice crackled through a distant loudspeaker as the telltale red and blue lights of a patrol car flashed.

Gus and Schuyler gasped as a troop of uniformed policeman encircled them from all directions. "Nobody move," the cop with the gold braid on his visor said. "You're all under arrest."

"But officer, we've captured Sasquatch," Schuyler declared.

"Intriguing," Chief Latham replied as the three were led off in handcuffs. "I never imagined Sasquatch could afford a Rolex."

CHAPTER 20

Daphne paced the office floor as she spoke on the phone. "It's unacceptable!" she emphatically cried. "Vincent's been in jail since Friday night. I demand they release him right now!"

"They'll cut him loose just as soon as you put up his bail," Martin Farquhar advised.

"But you said there was going to be an arrangement."

"No," the lawyer corrected. "I said there was going to be an *arraignment*, at which time the judge would set bail. As soon as you put up the cash, Vincent will be released."

"And what if I refuse?" Daphne asked defiantly.

"Then Vincent will have to remain in jail until the trial," Martin Farquhar explained.

"When will that be?"

"The judge set the date for October 12."

Daphne considered this. "That won't work. We're supposed to go on a cruise to Grand Cayman in October."

"Mrs. Tremayne, I think you need to come to grips with the facts. Vincent is in a lot of trouble and you folks don't have any money."

"What are you talking about? We're rich!"

"Maybe you were at one time, but not anymore. You're going to have to think about liquidating some assets."

"Well, I'm sure Vincent has a better idea," Daphne rejoined.

"That's between you folks. In any event, you're going to have to post bail if Vincent is going to make it to the permit hearing on Friday."

As Daphne was speaking, Louis Nickels barged into the office, brandishing a copy of the *Stirling Harbor Gazette.* Moon ambled in behind and blew Rayette a kiss.

"What's the meaning of this?" Louis Nickels demanded.

Daphne distractedly took the paper and read the front page headline. "HERO RESEARCH SCIENTISTS CATCH LOOTER RED HANDED," she mumbled aloud. Her eyes widened when she saw the close-up photograph of Vincent holding a stone spear point.

"I beg your pardon," Martin Farquhar said.

"Uh…" Daphne murmured as she scrutinized the picture.

"Mrs. Tremayne, are you there?" the lawyer asked.

"How am I going to get paid if your old man is in the pokey?" Louis Nickels growled.

Daphne gestured for Louis Nickels to wait a moment. "I'm sorry, Martin. What was that?"

"I said you're going to have to post bail if Vincent plans to attend the permit hearing on Friday," the lawyer repeated. "He really needs to be there."

"OK. Where do I get the money?"

"Well, unless you have some secret bank account I'm unaware of, you'll need to contact a bail bondsman."

"A bail bondsman? Where in the world do I find a bail bondsman?"

Louis Nickels grumbled something under his breath as he fished around his pockets. He produced a business card and waived it underneath Daphne's nose.

Daphne took the card. "*Louis Nickels Cut-Rate Bail Bonds*," she mumbled.

"What did you say?" the lawyer asked.

"Martin, I'm going to have to call you back. Bye." She put down the phone and looked at Louis Nickels. "You can get Vincent out of jail?"

"Yeah," Louis Nickels replied. "But you'll need to put up something as collateral."

News of the permit hearing traveled fast, due in no small part to Gianna Fox reporting that the results of *yet another* Cultural Impact Survey would be made public in Village Court. Rumors abounded as to why the State Office of Cultural and Historic Preservation brought in European archaeologists to conduct the survey, fueling suspicion that an international conspiracy was afoot to cover up evidence of Indian contact with ancient extraterrestrials. As a consequence, that Friday, the Village Court was packed.

As spokesperson for the *Save the Bayview Woods Coalition*, Roxanne McGrath managed to secure seats for herself and Thomas just in front of the judge's bench, right next to Lisa Tavolaro-Hennessey and the Scandinavian archaeological team. Lisa was in the midst of making introductions when a defiant Vincent Tremayne swaggered into the courtroom. Accompanied by Martin Farquhar and Daphne, he took his position across the aisle just as the bailiff enjoined everyone to rise.

Judge Schulman shuffled in and, banging the gavel, called the hearing to order. Every eye in the courtroom was riveted on his careworn face as he silently studied the crowd. A palpable air of dread descended as the judge finally fixed his icy gaze on Vincent. "I'm angry," Judge Schulman said in a measured voice. "And I'm in no mood to be lenient."

"With respect, your honor, this is not a criminal trial," Martin Farquhar stated. "My client is here today regarding a civil matter pertaining to building permits."

"Duly noted, councilor," Judge Schulman replied. "And let me remind you that since these are civil and not criminal proceedings, a different set of evidentiary rules apply. I'm not out of order in observing that your client's recent conduct has been in clear violation of my previous directive not to tamper or damage the Country Squire property any more than he already has."

"Your honor, the presumption of innocence is a bedrock principle of our legal system. Shouldn't we wait for a jury to decide if my client is guilty?"

"In a criminal trial, yes," Judge Schulman agreed. "But as you said, this is a civil matter, and I'm convinced your client was looting an archaeological site in direct violation of my orders."

"How could it be looting if the Country Squire property belongs to me?" Vincent challenged.

"Be quiet," Martin Farquhar growled in Vincent's ear.

"Mr. Tremayne, I have been more than fair with you," Judge Schulman remarked.

"Fair? Is it fair that McGrath's been trying to steal the treasure right out from under me—and I'm not even allowed to walk on my own property?" Vincent blurted out.

"For God's sake, be quiet!" Martin Farquhar said for all to hear.

"Mr. Tremayne, you are a disgrace," Judge Schulman declared, waiving the familiar photograph of Vincent holding the Clovis point. "To think you would plunder the heritage of all mankind for the mercenary purpose of personal financial gain. Shame on you!"

"I don't see what the big deal is," Vincent said. "So you caught me with some old arrowhead. How much could *that* be worth?"

Martin Farquhar threw his hands up in frustration as the spectators gasped at Vincent's admission. Judge Schulman visibly quaked, fighting to keep his composure. Pangs of guilt flooded Thomas' soul as he watched matters unfold.

Daphne looked up from her magazine and sighed. "Can we go now?" she asked, tugging Vincent's sleeve. "This is boring."

"Your honor, it would be a sin for me to keep silent," Thomas said, rising to his feet. "But Mr. Tremayne is right. That projectile point is worthless."

Judge Schulman slowly turned to face Thomas with smoldering rage. "What did you say?"

"The projectile point in that photograph is worthless," Thomas repeated as murmurs rose in the courtroom.

"What makes you say so?" Judge Schulman inquired.

A hush fell over the assembly as everyone waited for Thomas' reply. "Because…" he stammered. "Because it's a fake."

The courtroom erupted in an angry uproar as Vincent wheeled to face Thomas.

Judge Schulman whispered to the bailiff, who promptly slipped out of the courtroom. The tumult continued as the judge brought down the gavel in an attempt to restore order. "Everybody, knock it off," he warned. As the din subsided he turned his attention back to Thomas. "Are you sure about that?"

"Yes, your honor," Thomas said with conviction. "I'm sure."

"Just from looking at a photograph?"

The shame Thomas felt overwhelmed him as he groped for words. "Well, you see, your honor, I have some experience making replica stone tools. It's something I do in my anthropology classes."

As Thomas spoke, the bailiff returned with a large manila envelope marked *Tremayne: Exhibit A* and handed it to the judge, who drew out the projectile point to the angry jeers of the assembled spectators.

"Order!" the judge exclaimed. As the assembly calmed, Judge Schulman handed the projectile point to the bailiff, who in turn handed it to Thomas. "Take a good look at it, Dr. McGrath. Are you sure it's a fake?"

Thomas took the familiar object and examined it. "I'm absolutely certain of it."

One of the Norwegian archaeologists stood up. "May I see that?" he asked with a heavy accent. Both Lisa and the Swedish archaeologists looked on with keen interest as Thomas handed over the stone projectile point.

After passing the object back and forth a number of times, one of the Swedes chuckled dismissively. "Is this some kind of joke?"

"I beg your pardon," Judge Schulman said.

"This… this is a piece of garbage," the Swedish scholar scoffed. His Norwegian colleagues nodded in ascent as they chattered amongst themselves in a foreign tongue.

"How can you be sure?" the judge asked.

Thomas looked on with apprehension as Lisa Tavolaro-Hennessey held the point up and scrutinized it. Her eyes narrowed as she cast her former professor a knowing glance. "Your honor," she said, "It's clear to the trained eye that this is a modern knockoff."

"You mean it's a counterfeit?" Judge Schulman asked. "You're absolutely certain?"

"Yes, your honor," Lisa said as she looked back towards Thomas and scowled.

"But… how? How do you know?"

"Just look at those striations," Lisa said with disgust. "Whoever made this piece of crap probably used a steel mallet from a hardware store."

"And the absurd proportions," one of the Norwegian archaeologists added. "It looks like a bad movie prop."

"And that ridiculous fluting," one of the Swedes added. "A child can see it lacks aerodynamic stability. A spear with this point would fly as straight as a corkscrew."

"So it's a modern fake," Judge Schulman remarked.

"That's correct, your honor," Thomas replied.

Lisa gritted her teeth as she looked at Thomas sidelong. "Not just a fake, your honor, but a very *bad* fake. The work of a truly ham-handed amateur."

Thomas nodded his ascent with downcast eyes.

"Ya, perhaps it was not plunder this man was after," one of the Swedish archaeologists added, pointing at Vincent. "Maybe he was intent on sabotage."

"Sabotage?" Judge Schulman gasped as the crowd of spectators once again grew restive. "This information changes everything."

The spectators in the courtroom broke into catcalls and jeers directed against Vincent Tremayne, who looked about in utter confusion. Both Roxanne and Lisa glared at Thomas angrily while the Scandinavian archaeologists huddled around the bogus Clovis point, derisively confirming its inauthenticity.

Daphne leaned over towards Vincent. "I'm going to the juice bar for a smoothie. Call me when this is over."

The ruckus began to subside when the sound of Indian war cries suddenly filled the courtroom. A reverent hush descended as a small group of men with painted faces slowly advanced up the middle aisle, rhythmically chanting a dirge in the Makanhassett language. Leading the way was Old Earl, bedecked in feathers and turquoise, carrying a large shaman stick. As the group drew closer, Old Earl began shaking the stick at Vincent.

Judge Schulman looked down from the bench and smirked. "What the hell are you doing, Earl?"

Old Earl's eyes twinkled as he looked at the judge. "Our ancestors have no peace," he moaned theatrically. The men clustered around him resumed their rhythmic chanting in hushed tones.

"Oh yeah?" Judge Schulman asked skeptically. "Why is that?"

The spectators in the courtroom gasped as Old Earl held the shaman stick heavenward and danced in a circle. At length, he pointed the stick at Vincent again. "Because of this one!" Old Earl growled. "He stole the sacred land where our people met with the Sky Gods."

"He's full of crap, your honor," Vincent exclaimed. "I paid eight hundred thousand bucks for that land, fair and square."

"*Oy vey!*" Judge Schulman exclaimed. "You really paid eight hundred grand for that swamp?"

"And now he desecrates the graves of our ancestors," Old Earl added, shaking the shaman stick again for emphasis.

"Your ancestors?" Judge Schulman asked. "Are you sure about that, Earl?"

Old Earl looked at the judge with mild confusion. "Uh... And now we come to give him a chance to make peace." Old Earl turned to Lance Fairchild, who stood nearby holding a peace pipe. Lance's shoulders were shaking almost imperceptibly as he bit his lip and looked away. Bix elbowed his brother in the ribs, who then stepped forward and held up the peace pipe. "Yes!" Old Earl continued. "The peace pipe. If the blasphemer Tremayne will only return the land, the curse will be lifted and there will be peace."

Lance bit his lip even harder as he vainly fought to contain his mirth. Soon, his whole body convulsed spasmodically as tears streamed down his cheeks. If Old Earl did another absurd little jig he thought he's scream out laughing.

Casey stood up among the spectators. "Look!" he exclaimed, pointing at Lance. "That bastard Tremayne made this poor Indian cry. Oh, the injustice!"

Sibyl, who had been sitting towards the back of the courtroom, stood up shaking her fist. "No justice—No peace!" she cried repeatedly. "No justice—No peace!" Soon, half the courtroom spectators joined the protest, waiving their fists in the air. "No justice—No peace!"

Judge Schulman brought down the gavel forcefully. "Shut up! Shut up, every one of you, damn it!" The chanting subsided as the judge's wrathful expression filled everyone with fear. "I've had it! No more outbursts. If another person speaks before spoken to I'll throw 'em in jail for contempt of court."

Old Earl looked up at the judge stone-faced.

"Earl, take your little circus act out of my courtroom," Judge Schulman ordered.

"But Al—I mean *your honor*—we have a duty to our ancestors," Old Earl replied.

"Not unless your ancestor was Eric the Red."

A murmur of confusion arose among the spectators. "Eric the Red? I don't understand," Old Earl confessed.

"That's not an Indian grave on the Country Squire property," Judge Schulman explained. "It's a tenth century Viking ship burial."

"No kidding?" Old Earl chuckled.

"That's the big news, everybody," Judge Schulman announced. "The international archaeological team sent in by the State Office of Cultural and Historic Preservation has verified that a Viking ship burial has been discovered right here in Stirling Harbor. It's the first of its kind discovered in North America."

As the spectators began chattering amongst themselves over the significance of this disclosure, Old Earl turned to the members of the Makanhassett Tribal Council. "You can't win 'em all, boys, but it was worth a try."

"We're still up eight hundred grand," Bix reminded.

Judge Schulman tapped his gavel twice. "Clam up!"

"So I wasn't looting an Indian grave," Vincent Tremayne chortled.

"The court concedes that, Mr. Tremayne," the judge declared.

"Your honor, in light of this new information, we request that criminal charges against my client be dropped," Martin Farquhar said.

"Not so fast, councilor," Judge Schulman replied. "Mr. Tremayne might not have been looting an Indian grave, but in direct violation of my orders he was caught tampering with an archaeological site."

"But the artifact in question is not genuine," Martin Farquhar protested. "These experts confirmed it just a few minutes ago."

Judge Schulman looked at Vincent through narrowed eyes. "Which is precisely why Mr. Tremayne is being brought up on a whole new set of charges."

"New charges?" Vincent cried. "What did I do now?"

"I think it's pretty clear," Judge Schulman opined. "You were caught in the act of planting a Neolithic spear point on top of an Iron Age burial site. You were hoping to cast doubt on the authenticity of one of the greatest archaeological discoveries of all times just so you could get the '*go ahead*' to build your condominiums."

Thomas' guilty feeling was unbearable. "Your honor," he said, rising to his feet. "If I may…"

"Shut up!" Judge Schulman barked.

Roxanne grabbed Thomas by the shirt tail and yanked him back into his seat. "Shhh," she intoned, holding a finger to her lips.

"All I was trying to do was beat McGrath to the treasure," Vincent said.

"I guess that's why you had the pick ax and the shovel, huh?" the judge asked.

"Well how else was I supposed to dig for treasure?" Vincent rejoined.

Martin Farquhar stepped forward. "Your honor, I object…"

"Overruled," Judge Schulman replied. "This isn't criminal court. It's a building permit hearing. Our purpose is to determine an equitable solution regarding the disposition of the Country Squire property."

"So, do I get to build my condos or not?" Vincent asked.

Judge Schulman sighed. "Mr. Tremayne, I'm going to give you a choice. The Commissioner of Cultural and Historic Preservation has notified my office that the State has initiated *eminent domain* procedures for the purposes of acquiring the Country Squire property."

"What?" Vincent cried. "Those bastards are seizing my land?"

"Hear me out, Mr. Tremayne," the judge advised. "The State intends to deem the Country Squire property as parkland and commission an extensive archaeological study of the site."

Vincent thought for a moment. "You said you were offering me a choice. So what choice do I have?"

Judge Schulman took a deep breath. "Mr. Tremayne, just to be clear, you do have the option of fighting the eminent domain action in the State Court of Appeals."

"I'll fight all the way to the Supreme Court if I have to!"

"Vincent, be serious," Martin Farquhar whispered.

"That is your right, Mr. Tremayne," Judge Schulman said. "But if you choose *not* to fight the eminent domain case and relinquish ownership to the State right away, I'll drop all criminal charges against you stemming from your violation of my previous order. That's the choice I'm offering you."

"No criminal charges, but in the end I'm left high and dry, right?" Vincent asked.

"No," the judge explained. "The State will pay you the assessed value of the land in compensation. You get paid what the land is worth *and* you walk out of here scot-free"

"And if I fight it?" Vincent asked.

"Well, you might win—but only after months of costly litigation," Judge Schulman conceded. "But then you'll have a criminal case hanging over you as well."

Martin Farquhar pressed in close. "Take the deal," he growled in Vincent's ear.

Vincent looked about the angry faces in the courtroom, searching in vain for Daphne. *Oh, hell*, he thought. *A bird in the hand…*

"Take the deal, you dope," Martin Farquhar whispered urgently. "This is the best offer you're going to get."

Vincent sighed. "All right, your honor. I'll take the deal. The State can have the stupid land."

Cheers erupted in the courtroom as residents from *Von Däniken Village* hugged perfect strangers from the *Save the Bayview*

Woods Coalition. Thomas looked at Roxanne with a pained expression. "Roxy, what should I do?"

"You dodged a bullet," Roxanne replied. "Shut up and go with the flow."

Judge Schulman waited about a minute, allowing the cheering to subside on its own before tapping the gavel. "Alright. Simmer down," he urged the spectators with much less force than earlier.

"So, your honor, when am I going to get paid?" Vincent asked.

"Just as soon as we determine that all liens against the property are cleared and all outstanding debts of the Country Squire Development Corporation are settled."

"Yeah? Well Country Squire doesn't owe anyone a dime," Vincent affirmed.

"Like hell!" a voice barked from the back of the courtroom.

All eyes fell upon the gaunt man standing near the rear entrance. Old Earl's jaw fell open in recognition. "Ten-hut!" he exclaimed, snapping to attention. About a dozen elderly men interspersed among the spectators shot to their feet and saluted.

Louis Nickels made his way up the center aisle followed by Moon and Rayette. "At ease!" he growled as he approached the judge's bench.

Judge Schulman gasped, and rising to his feet, saluted smartly. "Good afternoon, sir!" the judge said as he threw his chest forward and tucked in his chin.

"As you were," Louis Nickels ordered.

Judge Schulman exhaled with relief. "What brings you here today, sir?"

Louis Nickels cast a glance at Vincent and gritted his false teeth. "Did I hear this deadbeat say Country Squire had no debts?"

Vincent looked Louis Nickels over from head to toe and smirked. "Your honor, what's this guy got to do with any of this?"

"For starters, smart-mouth, I'm the guy who put up your bond," Louis Nickels remarked.

"What are you talking about?" Vincent scoffed. "My wife paid my bail."

"You wife hasn't got enough money to buy a gumball." Louis Nickels rejoined. "The only reason you're walking around free is because I posted bond after she put the Country Squire property up as collateral."

"Aw, baloney!"

"And as far as not owing anyone money—you shouldn't be telling fibs. You're in debt up to your eyeballs."

"You're a liar!" Vincent rejoined.

All the old veterans gasped in unison. "What did he say?" Old Earl asked incredulously, raising the shaman stick. Bix placed a hand on Old Earl's shoulder, preventing him from slamming Vincent over the head.

Hearing Vincent's defamatory remark, Judge Schulman turned red. "How dare you! Do you have any idea who you're speaking to?"

"Who, this old coot?"

"That's Louis Nickels!" Judge Schulman exclaimed. "Have some respect!"

Martin Farquhar cleared his throat. "Your honor, with respect to the gentleman, his claim against my client is just hearsay."

"Oh yeah?" Louis Nickels challenged, handing Martin Farquhar a manila folder. "Take a look at this."

Martin Farquhar turned pale as he looked through the folder's contents. Vincent glanced over his shoulder and snatched up one of the bills. "What's all this supposed to be?" he challenged.

"Those are a stack of Country Squire's outstanding bills," Louis Nickels replied as he handed an identical folder to the judge.

Judge Schulman read aloud as he leafed through the documents. "*Louis Nickels Cut-Rate Excavations*, *Louis Nickels Cut-Rate Fencing*, *Louis Nickels Cut-Rate Real Estate Appraisers*, *Louis Nickels Cut-Rate Hydrology*, *Louis Nickels Cut-Rate Surveyors…*"

Vincent kept a mental catalog as Judge Schulman ticked off each invoice.

"*…Louis Nickels Cut-Rate Aerial Photography*, *Louis Nickels Cut-Rate Stonemasonry*, *Louis Nickels Cut-Rate Title Search…*"

"Title search?" Vincent queried. "What's that about?"

"We always commission a title search before accepting real estate as collateral," Louis Nickels explained.

Vincent burst into feigned laughter. "Your honor, this proves nothing!" he mocked. "He's just trying to get his hooks into me now that he smells money. Isn't it interesting how *he's* the only claimant?"

"There's a petition here from one *Candice Brennan* for settlement of back pay," Judge Schulman observed. "And here's quite a hefty bill from some outfit in Italy named *Giambologna and Sons.*"

"This guy doesn't know what he's talking about," Vincent remarked. "These must be forgeries."

"Oh yeah?" Louis Nickels growled. "Take a look at that signature."

Martin Farquhar glanced at the signature scrawled at the bottom of one of the invoices and groaned in recognition.

Vincent craned his neck slightly. "That ain't my signature."

"I never said it was," Louis Nickels rejoined. "These invoices were signed by the blond girl who runs the Country Squire office."

"Who, my wife? That's not Daphne's signature either."

"Take another look," Louis Nickels advised. "Are you sticking to that story?"

"I have never seen that signature before in my life," Vincent adamantly claimed. "You've got no proof Daphne signed these invoices."

"She signed them alright," Louis Nickels affirmed.

"Well, since that signature's illegible, it's your word against mine," Vincent claimed defiantly.

"And mine," Rayette squeaked confidently.

"Who are you?" Judge Schulman asked.

"I'm Rayette," the secretary explained. "I work at Country Squire."

"Your honor, I don't know this woman," Vincent stated. "She doesn't work for me."

"I was hired by Candice," Rayette explained. "I used to work for her when they were building *Von Däniken Village.* Candice was really nice."

"And now you work for Country Squire?" Judge Schulman asked.

"Yes," Rayette affirmed in a nasal voice. "When Candice quit, I stayed on as Mrs. Tremayne's secretary."

"Your honor, this is nonsense," Vincent said dismissively.

"Be quiet," Judge Schulman ordered.

"And this kid has a file full of duplicate copies of everything that blond girl signed," Louis Nickels stated.

"Hand it over, young lady," Judge Schulman directed. Rayette stepped forward and passed a file folder to the bailiff, who in turn handed it to the judge. After a moment of cross-checking, the judge looked up. "The signatures match. These are carbon copies."

"And that's Mrs. Tremayne's signature on every one of them," Rayette said.

"Are you sure?" Judge Schulman asked.

"Yes," Rayette said. "I was there when she signed each of those invoices."

"She's a liar!" Vincent challenged. "She's conspiring with this old coot to cheat me!"

Moon leapt out of his seat with murder in his eyes. "Sit down, son," Louis Nickels said, catching Moon by the arm. "The truth is its own best defense."

"Are you saying this woman doesn't work for Country Squire?" Judge Schulman asked Vincent.

"That's right," Vincent replied.

At that moment, Daphne stormed into the courtroom through the back door and strode up to Vincent. "Can we leave now?" she demanded.

Judge Schulman regarded the blond woman quizzically. "And who might you be, young lady?"

"I'm Daphne," she replied. "Senior Sales Agent."

"Nice outfit," Judge Schulman observed.

"Do you think so?" Daphne asked as she pirouetted in front of the judge's bench. "It's my own design. What do you think of the crest?"

"It's swell," the judge replied. "Does everyone at Country Squire wear a uniform?" he asked, motioning to Rayette.

Daphne scowled. "Yeah," she said. "But I wish Rayette would lose a few pounds. She told me she was a size 12."

"A size 12?" Judge Schulman questioned. "Are you sure?"

"Yeah," Daphne replied. "That's what she said when I fitted her for the Country Squire uniform."

"So, she works for you?" Judge Schulman asked.

"Duh!" Daphne replied rhetorically. "Haven't you been listening?"

"I'm convinced," Judge Schulman said. "These invoices are legitimate."

"Damn!" Vincent exclaimed.

"Enough, Vincent," Martin Farquhar urged. "You're making matters worse."

"Listen to your lawyer, Mr. Tremayne," Judge Schulman advised.

"Alright," Vincent relented. "I give up. I'll pay the bills."

"That's a wise choice, Mr. Tremayne," Judge Schulman said.

"So, when do I get my money?" Vincent asked.

Judge Schulman whispered something to the bailiff, who slipped out a side door. "I've just sent for the Village Assessor," the judge explained. "Once we determine the value of the Country Squire property I'll authorize the transfer of ownership to the State."

"And *then* I get the money?" Vincent asked impatiently.

"No," Judge Schulman replied. "Then the Clerk of the Court will supervise the disbursement of funds to settle Country Squire's debts. Once all your debts are paid, then you get what's left over."

The bailiff returned, followed by the Village Assessor and the Clerk. "Here you go, your honor," the Village Assessor said, handing the judge a sheet of paper. She handed a duplicate copy to the bailiff who in turn passed it to Vincent.

Vincent looked at the document incomprehensibly. "What the hell is this?"

"It's a copy of the Village tax map along with the assessed value of the Country Squire property," the Village Assessor replied. "The property value is on the bottom of page two, in bold print."

Vincent flipped to the second page and gasped. "This can't be… This can't be right. This says the assessed value of the property is only three hundred and forty thousand dollars."

"That's right," the Village Assessor replied.

"But I paid eight hundred grand for that property!" Vincent exclaimed.

"But you filed a petition for reassessment just last week," the Village Assessor explained. "We expedited the filing, as requested, and you'll be happy to know your property taxes have been reduced."

Vincent turned to Daphne with a look of purple rage. "This… this… this is all your fault!"

"My fault? I did exactly what you said, grouchy!" Daphne shot back defiantly. "And now we're going to save a ton of money, thanks to me."

Vincent staggered backwards, and falling into his seat, buried his face in his hands. Judge Schulman summoned Martin Farquhar to the bench. Assisted by the Clerk, the three went through the folder of property liens and invoices, and with the aid of a calculator, arrived at a sum. Vincent finally looked up as Martin Farquhar resumed his place by his side.

"Mr. Tremayne," Judge Schulman said, "according to our calculations, after all Country Squire's debts are settled, you are going to walk away with the net sum of… uh… four dollars and twelve cents."

Vincent Tremayne blinked. "Huh?"

"Four dollars and twelve cents," the judge repeated.

"That's all?" Vincent asked sheepishly.

"Yes. The settlement includes back pay for all Country Squire employees as well as final payment for legal services owed to the firm of Walsh, Farquhar and Dunn, Attorneys at Law."

Vincent turned to his lawyer. "Martin, what… what should I do?"

Martin Farquhar stepped forward and cleared his throat. "Your honor, may I make a statement?"

"Alright," Judge Schulman replied congenially.

"Your honor, I would like to go on record that the legal firm of Walsh, Farquhar and Dunn is no longer serving as legal counsel for either the Country Squire Development Corporation, nor for Mr. Vincent Tremayne."

"Very well, councilor," Judge Schuman replied.

Martin Farquhar turned to Vincent. "Here's my last bit of advice, and I'm offering it for free—accept this settlement and quit the real estate business for good." With that, Martin Farquhar picked up his briefcase and left the courtroom without looking back.

"Can we go now, Vincent?" Daphne whined. "I have a three o'clock appointment for a bikini waxing."

"We'll have you on your way in just a few minutes, Mrs. Tremayne," Judge Schulman announced. "Your husband just needs to sign this document."

"What is it?" Vincent asked as the bailiff passed the paper to him.

"It's an affidavit notifying the Commissioner of Cultural and Historic Preservation that you've accepted the State's offer in settlement of its eminent domain acquisition of the Country Squire property," Judge Schulman explained. "Once you sign it, we'll forward it to the Commissioner."

"Then what?" Vincent asked.

"Then the State will authorize payment," the judge replied. "Disbursement will be made through the Clerk of the Court. I expect you'll be able to pick up your check in about a month."

Vincent sighed. "Where do I sign?"

"Right by the X," Judge Schulman instructed. Vincent pulled out a pen and scrawled his signature on the document.

Vincent passed the document back to the bailiff. "Can I go now?"

"Oh, I almost forgot," the judge added. "That form needs to be notarized. Is anyone here a Notary Public?"

Louis Nickels cleared his throat, drew a business card from his pocket, and passed it to the bailiff. "*Louis Nickels Cut-Rate Notary Public*," the bailiff read aloud.

"Would you be willing to notarize Mr. Tremayne's signature?" Judge Schulman asked.

Louis Nickels scowled. "Yeah," he said as he pulled out his official rubber stamp. He snatched the paper away from Vincent and with painstaking and deliberate strokes of the pen, added his signature to the document.

"Thanks," Vincent said as Louis Nickels flippantly tossed the paper at him.

"That'll be seven bucks," Louis Nickels said. "Cash!"

Vincent checked his wallet and pulled out a five dollar bill. He counted his loose change and glanced over at Daphne. "Do you have thirty five cents?"

As Vincent and Daphne were settling Louis Nickels' fee, the Village Assessor approached. "Mr. Tremayne, while you're here, I thought I'd save a stamp and hand-deliver this to you."

"What is it?" Vincent asked sullenly.

"It's your new tax bill," the Village Assessor explained. "You know, for the Country Squire property—after the reassessment. The amount you owe is there—on the bottom line."

Vincent felt a lump in his throat as he read the sum. Daphne looked over his shoulder and giggled. "See!" she exclaimed as she backhandedly slapped his shoulder. "I told you I'd save you a lot of money!"

POSTSCRIPT

The forecast promised perfect Indian summer weather for Columbus Day weekend, and Saturday was shaping up better than expected. Thomas and Roxanne planned to make the most of the day and looked forward to attending a cocktail party that evening in honor of Gianna Fox, whose recent book chronicling the discovery of the Bayview Viking burial had meteorically shot to number one on the *New York Times* best seller list.

"Things turned out better than expected," Roxanne opined as Thomas navigated the pickup along the bumpy private road. "With the Bayview Woods, I mean."

"You can say that again," Thomas agreed as he considered the autumnal hues of the newly designated parkland.

"How is Lisa taking to her new position as director of the Bayview dig?"

"Things couldn't be better. This project will really establish her reputation as one of the leading archaeologists of her generation. She'll be able to write her own ticket after this."

"It's really nice that you're able to help by sending her so many interns, too," Roxanne said.

"I couldn't keep people away if I tried. Volunteers from the archaeology club are climbing over themselves just to do the spadework. We've had to set up a rotation just to give everyone a chance to participate."

"That's great. By the way, how's that new biology professor making out? Wasn't he involved with the archaeology club before the college hired him?"

Thomas chuckled. "Dr. Schuyler, you mean. He was one of the club's founding members. His role in Vincent Tremayne's arrest really impressed the college bigwigs. The president thinks he's a genius."

"Speaking of Vincent Tremayne, you'd better get a move on. The unveiling is in half an hour."

"We'll make it," Thomas replied. "We might even have time to grab a coffee at Silvio's first."

Thomas and Roxanne took two coffees to go and stepped onto Silvio's back patio. In the park, a small crowd gathered around what, from a distance, appeared to be a towering, two-storied teepee. As Thomas and Roxanne drew closer, they noticed a number of men milling about wearing capes and bicorned chapeaus, signifying their membership in the Knights of Columbus. Knowing that Vincent and Daphne Tremayne were somewhere near the center of this gathering, Thomas and Roxanne thought it best to hang back and watch the proceedings from a distance. At length, the mayor of Stirling Harbor stepped up to the speaker's podium and cleared his throat.

"Ladies and gentlemen," the mayor began, "on behalf of the Village Trustees, the Rotary Club and the Stella Maris Council of the Knights of Columbus, I'd like to thank Vincent and Daphne Tremayne for their generous bequest and welcome you all to the dedication of…"

Roxanne leaned in close. "Thomas, I don't get it. Why in the world did the Village Trustees agree to accept this nightmarish pile of crap?"

"They took it in settlement of Tremayne's property tax bill," Thomas explained. "Apparently this thing set him back quite a bit of money and someone on the Village Board thought it would add an artistic flourish to the park. Tremayne gets to fob it off as a *donation* to the Village while actually clearing up his tax debt."

"But it looks so awful in the photographs. Now we'll be subjected to this eyesore every time we stroll through the park."

"It's better than having to stare at it from our own back porch."

"You've got a point there," Roxanne conceded.

"…so in celebration of our maritime heritage," the mayor continued, "and in recognition of our to debt to Italian civilization and culture, on this Columbus Day I present to you the *Fontana di Nettuno*."

Daphne Tremayne stepped forward and pulled a braided cord. The crowd applauded as the drape-like tarpaulin fell away, revealing the ornate fountain in all its glory.

"Good God!" Roxanne exclaimed, cringing.

Daphne Tremayne, ebullient and beaming, posed before the fountain as a photographer from the *Stirling Harbor Gazette* snapped a series of pictures.

Thomas cocked his head to one side as he took in the spectacle. "Hmmm…" he intoned thoughtfully.

After some consideration, Roxanne arched an eyebrow. "You know, in this setting, that thing doesn't look half bad."

"I was thinking the same thing," Thomas said. "Give it some time and it could grow on you."

Roxanne checked her watch. "We still have a few hours before the cocktail party."

Thomas turned to her and smiled. "You know, we haven't been out to Anatoli Point in a while. Are you up for a leisurely drive? We could stop at a farm stand and pick up some pumpkins."

"That sounds like fun," Roxanne replied.

Thomas and Roxanne turned onto the North Road, passing farms and vineyards as they headed east. The balmy warmth made it feel like summer, but the lower angle of the sun and the changing color of the leaves signaled the unmistakable arrival of autumn. Even so, Indian summers in these parts were known to linger, sometimes as late as Thanksgiving, extending the tourist season well beyond Labor Day. Columbus Day weekend always drew crowds, especially if the forecast called for sun, and the pumpkin pickers and leaf peepers came out in force.

"I haven't been out this way in a long time," Roxanne stated.

"Me neither," Thomas said. "It sure is pretty in the fall."

They drove in silence for a short while enjoying the scenery. "Hey, Thomas," Roxanne said. "Look at that place on the left. I don't remember *that* being there."

"Wow!" Thomas exclaimed as he hooked the truck into a U-turn. "Lets' go back and take a look."

"This place is really crowded," Roxanne observed as they parked the pickup. She grinned as they approached the entrance on foot. "Hey! That house is shaped like a cupcake."

Thomas read the brightly colored sign. "*Welcome to the Fairy Glen Miniature Golf and Family Fun Center.* Wait a second," he said. "I've been here before."

"Really?"

"Yeah. It's all coming back to me. My grandparents used to bring me here when I was little."

"I must have passed this spot a hundred times," Roxanne said. "How come I've never seen it before?"

"It must have fallen into disuse years ago and become overgrown with weeds and brambles. I'd forgotten it was even here. Man, I used to love coming to this place."

"I bet. Look at all these kids. Everyone seems to be having a ball."

Thomas beamed with delight. "Look over there," he said, pointing. "I remember trying to knock golf balls through the legs of that wizard when I was kid. Gosh! He seemed like a giant to me back then."

Thomas and Roxanne wandered amongst the happy families and watched as children scurried amid gnomes and fairies, negotiating the challenges of the maze-like golf course.

"Hey, Roxy," Thomas said with boyish excitement. "How'd you like to play a round of golf?"

"I'd love to, but can we get a snack first?"

Thomas and Roxanne made their way to the cupcake-shaped concession stand. "Hi!" a chubby woman greeted them cheerily. "What can I get you?"

"Howdy," Roxanne replied. "Ya'll got cotton candy?"

"We sure do," the woman replied with the approval of a connoisseur.

"I'll have a cotton candy, then."

"And I'll take two hot dogs," Thomas added.

"Hey, Moon," the woman called to man working the fryer. "Order in—two hot dogs!"

Thomas scrutinized the woman's face as she handed Roxanne the fluffy confectionary. "Forgive me, but you look very familiar. Have we met before?"

"Maybe," the woman said with a broad smile. "I'm Rayette. I used to be a secretary, but I've been working here since the grand reopening." The fryer chef stepped forward with two steaming hot dogs on a cardboard tray. "This is my 'Prince Charming'," Rayette said. "His name is Moon."

"Matrimonial plans for the forthcoming spring commence," Moon said with a twinkle in his eye. "Please regard the ring."

"Isn't it lovely?" Rayette warbled as she held forth her hand.

"That's mighty fine," Roxanne gushed. "We wish you years of happiness together."

Having scarfed down the hot dogs and cotton candy, Thomas and Roxanne ambled about the Fairy Glen, admiring the restoration. As they walked, Thomas reminisced about his childhood and of the happy times spent with his grandparents at this long-forgotten place.

"They sure did a lot of work putting everything back together," Thomas remarked. "It must have cost a fortune." At length, they came upon what appeared a miniature railroad crossing and train station.

"My God, Roxy! Now *this* really brings back memories."

"What is it?"

"They used to call this *Lilliput Junction.* I remember we used to ride on a little train that made a circuit around the golf course. I wonder if..."

As Thomas spoke, a train whistle sounded somewhere in the distance. "Thomas, look," Roxanne said, pointing to an approaching midget-sized locomotive followed by a dozen open-air cars, each packed with smiling parents and children.

Thomas gasped. "There it is, Roxy! That's it!"

"Last stop, kids," the elderly engineer announced as the train rolled into the station. "Be careful getting off." The gaunt man set the engine at idle and helped the littlest children climb down to the platform. "The *Gwydir Castle Express* departs again in five minutes!"

"Please, Roxy. Can we take a train ride?"

Thomas and Roxanne fell in line behind a family with two little children. Once the first group of passengers had cleared the platform, the old engineer stepped up and opened a gate. "OK, kids. All aboard!"

Thomas watched as the elderly man assisted the family into the first car behind the locomotive. "Hey, mister," the little girl squeaked. "Are we really gonna see fairies on this trip?"

The old man gritted his false teeth and smiled. "Yeah," he said, holding the girl's hand as she climbed aboard. "If you look really hard, you'll see them everywhere."

Thomas was overcome with emotion as the old engineer blew the whistle. Evening twilight had crept upon the Fairy Glen and the electric lights above the mini-golf course flickered on automatically. As the train pulled out, Thomas put his arm around Roxanne.

"Hey, mister," the little girl called to the engineer over the low growl of the locomotive. "Is your name Choo-Choo Charlie?"

"No," the old man said over his shoulder. "I'm Choo-Choo Louis. Charlie has the night off."

"Are you sure we're going to see fairies?" the little girl asked guardedly.

"Yeah," the old engineer replied. "Keep your eyes peeled. They might pop out at any time."

"There's no such thing as fairies," the girl's older brother taunted.

"No!" the girl whined. "There *are* fairies!"

"Of course there are fairies," the mother interjected. "Leave your sister alone."

The *Gwydir Castle Express* chugged along at a leisurely pace, making a great arc around the perimeter of the Fairy Glen. Roxanne turned towards Thomas and smiled. "By the way, doll," she said, "I've been meaning to ask you. How are things going with your sabbatical application?"

Thomas thought about it and shrugged. "It's hard to say," he replied. "I submitted all the paperwork, and I'm just waiting to find out if it's approved."

"You mean *when* it's approved."

"Well, I'm not counting my chickens just yet."

"Oh, come on! They can't turn you down, can they? Between publishing a new book and serving as the archaeology club advisor, I would think the college president owes it to you."

"It's not that simple. I know the college president is pulling for me, but in the end, it's really not up to him. Ultimately, all sabbatical requests must be approved by the Board of Trustees."

"When will that be?"

"It's hard to say. Rumor has it three of the trustees are facing indictment and will be forced to step down. God only knows when the county legislature will fill the vacancies."

"Gosh!"

"And under the best of circumstances, the board's vote will be delayed for months. Hopefully, when all is said and done the new trustees will defer to the president and grant my request, but there's just no telling."

"So, what are you going to do in the meantime? Just sit and wait?"

"Not a chance," Thomas replied. "I'm applying for research grants from the New Mexico Office of Archaeological Studies and the Guy St. Lawrence Foundation. If I'm awarded the sabbatical, I'm still going to need money to finance the dig."

Roxanne nodded pensively. "You know I love the desert, Thomas, but I don't understand why you have to go all the way to New Mexico to excavate. You've got a major archaeological site right in your own backyard. Why can't you spend your sabbatical at home, working on the Bayview dig?"

Thomas wagged his head. "That would be a really bad idea, Roxy. Lisa still hasn't fully gotten over my... uh... little prank, and I think it would be best if I limited my involvement to just sending her interns from the archaeology club. Besides, I've had my sights set on this area near Bad Penny, New Mexico for some time. All I need do now is present evidence supporting my initial hypothesis and the grant money should come pouring in."

"I don't understand. Are you saying you need to go out to New Mexico and excavate *before* they award you any grant money?"

"Kind of. I don't want to bore you with the technical details, but I'll need to spend a few days excavating a test pit to see if my proposed site turns up anything justifying a more extensive dig."

"A test pit?" Roxanne asked skeptically. "When are you going to have time to do that?"

"I thought we might spend some time in New Mexico over the winter recess," Thomas replied. "Bad Penny is only a few hours' drive from El Paso. Once I'm done excavating the test pit we could stop by and see your folks."

"Well, alright," Roxanne said, frowning. "But this whole test pit thing..."

"What about it?"

"It seems like an awful lot of trouble to go to. Why can't you just do a surface survey the way Lisa did with the Bayview site?"

Completing its circuit around the Fairy Glen, the *Gwydir Castle Express* slowed to a stop as it rolled into *Lilliput Junction*. By then, darkness had fallen and the Fairy Glen was fully illuminated by electric light.

"It doesn't always work that way, Roxy. Judging what's on the surface can be misleading..." Thomas began.

"Fairies! Look at all the fairies!" the little girl in the first car cried, pointing to the swarms of moths dancing around the floodlights which hung overhead. "Choo-Choo Louis was right! The fairies are everywhere!"

"I told you we'd see fairies," the old engineer said as he helped the little girl down to the platform. "Just look at them all flying around up there!" The old man laughed heartily and waived as the little girl scampered off behind her brother. "The *Gwydir Castle Express* departs again in five minutes, kids. All aboard!"

Roxanne and Thomas watched from the platform as the old engineer helped a new group of people onto the train. "What were you saying, doll?" Roxanne asked.

"Hm?"

"About surface surveys?"

"Oh, right," Thomas replied. "As I was saying.... Things don't always add up if you judge by what's on the surface. What's hidden below is always a mystery. What you find when you dig down may thoroughly surprise you."

-The End-